RANDOM HOUSE

LARGE
PRINT

Also by Elizabeth Berg
available from Random House Large Print

The Art of Mending

THE YEAR
OF PLEASURES

The

YEAR OF
PLEASURES

A NOVEL

ELIZABETH
BERG

RANDOM HOUSE
LARGE PRINT

Copyright © 2005 by Elizabeth Berg

Published in the United States of America by Random House Large Print in association with Random House, New York.
Distributed by Random House, Inc., New York.

Library of Congress Cataloging-in-Publication Data

Berg, Elizabeth.
The year of pleasures : a novel / Elizabeth Berg.
p.   cm.
ISBN 0-375-43456-9 (lg. print : alk. paper)
1. Widows—Fiction.   2. Middle West—Fiction.
3. Loss (Psychology)—Fiction.   4. Female friendship—Fiction.   5. City and town life—Fiction.
6. Large type books.   I. Title.

PS3552.E6996Y43   2005b
813'.54—dc22
2004060925

www.randomlargeprint.com

FIRST LARGE PRINT EDITION

10   9   8   7   6   5   4   3   2   1

This Large Print edition published in accord with the standards of the N.A.V.H.

For those who have gone before us

You get the hovering gray of early morning,
or late afternoon—the hours of yearning.

—REGINA SCHRAMBLING,
The New York Times, June 27, 2001

Again the pyrocanthus berries redden in rain,
As if return were return.
It is not.
The familiar is not the thing it reminds of.

—JANE HIRSHFIELD, "Red Berries"

Today, like every other day, we wake up empty
and frightened. Don't open the door to the study
and begin reading. Take down the dulcimer.

—RUMI

THE YEAR
OF PLEASURES

I had been right to want to drive to the Midwest, taking only the back roads. Every time my husband, John, and I had taken a trip more than a few miles away, we'd flown, and had endured the increasingly irritating airport protocols. I'd finally begun to wear what amounted to pajamas so that I wouldn't have to all but strip before security guards who seemed either worrisomely bored or, equally worrisome, inflated with a mirthful self-importance. It was hard to believe that air travel had ever been considered glamorous, when now what most people felt was a seesawing between anxiety and exasperation. "Well, folks, looks like our time has been pushed back again," the captain would say, and everyone would shake their heads and snap their newspapers and mutter to their neighbor. And if there was unexpected turbulence, a quivering silence fell.

Now, on this road trip, my mind seemed to uncrinkle, to breathe, to present to itself a cure for a disease it had not, until now, known it had. Rather than the back of an airline seat or endless, identical rest stops on the interstate, I saw farmhouses in the middle of protective stands of trees, silos reaching for the sky, barns faded to the soft red of tomato soup. The weather everywhere stayed stubbornly warm, and people seemed edgily grateful—what could this mean, sixty-degree weather in November? I drove through one small town where old people sat on rockers on front porches and kids tore around corners on bikes and young mothers, jackets tied around their waists, proudly pushed babies in strollers.

I passed white wooden churches, red brick schools, stores with names familiar only to the locals, and movie theaters offering a single choice. I saw cats stationed at living room windows, horses switching tails against clouds of gnats, cows in pastures grouped together like gossips. These scenes seemed imbued with a beauty richer than normal; they seemed so perfect as to have been staged. I felt as though I were driving through a museum full of pastoral bas-reliefs, and I took in the details that way, with wonder and appreciation. That was the tolerable part of my new vulnerability, the positive side of feeling my heart had migrated out of my body to hang on my chest like a necklace.

There was an infinite variety of trees, and I felt ashamed to know the names of so few of them. John and I used to talk about how the current phase of the moon as well as the names of trees and flowers and birds—at least the local ones!—should be front and center in people's brains; maybe such a connection to nature would help to make us more civilized. But I was as guilty as anyone; the only tree I knew beyond pines and willows and birches was the black locust, and that was because I liked the way John had described the blossoms' scent: like grape lollipops. I passed massive-trunked trees standing powerful and alone, and imagined how in summer their leafy canopy would provide a gigantic circle of shade. I passed a group of reedy saplings bending like ballerinas in the wind. Willow trees dipped their bare branches into pond water like girls testing the temperature with their toes.

I felt a low and distinct kind of relaxation. Time became real. Nature became real: the woods, the sky, the lakes, the high bluffs and low valleys, the acres of spent fields, the muddy riverbanks. Live photos flashed before me: Here, a construction worker eating a sandwich, one foot up on the bumper of his truck. Here, a woman in curlers loading groceries into her car. Here, a child glimpsed through a kitchen window, standing on a stool to reach into a cupboard; there, a beauty operator giving an old lady a perm.

I saw in a way I never had before the beauty and diversity of our earnest labor on the earth, and also our ultimate separateness. This helped my pain metamorphose into something less personal and more universal, something organic and natural. And that helped give me strength. Someone had to die first. It turned out to be John. Nothing more. Nothing less. What fell to me now, what I was driving toward, was the creation of a new kind of life, minus the ongoing influence of what I had loved and depended upon most in the world. In a way, my situation reminded me of a little girl I'd once seen exiting a roller coaster at a state fair, all wide eyes and pale face and shaky knees. When her brother asked if she'd like to ride again, she said, "Not until I'm way readier." I felt myself trapped in line for a ride I was not nearly ready for, looking back but moving forward in the only direction I could go.

Mile by mile, the country unfurled before me—in bright morning light, throughout golden afternoons, under the pastel-colored skies of evenings. Once, just outside of Cleveland, when the sky was lavender and the clouds pink, I pulled to the side of the freeway to watch until darkness smudged the colors into night. Land rushed up, then fell away; rushed up, then fell away. I became intimately aware of the lay of the land, felt the rise and fall of it in my stomach as I drove up and down steep hills. I deliberately pushed everything out of my head but what was before me. Still, every now and then a quick thrill raced up my spine in the form of a thought: **I am my own again.** Sorrow that lay pooled inside me gave over to a kind of exhilaration in those moments; the relief was stunning.

Though impermanent. One night, I checked into a motel at around ten o'clock. Next door, I heard a couple making love. Their sounds were sloppy and slightly hysterical—**Drunk,** I thought. I turned the radio up loud, ran a bath, and while sitting at the edge of the tub unwrapping the absurdly little bar of soap, I felt the weight of my loss move slowly back into me. After I dried off, I sat before the television and marveled at the drivel that passed for entertainment. I turned it off, finally, then sat at the side of the bed and stared out at nothing. I picked up the telephone and dialed my home number. I heard the characteristic tones, then, **The number you have reached has been disconnected.** I hung up, closed my eyes, and took in a deep breath. Then I knelt at the side of the bed and pushed my face into my hands.

Late in the afternoon of the third day, I pulled over to a frozen-yogurt stand near the center of a small town that looked particularly attractive to me. A tall, early-thirtyish man waited on me. He was beginning to bald already and had a distressing complexion. But his eyes, as though in compensation, were a brilliant blue. "That'll be a dollar sixty-five," he said, handing me the raspberry cone I'd ordered. I pulled two dollars from my wallet and handed them to him, then took a lick of the yogurt. "Delicious," I said, and smiled at him. He smiled back, hesitantly, then fussed with the register for a long while as I watched, first in mild annoyance, then in sympathy, finally in utter fascination. Eventually, the man turned and called to someone in the back room. "Louise?" he said, apparently too softly, for then he called a bit louder, "Louise?"

"WHAT?" she yelled back.

The man straightened the paper hat on his head. "Could you come out and help me?" he asked. "Please?"

Louise came out to the cash register, scowling. She was wearing a maroon sweat suit and was massively overweight. She wore her hair in a high ponytail. It was beautiful hair, thick and auburn-colored; I concentrated on it while she concentrated on me. Finally, I looked at her face. "Hello," I said.

She jutted her chin at me. "How you doing." There was mischief in her eyes.

"Was that you yelling back there?" I asked.

She grinned. "Yeah, that was me, whistling while I work." She jerked her head toward the man. "**This** goes on all the livelong day."

"Oh, well," I said. "That's all right."

"Easy for you to say." She turned to glare at the man, who studied his shoes. Then she fixed the register and stomped off.

"Okay!" the man said. "Says here I owe you thirty-five cents!" He handed me the change.

I thanked him, then, laughing, said, "Though I think you could have figured that out on your own."

He looked doubtful.

"Oh, come on," I said. "Don't you think we're getting way too dependent on these damn machines?"

Now he looked grateful. "Idn't it?"

I thanked him again and headed for the door. But I turned back before I opened it. "Could you tell me what town this is?"

He pointed to the floor. "This here town where we're at now?"

"Yes."

He straightened, made himself taller. "This is Stewart, Illinois, and I'll tell you what, it's only forty-nine miles from Chicago. Exactamento. I been here my whole life. It's a good town, Stewart. Is this what you're looking for?"

I hesitated, then answered, "Yes."

As I started to open the door again, I heard him clear his throat and say, "Miss?"

I turned back. He was blushing, but with a kind of borrowed confidence, he said, "Would you like to be on my radio show?"

I tried hard not to let my astonishment show. "You have a radio show?"

"Yes, ma'am, **Talk of the Town.** I get guests from town on, and we talk. That's the show."

I thought of the empty miles I'd driven through to get to this town, the few places of business I'd seen thus far. I didn't recall anything that looked like it might be—or house—a broadcasting studio. "Where?" I asked.

"Right at WMRZ a few blocks over. It's above the drugstore. I've had Louise on my show—we talked about yogurt: Where has it been and where is it going? Louise liked being on a lot, you can ask her. She got dressed up and every-thing, got herself a new purse for that show." He lowered his voice and leaned over the counter to say, "Louise is the one sponsors me. Her bite is way worse than her bark, if you know what I mean."

I hesitated, then refrained from correcting him. Instead, I said, "Yes, I know exactly what you mean."

"So do you want to be on? I tape every Sunday morning. Six-thirty. You'd have to get up early, but you're going to church, anyways, just get ready sooner."

"Well, I . . ."

"You don't need to answer now," the man said. " If you want to do it, just come back and see me here. Or you can call me. My name's Ed Selwin. My number's in the book. It's spelled exactly more or less like it sounds. You can think on it. Just, I figured if you's moving here, it'd be good to interview you. You being a new person and all."

"But I . . . did I say I was moving here?"

"Not exactly. I just saw your loaded-up car with out-of-state plates, and then you said this is the town you were looking for . . ."

"I see."

"And since you'd be a new person here, it'd be interesting to see where you came from and such. Like that. And don't worry—people get nervous being on the radio, just a natural thing, but I'll settle you right down."

"Okay, well . . . . I'll let you know." I waved goodbye and began licking the quickly melting yogurt. Inside the car, I started the engine, turned on the heat—the weather had finally become seasonally appropriate—and finished eating. I had an odd but familiar feeling inside, a kind of surety without grounding. It was something I often felt as a child, and it drove me to do things very quickly and without regret. I wondered if I should say, **Yes, here, this is the place,** just like that, and then go in search of somewhere to live. Why not? What had I to lose, really? I was in the middle of the country, as I'd wanted to be. It looked to be a charming little town. And anyway, I wouldn't mind moving back toward a certain boldness of spirit, a reliance on a kind of luck I'd always enjoyed. I remembered a story I once heard about a couple from a farm in Iowa looking for a place to live in Washington, D.C. They weren't having any success; everything was incredibly expensive, and to make matters worse, they had three dogs. They became greatly discouraged, and then one day the woman threw up her hands and said, "All right. Let's just drive ten minutes one way and then turn left. And then drive ten minutes more and turn right. And then ten minutes straight, and if we don't find something, we'll give up." What they drove to was a huge farmhouse just outside the city, and a man was standing outside of it. Feeling more than a little foolish, the couple asked if the man happened to know of anything around for rent. Turned out he had a little house on his property he used for hired hands that was newly vacated. Freshly painted. They could have it for next to nothing if they'd help a bit with chores. And three dogs? No problem. John once said, "Sometimes serendipity is just intention, unmasked." I think I answered him with some sort of vague

Mmm-hmm, right, hidden as I was behind the **Globe**'s book review. But I'd always remembered it. And now I thought I knew what he'd meant. When you were willing to say what you really wanted, something just might help you along.

I got out of the car to throw away my napkin and then headed farther into town. I'd look at some neighborhoods and see what happened.

For the most part, the houses were old and large and well cared for. Alleys ran behind them—the wide, old-fashioned ones I'd always loved for the way they offered views of the backs of people's houses. In alleys, things were more casual and more intimate—and therefore more revealing. In summer, you saw things like colorful plastic glasses left on little outdoor tables, rugs draped over back-porch railings, toys strewn across lawns or homemade sandboxes, laundry on the line with the sleeves of upside-down shirts seeming to wave. There might be hollyhocks and snapdragons and gigantic sunflowers, tomatoes hanging heavy on the vine, green peppers hiding in the shade of their own leaves and waiting to be found like Easter eggs. There might be sugar snap peas climbing chain-link fences with curly abandon, children's gardens with leggy printing on Popsicle sticks identifying dependable and forgiving crops: zucchini, carrots, marigolds. In winter, you could find families of snowmen, sleds resting against walls like tethered horses, imprints of snow angels, lopsided circles with wedgelike lines stamped out for a game of snow pie. And no matter what the season, I always liked seeing what was left by the big garbage cans: boxes from new purchases, kitchen chairs with broken rungs, refrigerators with the doors removed, suggesting an odd kind of nakedness.

Alleys sparked other pleasant memories from my childhood: visiting my aunt Lala in Worcester and playing in those narrow little streets behind the houses with my cousins. We played old-fashioned games like tag and hide-and-seek and capture the flag, games I thought had been eclipsed by electronics and technology and the fear of leaving children alone outside. But here, despite the nip in the air, I saw a lot of children, though they were on sidewalks rather than in the alleys. A group of little girls jumped rope, calling out singsongy rhymes familiar in cadence if not in lyrics. Older boys shot baskets at the end of someone's driveway, dribbling furiously through piles of leaves that had lost their colors to a uniform brown. I saw towheaded girls somewhere between the ages of seven and ten who looked like sisters, dancing in a circle around a tiny brown dog who continually charged them, biting at the hems of their pants. "**No,** Tootsie!" they shouted, laughing.

"The town that time forgot," I said out loud, perhaps to John, who perhaps heard, and I turned off the radio and cracked the window, the better to hear the indigenous sounds of this place so different from what I'd left behind. Even the air was different: clean and apple-scented.

I turned down a wide street lined by tall and stately trees and saw what looked like a FOR SALE sign in the middle of the block. And indeed it was that. I pulled over to the curb next to a white wooden sign reading HENCKLEY REALTORS, a phone number stenciled neatly below. The house was a beautiful Victorian, complete with a wrap-around front porch. It looked empty: There were no curtains, I could see no furniture or artwork through the windows, and the dying grass was longish. My heart sped up; this was exactly what John and I had fantasized finding when we planned our trip. I sat for a long minute in the car, hesitant to get out. I knew if I loved the house, I'd buy it, and I was afraid, suddenly, to follow through on what I'd thought I was so sure of. If John were here, he would be the stable force against which I could play out my daring and my spontaneity; now I wondered if this whole trip had been such a good idea after all. "Don't do **anything** for at least six months," one woman had told me. But another had said, "Get right back into the swing of things. You're not twenty, you know." Then she'd all but covered her mouth and added, "I didn't mean that like it sounded."

I decided to go up and ring the doorbell. If the house was empty, I'd have a peek through the windows. If it wasn't . . . well, I'd think of something. I turned off the engine and checked myself in the visor mirror. I didn't look deranged, as I feared I might: I could feel my overeagerness knocking about inside me. I thought surely I would look at least somewhat exophthalmic. But no, I looked normal: a fifty-five-year-old woman with clear green eyes that were just the slightest bit asymmetrical and a nose that was just the slightest bit crooked, traits I'd wept over in high school but had come to accept, even love, because John had. I was a redheaded, freckle-faced woman in need of a haircut but wearing decent clothes and diamond studs, a gift from John on our fifteenth anniversary. They were not so large as to be gross, but I thought they would signal to the Realtor that I had some money. That seemed important. I anticipated him being annoyed having to show a house of this size and quality to a single woman—my opinion was that when it came to women being taken seriously, the world had not advanced so very much.

When I got to the door, I saw that the house was indeed empty. I looked around to make sure no one was watching, then moved cautiously over to a large front window to peer inside. What I saw took my breath away: egg-and-dart mold-ing, a fireplace with a carved mantel, polished wooden floors in a tiger oak pattern. The stairs curved around to go up; at the landing was a large stained-glass window in the striking form and colors of Frank Lloyd Wright. I pulled my cell phone out of my purse and noticed that my hands were trembling—out of fear or out of eagerness, I wasn't sure—but I dialed the number on the sign and prayed that someone could show me the house, **now.**

I asked the receptionist who answered for a Realtor—in fact, was Mr. Henckley there? I asked. I wanted the owner of the company. I thought that was probably the way to do it. "This is **Mrs. Henckley**," the woman said, "and I am the Realtor. The only one."

"Oh!" I said. "I'm sorry, I thought you were the receptionist."

She laughed. "There's no receptionist here! It's just me and the cat. What can I help you with?"

I took in a breath. "I'd like to see a house you have listed. It's a white Victorian—"

"Oh, the Samuels place. Three-eleven Maple?"

I looked at the number beside the door. "Yes, that's it. I'd like to make an appointment to see it."

"Well," she said, "how about now? Do you want to see it right now?"

I nodded vigorously, then realized what I

was doing. "Yes!" I said. "Please. That would be great." I sat down on the top step. "I'll just wait right here. I'm right here on the front porch."

"It'll take me about fifteen minutes to get there," she said. "Take a walk around the place. Look at the garden in the back. There's not much there now, of course, but you'll get an idea. Lydia Samuels made a bargain with the devil to get a garden like that one. I'll show you pictures of it in bloom when I get there. What's your name, anyway?"

I told her, then added, "I'm from Boston."

Silence.

"But I'm moving. Here. Maybe. I mean, I **am** moving, for sure. I just don't know if it's to this house."

A moment, and then, slowly, "Well, of course you don't, hon. You haven't even seen it yet. You just have a look around and I'll see you soon. I'm Delores, okay?"

So much for not seeming deranged.

I looked through the window a while longer, then headed for the back of the house. There was a narrow strip garden along the side, but in the backyard was a magnificent plot, gently curving in and out, taking up fully half of the yard. A white stone birdbath was stationed in the center, the pedestal plain and solid, the bath in the form of a shell. Dried leaves had accumulated at the bottom, and I brushed them out with proprietary license. At the far end of the garden there were two birdhouses stationed side by side, one slightly taller than the other. They were sturdy and handsome and huge, made from a dark green metal. Judging from the cobwebs, they'd been long without seed; I hoped this meant the house had been empty for some time. Then the owners would be more eager to sell.

There was a garage, painted the same cream color as the house, with a multipaned window complete with shutters and a window box. I looked through the glass and saw rakes and shovels neatly lined up, flowerpots stacked high on wooden shelving, plastic bags full of something I couldn't identify, freestanding pieces of latticework, tightly bound piles of garden stakes in all sizes. This was not a backyard garden, I thought; it was the Kennedy compound! I couldn't possibly take care of it. But I wanted it with the fierce longing and determination of a child fixated on a toy behind glass. It was more than the beauty of this house making me want it. It was that I thought acquiring it would somehow empower me to do more of what I needed to do. There was so much more I would need to do.

I went to the middle of the yard and stood before the barren garden, imagining myself here in the summer. I saw myself lying on a chaise on a warm afternoon, drinking lemonade, a fat novel open in my lap. Bumblebees, weighted with pollen, would fly from blossom to blossom, drunk-looking with their loopy flight patterns. Or I would lie out at night, watching fireflies; there were fireflies in the Midwest.

And then I realized I was having this fantasy thinking that John would be there, too; in my mind's eye, I'd seen the end of the chaise he lay on, his ankles crossed, his feet bare and tan.

I sat down on the ground and wrapped my arms around my knees. "What do you think?" I asked. Overhead, an airplane flew by. The pilot did not dip his wings. A breeze did not caress my cheek. A bird did not land on a bare branch and sing a song of pointed assent. No whispered words came into my ear, made-up or somehow real. But I did not need such assurances to know what his answer would have been. I had not lost him that much.

I went up to the door on the back porch, hoping I'd be able to see the kitchen, but faded yellow curtains covered the glass completely. And then I heard the sound of someone calling, **"Yoo-hoo!"**

I'm taking it, I thought. **Yoo-hoo, indeed.**

A heavyset woman with short white hair came around the corner. I put her in her late sixties, early seventies. She wore an ill-fitting mustard-colored Realtor's jacket over a black-and-white print dress—you could see that a patch had been removed from over the front pocket of the blazer. Her shoes were red and badly worn. She had been a good-looking woman, in her time; she had beautiful, widely spaced, dark blue eyes and a generous mouth, deep dimples. "I'm Delores," she said, and pressed her hand flat against her chest. "Whew!" She was apparently out of breath from her short walk from the car.

"Betta Nolan." I held out my hand to shake hers. Her grip was surprisingly strong, nearly painful. "Glad to meet you," I said, and had to work hard not to massage my hand.

"How do you like the place?" she said. "Isn't this garden something? I mean, you can just imagine what happens in the summer. Did you see the Miss Kim lilac bushes in the front? Right up next to the front porch?"

"I saw bushes," I said. "I didn't know what they were."

"Well, they're Miss Kim lilacs, and you know they're the ones with the **most** potent scent, knock you right on your keester. I have them myself, just love them. I believe she's got mountain laurel somewhere back here, too; I'm not real sure where." Delores moved over to some bare bushes, frowned at them through the lower part of her bifocals. "This might be it, I don't know. But let's go inside, there's some pictures of the yard in there."

I started toward the back door, and Delores said, "Oh, no, let's go in the front. I like to do it that way."

I followed her around to the front and then up the steps. She was puffing hard by the time she reached the door and began digging in her purse for the keys. "Do you smoke?" she asked, turning around and sizing me up as though she might find the answer by looking.

"No," I said.

"'Jever?"

"Nope."

"Well, you're smart. I finally quit. I've got the lung capacity of a flea on account of those things." She unlocked the door, then pushed it open. "Go ahead," she said.

I stepped into the front hall. There was a musty smell, but it wasn't bad. It reminded me of the old library I'd gone to as a child, so the association for me was one of pleasant anticipation. There were art-glass windows in the entryway that I'd not noticed before. They were lovely, but much simpler in style than the one by the staircase.

"Let me give you the tour," Delores said, stepping around me.

I followed her through a formal dining room, complete with shoulder-high wainscoting. The kitchen had not been updated; the stove and refrigerator were old, and I saw no dishwasher. But why would I need one, for myself alone? The truth was, I had always enjoyed the meditative quality of washing dishes, the scent of soap and the squeak of the sponge, the goings-on outside the kitchen window. Anyway, there was a fine farmer's sink and a generous-sized pantry, both back in vogue.

Upstairs were four relatively small bedrooms with fading cabbage-rose wallpaper—again, old enough to be new. There was a very large bath-room with vintage tiles and a claw-foot tub. In my mind, I was already placing my things. Here would be a library, there an office, there my bedroom, and there a combination guest-and-television room.

"Did you want to see the basement?" Delores asked as I stood cross-armed before the bathtub, imagining myself shoulder-deep in bubbles.

I knew what this question meant. Only serious buyers went into the basement. I wondered what I'd look for. John was the one who knew about electrical systems, heating systems. For one long, wavering moment, I thought, **What am I doing? I can't do this! I need a condominium with water views and a grocery store on-site and a balcony with a container garden and a man wearing a tool belt who's only a phone call away. I need neighbors on the other side**

of a wall so that I won't feel so alone. But that fantasy, though it felt safer, also felt lifeless. And so I said yes, I would like to see the basement.

We started down the stairs, Delores ahead of me and gripping the handrail tightly. At the bottom, she turned, smiling, to ask, "How many's in your family?"

"It's . . . just me." I felt terrible, suddenly. Greedy and foolish.

Delores stared at me. "You would want a house this size all by yourself?"

"You know, it looks bigger from the outside," I said.

"Well, that's true." She stood hesitating for a moment, then said, "Now, listen. I'm going to send you into the basement by yourself for one reason and one reason only. And that is that I can't walk up the dang steps. Would you mind going by yourself?"

"Not at all."

Delores directed me to the door and flipped on the light, and I went down narrow wooden stairs. There was a strong scent of earth; this was an old basement.

Off to the right was a finished laundry room with a high window. There were wooden storage shelves and a deep divided sink. That would do. To the left and beyond were the furnace and the electrical box. I went over to them, my arms crossed over my chest. I had no idea what to look for. Well, there'd be an inspection. That man would know what to look for. I proceeded no farther in the dimness; I wouldn't be needing the space except for storage of the most basic kind.

I came back upstairs quickly and nodded at Delores. "Looks just fine," I said.

"You know what you're looking at down there?"

I laughed. "No."

Delores smiled, a kind and sympathetic smile. "I didn't think so." She reached out to touch my arm. "You divorced, hon?"

"No. I'm not." I moved away from her, into the living room, then to the bottom of the stairs, where I focused on the art glass there, willing myself not to cry.

From behind me, I heard Delores say, "Not a thing in the world wrong with being single. You ask half the married women in the world, they'll tell you that. Probably more'n half, let's face it!"

I turned around, and before I could speak, she said, "Oh. I see." She moved one step closer, then two. "When did he die?" she asked, and when I told her mid-October, she inhaled sharply. "Oh, sweetheart," she said. "This is way too soon for you to buy a house."

"No," I said. "It isn't. Can we go to your office now?"

"'Course we can," she said, though she made no move at all. I walked past her, out the door, then waited for her to follow me. After a few moments, she did. She closed the door and locked it, checked to make sure it was secure. Then, "You just come along with me," she said. "It's not far. It's easy. Just stay right behind me."

I got in the car, wiped away two tears, only two, and pulled away from the curb to follow her ancient white Cadillac. I looked back at the house in the rearview, and claimed it.

My husband, John, age fifty-five, was handed his diagnosis of liver cancer by a newly graduated doctor—John's own had just retired. "As I'm sure you know," the young man had blushingly begun, and John said simply, "Yes." We walked out of the office holding hands and cold to the marrow.

Near the end, I started looking for signs that the inevitable would not be inevitable. I watched the few leaves that refused to give up their green to the demands of the season. I took comfort in the way the sun shone brightly on a day they predicted rain—not a cloud in the sky! I even tried to formulate messages of hope in arrangements of coins on the dresser top—look how they had landed all heads up, what were the **odds**?

I prayed, too, in the way that agnostics do at such times. **Sorry I doubted you; Dear God,**

help us now. I stood shivering on our back patio in the early mornings with my mug of coffee and told whatever might help us that now would be the time. I tried to believe with all my heart that a miracle would come—I knew I needed faith to stand alongside belief. I thought of how after John recovered I would tell everyone that I never gave up hope, and see? But my dreams betrayed me: John, shrunk to the size of a thumb, fell from my purse where I'd been carrying him and was stepped on. In another dream, I took a walk around the block and when I came back, my house was gone.

Three days before he died, John wanted to go to the hospital. In his pleasant private room with a river view, I sat beside him or lay in bed with him, leaving him only to shower or to use the bathroom. The sky stayed gunmetal gray; clouds hung low and threatening; birds flew by in formation, on their way to a kinder climate. Much of the time, John slept, and I studied him as I might a painting: his high cheekbones, his thin but sensuous lips, his overly large earlobes on which he'd once clipped old-lady rhinestone earrings as a finishing touch to his Halloween costume. I watched the subtle play of light on the folds of his blue pajamas—he'd insisted on wearing his own rather than the silly patient gown offered him on admission. In sleep, he kicked off the covers as always, and his winter-white feet were so innocent-looking. I felt fiercely protective of John but utterly helpless as well; when they came to draw blood, my only protest was to look away.

When he was awake, John was lucid, and he returned again and again to making a certain request. He wanted me to move to the middle of the country, to drive on the back roads to a small town I'd never heard of, and start over.

It was something we'd talked about doing together, and just before John got sick we'd invited a Realtor over to our Beacon Hill brownstone for what turned out to be a thrilling appraisal. We'd been ready to put things into motion, and we were excited in some fundamental way we'd not been for a long time. We appreciated the rich contentment of a good marriage and old habits; but there was something evocative and irresistible about our new plans; even the minor anxiety we felt about leaving Boston, where we'd always lived but for our college years, was more compelling than disturbing.

All of this had been my idea originally; born of what I'd call midlife stirrings. By that I mean there'd been no crisis, just a growing awareness that there were other ways of living that I longed to explore. I'd had my head down for a long time, doing something satisfying but ultimately repetitious. Now I wanted to go in a different direction. John had similar feelings and so had warmed quickly to my idea. We agreed that he would give up his psychiatric practice, and I would stop writing children's books. We had both done well in our careers; we could afford to retire early if we wanted to, or we would find something altogether different to do.

We knew little about the Midwest—we had confined our travels to either coast and to Europe. But we had always been charmed by the people we'd met from there, and it seemed the right place to start a new life: exotic, at least to us, but not as difficult as, say, Prague. John confessed that he'd always wanted to own a little neighborhood grocery store and be on a first-name basis with all the customers—the Midwest seemed the right place for that. For my part, I told John I'd always fantasized about owning a store with a wide variety of beautiful and disparate things: unusual jewelry, handmade quilts and pottery, beautiful cookware and vintage kitchen linens, ultra-luxurious bath products, journals made of handmade paper, and small watercolors, exquisitely framed. What a Woman Wants, John suggested I call it. He leaned back in his chair that night, smiling and dreamy-eyed. "Maybe we really will open stores," he said. "Or maybe we'll sit around on some great big front porch and do not much at all." Either sounded good to both of us.

John wanted to be sure I did what we'd talked

about, even without him. "Follow through on this; it's a good idea," he told me. "It will be right for you. You're going to have all kinds of people giving you advice. You're going to be tempted to follow some script, to show some sense of propriety. Don't do it. It will give me peace to know that what you will do is exactly what we talked about." I began to cry and he took my hand and looked into my eyes. "You're stronger than you know, Betta; you can do this," he said. "I've seen it happen so often where one person dies and then the other dies in spirit. Don't let that happen to you."

"I won't," I said, though I did not exactly believe myself.

"And Betta? Try hard to make friends in the new place." He lay back against his pillow and sighed. "I took you away from people. We kept too much to ourselves. I let you neglect your need for others."

"No, you didn't," I said. But he put his hand over mine and said emphatically, **"I did."**

I reached up to smooth one of the wild hairs in his eyebrow and said softly, "I didn't mind it so much, you know."

On the last morning in the hospital, when we lay together in his bed holding hands and watching a glorious sunrise, he said, "I want you, even in sorrow—especially in sorrow—to find joy. Will you try?"

"Yes," I said, watching the clouds lighten and wondering how that could possibly happen.

"I'll help you," he said. He was reading my mind again.

"Okay." I leaned over and kissed the top of his head, thinking that if a forehead could look weary, his did.

A few hours later, he rested quietly as I sat in the Naugahyde chair next to his bed. I was reading aloud, poems by Neruda. A light rain was falling and you could hear the distant rumble of thunder. There was a name for such thunder, and I had been thinking I would ask John what it was as soon as I finished the poem. But I heard his breathing slow, then rattle. I looked quickly over at him, and he smiled at me, then closed his eyes. I watched for his chest to rise again. It did, several times, and then it did not. I took his hand and leaned closer to him. Inside my own chest, it felt as though someone were beating a rug. "John?" I said. I shook him. "John?" I felt a mounting sense of desperation. I had a question. I had one more question. **"John?"** One more question, and then if it would be all right, if I could just have him until the day was over. Just a few more hours. But he was gone. I clasped my hand tightly over my mouth and felt a trembling that started deep inside move out to make all of me shake. I had a mighty impulse, it truly was mighty, to rise to my feet and howl. To overturn the chair and nightstand, to rip at my clothes, to bring down the very walls around us. But of course I did not do that. I pulled an elemental sense of outrage back inside and smoothed it down. I forced something far too big into something far too small, and this made for a surprising and unreasonable weight, as mercury does. I noticed sounds coming from my throat, little unladylike grunts. I saw that everything I'd ever imagined about what it would feel like **when** was pale. Was wrong. Was the shadow and not the mountain. And then, "It's all right," I said, quickly. "It's all right." To whom? I wondered later.

I closed the slender volume of poems and sat still for a long moment. Then I leaned over to lay my head in the familiar hollow below his shoulder. After a while, I rang the bell for a nurse. I hoped Lonnie would come. She had been his favorite. And indeed it was Lonnie who came, and before she did anything, she embraced me. "He was such a gentleman," she said.

"Yes," I answered.

"You were very lucky," she said, and to this I did not reply.

They let me say a final goodbye, and I put his clothes into the little suitcase we'd brought with us. I opened his bedside drawer and took out his watch and his glasses and his wallet. There was also a blue plastic denture cup, which was odd, because he had no dentures. When I looked inside it, I found three slips of paper. One said **green bowl.** Another, **carbon.** And the third I wasn't able to quite make out, but I thought it said **gingerbread.** All of this I put into the suitcase as well.

I took a cab home because I did not trust my driving. It had stopped raining; the sun was bright. "Finally nice out, huh?" the driver asked. He was a middle-aged man, probably close to John's age, wearing a Harvard sweatshirt.

I swallowed, mumbled agreement, and pulled John's suitcase closer to me on the seat.

The driver's eyes sought out mine in the rearview mirror. "Let me tell you, **I've** had better days," he said, and waited for me to ask why. But I stayed silent, stared out the window at the beautiful synchronicity of the rowers on the Charles. They would not be out there much longer.

When I arrived home, I wept, of course, walked around from room to room sobbing from a place deep in my gut. I cried until my eyes swelled shut, and then I slept, a black, dreamless sleep from which I awoke amazingly refreshed, at least until I remembered.

I made calls to arrange for John's cremation and memorial service in a kind of removed way that I realized was necessary for performing such a task. I'd argued against his cremation even though I had asked that he do the same for me, should I be the one to go first. But that had been when our deaths were an abstraction. When it became clear that John was going to die, I'd changed my mind—I wanted him to be buried. "I want a place to **find** you," I'd told him, and he'd said, "In time, you'll find the place." He'd asked me to release him to the ocean as soon as I got the ashes, and I'd promised I would.

I stayed in the house for a week after that, wearing John's shirts during the day and John's pajamas at night. Sometimes I felt on the far edge of reality, unable to understand the simplest things: an exuberant voice on the radio, an advertisement in the mail. The phone rang and I would look at it as if I were a visitor from a distant planet, wondering what sort of animal was making that irritating, repetitive noise.

Other times, I went numb, as though vultures had landed inside and picked me clean. At those times, I did not quite taste or see or hear or touch or feel. And at those times, I thought cautiously, **Is that it, then? Am I through crying? Am I healing already?** And then would come another tidal wave of pain, nearly nauseating in its force, that had me pounding and pounding on the kitchen table. I knew it was a common story, the loss of a husband, widowhood, but it was of no use to me to know how many had experienced this before me. I remembered an

eighty-nine-year-old woman who'd lost her husband many years ago telling me in her shaky
voice, **You still sleep on your half of the bed.** I
learned that it was true.

Then around seven-thirty one evening, I suddenly became ravenously hungry. I didn't want
to cook and I didn't want to go somewhere I'd
been with John, so I walked to an Italian restaurant I'd never been to. It seemed darker outside
than usual, the light from the streetlamps moody
and insubstantial. I supposed this might be because of a thin layer of fog. But more likely, I
thought, it was because I was walking in the
dark by myself, something I'd not done in a long
time. I could smell the sweet decay of fall, but it
was warm, and I opened my coat to the moist
night air.

The restaurant was loud and bright, the tables
covered with the commonplace but always comforting red-and-white-checked tablecloths. Tiny
white lights ran across the ceiling and down the
walls. There were beautiful wooden booths with
wide benches and high backs, and I saw couples
sitting there together, some with their heads
practically touching, some ignoring each other
in the tired way of many long-marrieds. I concentrated on looking at the bored couples so that
I did not have to see intimate smiles, quick ca-
resses, the open joy of those who clearly appreciated the person they sat across from.

I ordered eggplant Parmesan to go, then leaned against the wall near the hostess station to wait for it. I checked my watch every few minutes. When thoughts of John and the resultant sting of tears came, I willed them away, thinking, **Later.** It was like trying to hold back a full-body sneeze.

When my order was ready, I paid and walked quickly toward home. Outside the Bank of Boston, I saw Burt the Bum (not an unkind appellation—it was what he called himself) sitting in his usual spot to the left of the door, wearing his usual outfit: a suit with a T-shirt, running shoes, and a battered fedora. I'd heard rumors that he'd been a very successful stockbroker at one time, but then he began having a little difficulty with that old bugaboo, reality. "Hey!" he called out. "Where've you been?"

I hesitated, then walked slowly over to him. "John got very sick."

"That's too bad. Is he okay now?" He leaned closer to the bag I carried, and sniffed. "Leftovers?"

"He died," I said, and the simplicity of it stunned me. Two words. Whole story.

Bert's eyes widened. He took off his hat. "Aw, man. That's a pisser. I always liked him."

"And he you." It was true. I used to grow impatient sometimes, waiting for John to finish his conversations with Bert so that we could go home. John had appreciated what he called Bert's clear-mindedness, though it seemed obvious to me that Bert's mind was far from clear. Still, he was unfailingly interesting, and he had the habit of truth about him.

"So . . . how are you doing?" Bert asked.

I shrugged, then handed him the bag of food. "Would you like this?"

He shook his head. "Just lost my appetite."

"Yeah, me too." But I opened the bag and looked inside.

"Probably pretty good, though," Bert said.

"Have you eaten today?"

"I had a donut."

"When?"

"Yesterday morning."

"That's not today." I took out the foil dish, lifted the lid, and handed him the plastic fork. "Here. Eat some."

He looked up at me, put his hat back on, and took a bite. "Not bad," he said. "Sure you don't want some?"

"No, you go ahead." It did smell good. I leaned against the building, pulled my coat closer around me.

"Too bad I drank all my wine," Bert said. He chewed thoughtfully, then leaned back against the wall, put his fist to his diaphragm, and belched. "Oh. Sorry." He looked up at me. "Guess life goes on."

"I guess it does." I smiled at him. And then, suddenly, I blurted out, "I'm going to move."

"Really. Where to?"

"I don't know. I'm going to sell my house and put my stuff in storage and drive to the middle of the country. When I find some small town I like, I'll buy a house."

"Uh-huh. You think that's a good idea?"

"John wanted to do it, too. We talked about it a lot. He asked me to do it without him."

"Oh. Well, that's all right then." He took another bite of eggplant, spoke with his mouth full. "This from Agostino's?"

"Yes."

"They're all right, but Donatello's is better. Donatello's puts a little something extra in their sauce, maybe allspice. Don't get me wrong, it's not that this isn't good."

"You enjoy it," I said, moving away from him.

"You going?"

"Yeah."

"What are you going to do tonight?"

"I don't know. I . . . don't know."

"You get lonesome, you get too sad, you come and sit with me. I wouldn't mind anything you did."

I smiled at him.

"I mean it!"

Something occurred to me. I had always thought maybe we should invite Bert to our house—to have a proper meal, to take a shower. But John had thought it was a bad idea, so we'd never offered. But then I said, "I live two blocks down, Bert. Would you like to come over?"

"Thanks, but I wouldn't enjoy it, Betta. No offense."

"I could offer you a guest room for a night."

"I'm used to this."

"I just thought you'd like—"

"I wouldn't enjoy it, Betta."

"Okay." I drew in a long breath. "So, I guess I'll get going then."

He struggled up from his sitting position and offered me his hand. I shook it, then wiped away tears that had begun spilling down my face.

"I'll tell you something, Betta. I'm not going to worry about you. You know why?"

"Why?"

"Because you'll be fine. That's why. You can't see it yet, but I can." He tapped the side of his head with his middle finger. "Psychic. Seriously."

"Okay, Bert. So long. Take care of yourself." I dug in my purse for my wallet and held out a twenty-dollar bill. "Here you go."

He looked at the bill, sadness in his eyes. "Betta. Don't insult me."

"What do you mean?"

"Put that away."

"We've always given you money!"

"Yeah, a five, that's all right, buys me a coffee

and a Danish. A twenty, you're saying you feel sorry for me."

"Would you like a five?" I asked.

He lifted his chin and pooched out his lips, considering. Then, "Yeah, sure," he said. And when I gave him the money, he shoved it in his pocket without looking at me.

"Goodbye, Bert." I turned to go.

"Hold on." He stood up, put his hat back on. "Good luck to you, Betta. And . . . I just wanted to say that I sure liked him a lot. He was a rare man. You know. Just . . . a rare man."

"Yes. Thank you." I walked quickly away. Some analytical and oddly interested part of me noticed the specific characteristics of my pain: centered in the middle, making for a weight that felt like someone was sitting on me. I squeezed my hands into fists and thought, **I'll go home and make some scrambled eggs. Maybe I'll put some cream cheese in there.** After that, a hot bath. Jasmine-scented oils. **Eine Kleine Nachtmusik** in the background, silk pajamas. I looked up into the night sky, at the shrouded stars. "How's that?" I asked.

The service for John near the end of October had been a small but elegant affair involving the usual mix of humorous and poignant homages. Everyone who attended—a few friends and a large number of people from the hospital where John practiced—knew of my plans to move right away, and everyone advised me not to. But their advice about staying had not seemed as right as the immediate acceptance I'd gotten from Bert about leaving. And it was not what John had advised.

After the service, I drove to the ocean to scatter John's ashes. But I didn't put them all in the water—I hoped he wouldn't mind a few alterations. I buried a pinch of him in the earth. I released a bit of him to the air. Some of him I put fire to again—I lit a match to a small pile of ashes. A little bit of him I swallowed. Then, weeping, I took off my shoes and walked to the shoreline to let the rest of him go. I stood shivering for a while, watching the water take him— despite the odd warmth of the day, the sand was ice-cold. I put my hand over my heart and said, "I love you." I said, "My sweet, sweet, sweetheart." Then I said, "I'll see you," and started back for the car. Behind me, I heard the raucous and eager cries of the gulls. I didn't turn around to see if they were near him. The ashes had not really been him, after all. And I understood, too, that he was right in asking to be cremated. For if he was nowhere, he could be everywhere. As in, with me.

On November first I listed the house with the agency John and I had called, and it sold immediately, without advertising. The real estate market in Boston was crazy; there were waiting lists of people wanting brownstones. I received seven offers over my asking price, and all of the bidders seemed willing to try to top one another forever. One of the couples was in their late twenties. "Where did they get this kind money?" I asked Victoria, the Realtor, and she shrugged. Which I assumed meant none of my business.

By the end of the week, the house went to a late-thirtyish couple with a young child. One point nine million, a cash deal, when John and I had paid a hundred forty thousand. I didn't meet the people; for many reasons, I didn't want to. I arranged for the lawyer to represent me at the closing only three weeks hence, then made the call to a mover to pack up my things and put them in storage.

"You're lucky," the woman on the phone told me. "We've just had a cancellation. Do you want us to come on Thursday?" It was Tuesday. I thought Thursday was probably too soon, but when I cast about for reasons to stay longer, I couldn't think of any. It would feel good to keep moving, I thought. I didn't want to stay in a place that only reminded me of him. I wanted to go to a new place. I had been ready even before.

On my last night in Boston, my neighbor Sheila Murphy came over with a gift. It was beautifully wrapped—pink-and-gold floral paper and wide, satiny pink ribbon, and at first I worried about having to make a fuss over whatever it was. I felt at the bottom of my own resources; I had nothing to give. But it turned out the gift was not from her but from John. This was so like him, a corny, bighearted man who quoted aphorisms like "We make a living by what we get; we make a life by what we give." Even when he was very ill, he still had sent me flowers. I had once answered the door to a glorious bouquet, looked for a card and found none, then turned to see John sitting on the sofa, smiling. He had no longer been able to walk around very much, but he could still use the phone.

And now here was his final gift. I began to cry and winced as I put a tissue up to my face. My right eye had developed a minor infection from wiping away tears with everything from hankies to paper towels to envelopes from condolence cards. "Sit down with me for a minute," Sheila said.

We moved to the family room sofa, and I sat sobbing beside her, she patting my back awkwardly. It didn't last long—in less than a minute, I straightened up and took in a deep breath. "Sorry," I said, and she said, "Don't be ridiculous. You don't have to apologize." She had tears in her eyes, too.

I looked at the gift in my lap. "Do you know what this is?"

"Sort of."

"What is it?"

"Well, it's . . . you know, that one time when I stayed with him when you went out for groceries? He spent the whole time writing out things on little slips of paper. I don't know what they were. But that's what this is."

I thought of the papers I'd found in John's hospital drawer. "Just . . . words?" I asked.

She shrugged. "Don't know. He asked me not to read them, so I didn't. He just sat there and wrote these things and then folded the papers and put them in a cigar box. That's what this is, it's just a cigar box, but John asked me to wrap it in something beautiful—he said you liked pink."

I nodded, miserable.

"Well, anyway, I just wanted to bring you this." She looked around the room, then at me. "Oh, Betta. How are you?"

"Fine," I said, in a bright and automatic way that made us both smile. "Really," I said. "I'm okay."

"You've lost weight."

"Well, might as well have one good thing happening!"

"No, but seriously, you've got to take care of yourself. Did you eat today?"

"Yes."

"All three meals?"

"Uh-huh. Yup."

"What did you eat?"

I sighed. "I had bad cholesterol for breakfast, mad cow disease for lunch, and mercury poisoning for dinner."

She frowned, then said, "Oh, Wagner's? The salmon special?"

"Yes."

"How was it? Randy and I have been meaning to go there."

"It was all right." I tried not to resent her identifying herself as part of a couple in front of me, who no longer was.

"I can't believe you're moving so soon!" Sheila said.

"I know. It's hard to explain, but I think it's the best thing to do."

She stared into her lap and fidgeted with her watchband. "Betta, I have to tell you, I think it's just too radical. Randy and I were talking, and—"

"It's too late to change anything," I said. "I appreciate your concern—I know how crazy this must seem to you, but it's what I really want to do." I recalled the time Sheila and I had run into each other at Copley Place and then gone to lunch at Legal Seafood. We'd talked about a woman who lived in the building next to us who had lost her husband in a drowning accident. He was thirty-eight. It had been almost seven months, and Sheila and I—it chilled me to remember it—had apparently decided that the time for mourning was up. No more grieving; Annie needed to get **out there.** "I mean, couldn't she take a cooking class or something at the Cambridge Center?" I'd said. I saw it as though it were yesterday, the two of us having our sanctimonious lunch at Legal Seafood, the restaurant's blinds pulled against the bright sun, a table full of businessmen next to us, exulting over their **frutti di mare.** "They have wonderful classes there," I'd said, "and you get to eat the dinners. And it's too early for her to date, I suppose, but she could make some new friends."

And Sheila had said, "Well, of course. Or go to a movie with a girlfriend, or shopping, or anything but continue to stare at your own bedroom walls." "Exactly," I'd said. "This is just too long to . . . well, I don't know if **wallow** is the right word." "I think it **is,**" Sheila had said, around her bite of lobster roll. How cruel we'd been, sitting there with our shopping bags full of new fall clothes, deciding how someone else should repair the rent in her own heart. I wondered whether I would be able to live up to my own ruthlessly dictated standards.

In a more conciliatory tone—Sheila was, after all, only trying to help—I told her, "I can always move back if it doesn't work out."

"But not here. Not to this house. This is a beautiful place. I thought about buying it myself."

"Oh?" I looked at her, not quite sure how to respond, and we both laughed.

"I'm sorry," Sheila said. "That must have sounded—"

"It's okay," I said. And then, "Well, so . . ."

"Right." She slid her hands into her pants pockets. It was clear to both of us that there was nothing more to say. Again we smiled awkwardly at each other, and Sheila moved to the door. She started to open it, then turned suddenly to face me. "I just want to say . . . you know, I wish I could be more **with** you in all this. I wish we were closer. You're kind of hard to get to know—not your **fault,** I don't mean that, but you and John were sort of . . . well, you were complete unto yourselves. I guess that's what I'd say. We wanted to invite you to more things—other people did, too—but—"

"I know. I know how insular we were. I thought of calling you sometimes, to actually plan something, you know—lunch, a matinee . . ."

"I would have liked that. I know neither you nor John have family. It just seems like it might help, now, for you to have some really close friends. I mean, you have no one, right? Randy and I—"

"John and I do have really close friends, actually. They just don't live here." **Lie.** But this kind of talk was only making me feel worse. I wanted to go to bed. Well, I wanted John.

"Oh! Well, I'm **sorry**! I guess I never saw anyone—"

"Mostly we visited them." Again a function of writing fiction. In my mind's eye, I began seeing these friends clearly: friendly-looking people, all with good teeth. Permanent residents of Martha's Vineyard; we liked riding bikes with them there.

"I see. Well. I'd better go. Keep in touch."

"I will." **Lie.**

"Do you have a phone yet?"

"No, not yet. But I'll call you when I get a number." I doubted I'd even do that.

"Okay, so . . . good luck, Betta."

"Thank you." I closed the door behind Sheila and watched her walk home. There was nothing wrong with her. She was a perfectly nice woman. I had seen her carrying things into her house that I'd wanted to ask her about sometimes: a footstool I liked, a potted plant with beautiful feathery foliage that I'd wanted the name of. Once she came home with a ridiculous number of grocery bags, I didn't know why, and I'd stood at the window watching her carry them in and had made no move to help her. I was shy, but this did not absolve me. Sheila was right; it would have been nice to have a really good friend now, someone I could be completely and utterly myself around. But I was out of the habit. I'd met John right after I finished school and moved back home, and I'd given myself over completely to him without regret. People deeply in love almost always do that at first—abandon the rest of their friends in favor of being with each other—but John and I just never really stopped. It was the downside of having such a good relationship; we were so compatible that we were lazy about starting and maintaining outside friendships. My housemates in college had been as close to me as I imagine sisters might have been—closer, probably—but I had lost touch with all three of them soon after we graduated. It was a pity I'd let that happen, but there was no sense brooding about it now.

I went over to the sofa, picked up the present, and opened it. Inside the cigar box were more slips of paper with mysterious phrases written on them. **Eclipse,** I read. **Old CDs.** It looked like there were hundreds of them. **Mists. Split rail.** What did these mean? Nothing. I began to grow angry—why would he have left these things for me without making it clear what I was meant to do with them? And then it occurred to me that he had not been lucid to the end after all, as I'd told so many people, as I'd told myself. His last gift to me had been only precious bits of nonsense.

I stashed the papers in a deep drawer of the Chinese chest we kept up against one end of the living room. It was the piece of furniture John and I had always loved best of anything we owned, for its elegance and mystery, for its beautifully painted birds and flowers. Sometimes we'd hidden things in there to be found later as surprises—either to ourselves or to each other. I'd found a polished amethyst once, and hadn't remembered putting it there, nor had John. I'd put a tiny wren's nest in one drawer that John hadn't discovered for months, and a watch I'd meant for a Christmas gift that he'd found minutes after I'd hid it there. John had put in a jade necklace he'd bought for me, a poem he'd liked and torn out of **The New Yorker,** and once, tickets for us to go to a play, which he'd forgotten about and that I almost hadn't found in time. I looked now for something new, but there was only a feather, tucked so far inside a drawer I figured it had been there when we first bought the chest.

I turned out all the lights but one and headed upstairs. I felt my aloneness like a coat. You think you get used to death in the dying. But after the dying is done, you see how the end is the beginning.

I bathed, listening to Mozart, and wept briefly, the bathtub being a convenient place for tears. I climbed into bed and tried to read for a while, though I found it difficult to concentrate. Finally, I turned out the light, folded my hands over my chest, drew in a deep breath, and exhaled. And it came to me.

One Sunday, when John and I were browsing in an antiques store, I'd found a small green bowl I liked very much. It was just the right size for making scrambled eggs, and I told John this as I held it up before him. "Buy it," he said, and I said no. I had a great fondness for bowls, and I'd collected far too many already. Among those wrapped in newspaper in the attic were a tiny black-and-white-striped bowl, a butter-yellow antique mixing bowl, one that had been hand-painted with violets, and more than a few sets of nesting bowls. I put the green bowl back on the shelf, but I kept looking at it. "Buy it!" he said, but again I said no. He picked it up, ready to get it for me, but I told him not to. The next day, I decided I wanted it after all and went back to the store, but it was gone. It had cost two dollars.

So, what was his message to me, on that little slip of paper? Take the green bowl. Take all the green bowls; love what you love without apology. I went down to the chest and pulled out other slips of paper. Those that I had been unable to decipher, at least not then. But here was the glory: We were not done with each other yet.

Henckley Realtors was in a strip mall a few miles away, along with a pizza parlor, a pet store, an exercise club, a beauty shop, and a Laundromat. The place had the dispiriting air of all strip malls, but at least the businesses weren't chain stores. I sat in the car for a couple of minutes. Was I **sure**? Sure enough, I decided.

When I came in the door, I saw Delores seated at the only desk, her jacket slung over the back of her chair. Philodendrons grew down the sides of a filing cabinet. There was a card table covered by an embroidered tablecloth, holding a Mr. Coffee and various-sized ceramic mugs. One said I WORKED MY ASS OFF, BUT IT CAME BACK AND FOUND ME. A round wooden table had three chairs grouped around it—the conference center, I presumed. Delores was on the phone, and her brow was furrowed. "Now, that's not what I—"

she said. "Well, if you want, I—" She listened for a long while, then said, "No, I should think that—" She listened again, then leaned forward in her chair and yelled, "LYDIA! Stop your yammering and let me get a word in! Now, the woman who's interested is standing right in front of me. Do you want her to think that you're—" She sighed. "Yes . . . all right, Lydia. Hold on and I'll see."

Delores put her hand over the mouthpiece and looked up at me. "This is the owner, Lydia Samuels, I've got here on the phone. Just in case you hadn't figured that out. She wants to meet you. Won't sell the house to anyone she hasn't met. Would you be willing? She's over at the Rose McNair Home, it's pretty close by. Won't take us more than ten, fifteen minutes to get there."

"I guess that would be all right. But you haven't even told me the price!"

"Well, I know that. You forgot to ask and I forgot to tell you. **And** I forgot to show you the pictures of the garden in bloom! We're a hell of a team. The house is listed at three hundred and fifty thousand. We'll get to all the financing options, and there are some other things I want to talk to you about, too. But first I had to call Lydia. I promised her that if I showed it, I'd let her know who to. And now she's gone and—" She turned her attention back to the phone.

"What? . . . All right, yes, I suppose I could do that. What kind do you want? . . . With or without nuts? . . . All right. So let's say, five?" Delores looked up at me and I nodded. "Fine, Lydia, we'll see you then."

Shaking her head, Delores hung up the phone. "You know, she is something, that old woman. She's ninety-five years old now, and she still scares the bejesus out of me." She gestured to the chair in front of her desk. "Have a seat."

I moved to the chair and picked up a small pile of newspaper clippings that were resting there. "Did you want these?"

"Oh, that." She reached for the clippings and shoved them into a desk drawer. "Recipes. Clip them out every day and never make a single one. You do that?"

I nodded. "I used to."

"You will again," she said, and her words seemed so full of something beyond what she had said. I looked closely at her, both afraid and hoping she'd impart some particular wisdom, but she was busy reading a listing, I assumed for the house we'd just looked at.

But what she said when she looked up was, "Now, this is a condo, which I think might be much more appropriate for you. What do you say we have a look at it, before you make an offer on a three-hundred-and-fifty-thousand-dollar house that I know will not come down one cent."

I shook my head no.

She raised her eyebrows—I saw that one was drawn in longer than the other. "Don't like condos?"

"No, actually, I don't. I'm interested in the house. The price is all right."

"Well, let me just tell you about this one other little house I have. Just darling. I think you'd like it, too, and it's not so big. Or so much money."

I said nothing.

"You want to see it?" Delores reached for her jacket and began to put it on. "It has the cutest little kitchen—but fully equipped!"

"This will be a full-price offer," I said. "And it will be a cash deal. And I am ready to write a check."

Delores sat back in her chair, her jacket half on. She said nothing for a moment; we sat staring at each other. And then she finished slipping her jacket on and said, "You know, if I didn't already like you, I might not like you."

"That's all right," I said. "I understand."

"Everything will depend on what Lydia decides. I just have to tell you that. There'll be nothing I can do to influence her, one way or the other. Are you ready to meet her?"

I said I was.

From the back room, I heard a meow, and an ancient, overweight tuxedo cat wandered out, yawning. Delores hesitated, her hand on her hip, and said, "Let me feed Boodles, and then we'll go—as you can see, she's wasting away. And don't let me forget to stop at Mick's to get Lydia her turtle sundae. We might want to get one ourselves. Might as well be fortified."

Let the old lady be stubborn, I thought. **I am, too.**

We found Lydia Samuels in an otherwise deserted community room. It was a large multiwindowed space furnished with several big wooden tables and chairs and an ancient studio piano. The place smelled not unpleasantly of some sort of cleaning agent. Fake-flower arrangements sat on doilies at the center of each table, and glaringly amateurish artwork lined the walls: lighthouses, bowls of fruit, wicker chairs on front porches. A portrait of a girl with a potato-like nose.

Lydia sat slumped in a wheelchair near one of the windows, her back to the view. She was tiny; from a distance, she looked like a child impersonating an old lady. "Pleased to meet you!" she said loudly from halfway across the room. When we reached her, she squinted up at me and said, "There's not a goddamn thing wrong with my hearing."

"Good," I said. Or with her voice—it was surprisingly low and strong. A man's voice, almost.

"Just so you know and don't start shouting at me like I'm some old fool." She crossed her legs and leaned back in her chair. She wore a brightly patterned housedress, a tan cardigan sweater, and white sneakers with thick gray kneesocks—all of which looked long overdue for the laundry. The home was very clean, but I supposed it was a bit of a challenge to get Lydia Samuels to hand over her clothes—or anything else. Halfway down her nose was an ancient pair of cat-eye glasses, powder blue with rhinestone trim—they would work for stylish irony but for the grease stains on the lenses and the Band-Aid that had been wrapped around one stem for a quick repair. She smelled of baby food and, more distantly, of urine. Her hair, what little there was of it, had been pulled up into a ponytail with orange yarn. Crisscrossed bobby pins anchored the sides. She had several long white whiskers on her chin—they stood out in the strong light of the window.

"Here's your sundae," Delores said, and handed the rapidly melting dessert to Lydia, who ate it with astonishing speed. She handed the empty container to Delores to dispose of. Then, favoring the back of her hand over the napkin to wipe the chocolate off her chin, she told me, "Give me your hand."

I offered her my right hand, and she shook her head impatiently. "No, the other one."

I gave her my left, palm up, and she held it in her own hands, firmly but gently. Her skin was dry and papery but warm. She sniffed at my hand as a dog might, tentatively but knowledgeably, and Delores and I exchanged a quick glance. Then she took off her glasses and peered closely into my palm. "Long life. Given to dreaming. Oh, lucky in love, I see. And you . . ." She grew quiet, looking even more closely. She stayed so still I thought for a moment she had fallen asleep. But then she dropped my hand and sat back in her chair. "Price of the house just went up," she said, and cackled—there was no other word for it. She put her glasses back on carefully. Then she clasped her hands on her lap, and one thumb began rapidly tapping the other. A passerby might have thought, **Parkinson's.** I saw it for what it was: **I'm waaaaiting.**

"Lydia," Delores said. "You can't do that!"

Lydia gripped the sides of her wheelchair and turned a fierce gaze onto Delores. Her eyes were beady and dark, her mouth turned dramatically downward. "I can. I'm the owner."

"It went up to what?" I asked, and Lydia turned slowly to me, spider to the fly. She was sweet-faced now. "Went up to three hundred and sixty. Five."

"Sold," I said, though I could hear Delores's silent objection.

"I meant, three hundred and seventy," Lydia said, and I said no. And then she seemed to suddenly tire; she sighed and said, "All right. Take it, then. Three hundred and fifty."

"You mean . . . sixty-five?" I said, and heard Delores inhale sharply. Later, we would have a conversation.

"Three hundred fifty!" Lydia said. "And that's my last offer!"

I looked over at Delores, who shrugged.

"Deal," I said, and offered Lydia my hand to seal the agreement. But she waved me away.

"Take me back to my room," she said. "I want to watch the news."

After Lydia was settled in front of her television, Delores and I said goodbye and started out of her room. But then, "You," she said to me. "Come over here."

I went to stand before her, bracing for another price increase. She looked up at me, her brown eyes watery and searching. "He will come," she said finally. I felt a cold grip at the back of my neck.

"What do you mean?" I cleared my throat, smiled.

She leaned her head around me. "Don't block the television. Get out of the way." She sniffed, pulled a wadded-up tissue from her sleeve, dabbed at her nose, regarded with interest an ad for a sporty car. Then she yelled into the hall, "Thanks for the sundae, Dorothy! Bring me another one when you come with the papers for me to sign. Bring me two!"

"It's Delores."

"Oh, what's the difference? You know who I'm talking to!"

Delores turned wearily toward me. "What do you say we go and get some dinner? And a drink."

I nodded, then turned to Lydia. "Goodbye," I said. "I'm glad to have met you. I love your house, and I want you to know I'll—"

"Enough," she said.

Delores and I sat in an overly dark booth at the Chuck Wagon Round Up, chosen in part because it was right next door to a moderately priced motel where Delores had suggested I'd be comfortable staying. She pulled a tiny flashlight out of her suitcase-sized purse so that we could read the menu.

"That's handy," I said.

"You have no idea how often I use it," she said. "I've got a little bitty fan in here, too, and the **most** adorable tool kit." We placed identical orders for dinner: barbecue ribs, baked potatoes, salads with peppercorn dressing, and Bacardi cocktails.

"I have to apologize for Lydia," Delores said. "At the very least, I should have prepared you better. Still learning how to sell houses, I guess." She pulled off her clip-on earrings and threw them in her purse, then leaned in closer to tell me, "My shoes are off, too. And my girdle's not far behind."

"How long have you been in real estate?" I asked her.

"Oh, hell, it's just a hobby. Like macramé. I got into it a few years ago, after my husband died. I'm not very active, as I'm sure you've deduced. Don't have more than four or five clients at a time. Lydia will be my biggest sale. I got her house because nobody else would work with her."

"Was she ever married?" I asked.

"Yeah. Guy by the name of Lucifer Beelzebub."

I laughed, then said, "I hope you don't mind my asking, but what did your husband die of?"

"Heart attack. Out mowing the lawn one hot day, and that was that. I'd just gone in to make him some lemonade, and when I came back out, there he was. And do you know, I started laughing at him lying there, facedown? Thought he was goofing around." She shook her head, remembering. "First thing I thought when I turned him over was, **Damn it, I told him he was**

getting too old for a push mower! I was so mad at him! I tried CPR, but it was too late. I was crying and pushing on his chest and yelling at him, saying, 'You **stop** this! Now come on, come on!' Oh, it was awful. I ran in the house and called 911 and then ran back out to keep trying until they came—that was the longest wait of my life. Only good thing was that he died instantly— never knew what hit him. How about you?"

"Cancer," I said, and felt inside a curious puckering, a drawing inward and upward. I was grateful for the waitress coming to the table to deliver our drinks. She was a young and very pretty blond woman, an engagement ring sparkling on her hand. "**Here** you go," she said. And then, "Hey, Delores. A hundred sixty-eight and a half more hours."

"Good for you, sweetheart," Delores said. "Still time to change your mind."

"Oh, I'm not changing my mind," the woman said. She walked away toward the kitchen, the lightness of new love in her step.

"You know," Delores said, "her fiancé put her ring in a Kentucky Fried Chicken biscuit—that's how he proposed. I thought that was pretty dangerous—she could have swallowed it, for Pete's sake! But Cindy said he was watching her real carefully. In fact, she said she was worried he was going to break up with her—he kept staring at her in this really odd way."

I nodded, looking down into my drink. My own proposal had come at the end of a glorious Saturday. John and I had gone out to breakfast, then for a walk along the Charles, then to look in antiques stores out in the western suburbs, then to a funky restaurant in Cambridge for dinner. Just as we were getting ready to leave, John asked quietly, "Do I have anything in my teeth?" He raised his lips, chimplike.

"No, " I said, giggling. "Do I?" I showed him my own teeth.

"No," he said. And then his face changed and he rose quickly from his chair. I remember thinking that he'd gotten suddenly ill and was rushing off to the bathroom. But what happened was, he came to kneel beside me.

"What are you **do**ing?" I asked. "John?"

"Shhhhhh!" he said. "I'm about to propose!" And he pulled the black velvet ring box from his pocket.

"Yes," I said, and he said, "I didn't ask yet." And I said he didn't have to, and then I kissed him and the people sitting around us began to clap and I thought I might die of happiness on the floor of an Ethiopian restaurant.

"You okay?" Delores asked.

I sighed. "Yeah. It's just . . . I resent the time of John's dying. If I'd been older, I think I would feel more resigned—I'd hope to just enjoy what was left of my life. And if I'd been younger, I might have remarried and had children—John and I couldn't. As it is . . ."

"I don't imagine it's ever easy," Delores said. "For me, the hardest thing was not to turn bitter. At first, there's all this attention, casseroles and pies and cards and phone calls. But then it's just you, and it starts to sink in, all that you've lost. Funny, for the longest time it seemed like I was surprised that it didn't **all** go away, that Carson didn't come walking back in the door saying, 'Well, sweetheart, that was a real good job you did on my funeral, now what's for dinner?' But they don't come back and they don't come back and it takes a toll. You can get mad. And then you can take it out on the whole world. I've seen that happen often enough. But the alternative is . . . well, you can speak the truth and shame the devil. You can tell people you need a little help and then let yourself take what people offer—even though it's hard to do! It is **hard** to do! And you can let yourself be gentle, which takes a lot of strength. But look, honey, it seems to me that you are very strong—look at what you're doing!"

"Well, mostly I'm honoring a request my husband made, trying to fulfill a dream we had. That and . . . you know, John used to say, 'Never underestimate the power of denial.' I suppose that's what this is, in a way. Denial." I finished my drink, shrugged. "If nothing else, I'll sell the house and move back. You can be my Realtor again."

"That," Delores said, "would be a very pleasant change from Miss Lydia Samuels." She leaned back to make room for the large platter being put before her. "Oh my!" she said. "Doesn't that look good."

Outside of my elementary school **Dick and Jane** reader, I didn't think I'd ever heard anyone say "Oh my!" without being sarcastic. I liked that she said it with such clasped-hands sincerity.

After we finished dinner and were ready to leave, Delores said, "Now, listen. Why do you need a motel room? Why don't you just come and stay with me?"

I looked at her, considering, then smiled and said no.

"Why not?" she asked. Her voice was loud; she had ordered a second drink.

"I'll be fine," I said. "But thank you."

"Well . . . okay," Delores said. "But you come over to my office first thing in the morning and we'll get everything settled. Call your movers— I'll have you in that house in less than two weeks."

In fact, it was a bit over one week. Lydia agreed to rent her house to me for fifty dollars a day until I owned it. And I was lucky again with timing—the moving company was able to bring my things out four days after I called.

So it was that at ten o'clock on a Friday night, I wrapped a quilt around myself and sat on the top step of my new front porch. A few hours earlier I had watched the moving truck drive away, had watched the taillights grow smaller and smaller until they disappeared. It was as though Boston and John and all the life I'd lived thus far was contained in those glowing red circles. I thought of how the movers might go out and grab some burgers and coffee, how they might then jump up into the cab of the truck, turn on the radio, and start the long and bouncy drive back east. It was all I could do not to run after

the truck. It had been one thing to be on a jour-
ney that was stimulating and full of promise—
and distraction. But now here I was. Now what?
Should I really try to open a store?

I thought of the boxes of things I'd kept in
Boston and now had downstairs in the basement—the candelabra with birds and twisting
branches that I'd found in New Orleans, the glass
pens and bottles of sepia-colored inks I'd gotten in
Florence, the calligraphy sets once given to John
by a grateful patient, beautiful samples of lapis
lazuli that I'd meant to have made into a bracelet.
I had antique birdcages, lengths of kimono fabric, a small bench with ornate ironwork at the
ends, the seat covered in apricot-and-cream wide-
striped silk. I had yards and yards of many kinds of
fancy ribbons. One box held only dried bittersweet and silver dollars; another box once used
for wine now had a bird's nest in each divided
compartment. I had charms and beads, vintage
aprons, leopard-skin lamp shades, ornate doorknobs, small stained-glass windows. I had a Hopa-
long Cassidy child's dinner plate and matching
silverware, old black dial telephones, framed pictures of women from long ago, their hair in
Gibson girl upsweeps, a variety of funky kitchen
cannisters. John used to ask, early in our marriage,
what I was going to do with all the random things
I bought. But after he heard "I don't know, I just
like them" so many times, he stopped asking.

I looked up at the sky, gaudy with stars in a way I hadn't seen for a long time. It looked fake, like a backdrop for a stage play created by exuberant elementary-school students who might still believe stars were small, five-pointed objects that glittered in your hand, that you could take home and keep in a shoe box under your bed. In the first weeks after John's death, I felt closer to him whenever I looked at the sky. Now I felt no ethereal connection; rather, I felt my aloneness. I pulled the quilt closer around me, breathed in deeply. I could smell dampness in the air. Mid-November was still early for snow, but that morning I'd stood out in the backyard before the movers arrived and watched a few flakes swirl around as though scouting out the territory, then melt on the blackening stalks in the garden.

Delores had finally given me pictures of the garden in bloom. Come spring and summer, my senses would be pleasantly assaulted by roses and lilies and lilacs, by foxglove and peonies, by delphinium and phlox and zinnias and dahlias, and, best of all, by hydrangea in the glowing blue color I loved best. I envisioned a white pitcher in the center of my kitchen table, full of a bountiful mix. It made for a bittersweet rush of pleasure—John would have loved such a garden. He was often the one who would gather bouquets of wildflowers when we took walks through the countryside.

That afternoon, while the movers carried in box after box, chatting in Spanish and laughing at things I couldn't understand, I'd abandoned trying to keep up with them and instead went outside. The trees lining the block were mostly skeletal now, but there were still a few leaves in glorious reds and yellows lying on the lawn and sidewalk. I picked a few of the brighter ones and lined them up on my kitchen windowsill. I knew that the next day they would be dried out and curled at the edges, but I couldn't let them just lie there, they were too beautiful. It was a tradition for me to do this; from the time I was a little girl, I had decorated kitchen windowsills with gifts of the season. John joined in this tradition. He used to carve fearsome little faces in the miniature pumpkins every Halloween, for example, and we would light them with votive candles. In December we had branches of holly berries and mistletoe; in spring, forsythia in small, colored bottles; and in summer we would line up the three sand dollars John and I had found on our second date when we walked along the ocean holding hands, both of us taut with the knowledge that we had found The One— though neither of us admitted that until much later. It was the same beach where I scattered his ashes. It is good we don't know our own futures.

A small gust of wind rushed up under the blanket, and I shivered; but I wasn't quite ready to go back inside. I looked around at the houses up and down the block. A few porch lights were on, but otherwise it was all dark. I supposed people went to bed early here. I used to like doing that myself, though I was long out of the habit. The last few months of John's life, we'd both slept in fits and starts.

I rested my chin on my knees, huddled in closer to myself. I wished, suddenly, that I smoked—never mind the danger, what **wasn't** dangerous, anymore? I wished I could take in a long drag and then watch the exhalation dissipate into nothingness. I believed there must be a comfort in it.

In the late sixties, the three women I lived with when I was in college—those ones who'd been my last close friends—had all smoked. Almost every night, we sat in the kitchen and talked until very late, and the air would be thick and colored blue, the big orange ashtray we kept in the center of the table filled to overflowing. Sometimes I'd tried to smoke, too, but it never worked. If I inhaled, I'd have a fit of coughing. If I smoked without inhaling, I'd feel like an idiot. So I'd watched them, watched the lift of their chins and the whiteness of their throats as they blew straight up toward the ceiling, their long earrings dangling.

Also I'd helped drink the cheap bottles of Boone's Farm wine we bought and I'd helped change the records on the turntable so that we would never be without music. Odetta, we'd listened to. Dylan. Marvin Gaye. Joan Baez and Joni Mitchell. The Beatles, the Stones, Jimi and Janis. Also Lou Rawls's elevated version of "September Song" and Morgana King's "How Insensitive." Music had been more important then. We'd put on a record when we got up in the morning; we'd put on another to send us off to sleep. We played music to articulate our own wants and needs, to amplify our burgeoning political convictions. Musicians posed questions we didn't know we had until we heard them asked. It was understood that if certain songs came on, everyone stopped talking, no hard feelings.

Maddy, Lorraine, and Susanna, those were their names. Maddy was Italian, beautifully complected (it was the olive oil, she insisted), and she was always doing something for you, though she would never let you do anything for her. She was an exquisite cook, even at twenty; she embroidered with great skill, and she was a serious mountain climber—she kept the scary equipment she used in pillowcases at the back of her closet. Susanna wanted to be an actress and was very dramatic about everything—"Oh my **God, I've got a run**!!!"—and she had a kind of charisma that makes me think she probably did make it in theater. And then there was the beautiful, black-haired Lorraine, who, despite her inherent snobbishness and her dark moods, was the one I liked best. Lorraine once poured a drink down the front of a woman's dress, long before it had been done on film. She told the men she dated that her mother was a Hungarian Gypsy who had castrated her husband. This, strangely enough, seemed to attract them. Lorraine and I once gave our little Christmas tree a Viking funeral: On a railroad bridge, we set it on fire, all its ornaments still on it, and then we cast it into the Mississippi River. The idea, I think, was that a thing of such beauty should not suffer the indignity of being undone; let it go out in glory. I remember when Lorraine had proposed the idea, I'd said, "Wouldn't that be dangerous?" and she'd said, "Of course."

We lived in a house full of the smells of shampoo and White Castle and patchouli oil. Necklaces hung from window latches and doorknobs and closet pulls, rings were cast off onto saucers. No one had anything so practical as a jewelry box. Books and record albums and clothes were piled everywhere, and the phone rang all the time, often in the middle of the night. Once, a boy named Dan had called at 4 A.M. to tell me I was his Suzanne, and then he sang the lyrics of Leonard Cohen's new song to me. I was honored. Dan's roommate, Ron, had called me when their phone was first installed—neither of them had ever had his own phone, and they wanted me to call their number to make sure it worked. When I did, the phone rang thirteen times. Just as I was ready to hang up, Ron answered with a stoned "Hello?" "Why didn't you **answer**?" I said, and he said, "We were **lis**tening."

It was also Ron who once called me on a cold January night a little after midnight. I had just fallen asleep. "Come over," he said. "Dan and I were just talking about you, and we want to see you." I told him I had just gone to bed and I was tired; also, I had an eight o'clock class the next day. "Aw, come on," he said. "What we were saying about you is that you are real people. If you're real people, you'll come over." I told him I had no car. He said to take Lorraine's. I reminded him that I also had no driver's license. "Drive real slow," he said. I did take Lorraine's car, which was a '65 Mustang convertible, burgundy with a white interior—what I wouldn't give to have that car now! Its windows were coated with ice, and I had no idea how to work the defroster, so I put the top down and drove the mile and a half to Ron's house half sitting, half standing so that I could peer over the top of the windshield. I remember I had the radio up loud and was singing along. It was one of those moments you hold forever in your internal scrapbook.

It had been fun living there, yes, but mostly it had been comfortable, not so much physically as psychically. Lorraine had called it **safe,** meaning,

I think, **accepting.** You could station yourself at the kitchen table and someone would show up to talk to you with unflinching honesty about anything.

I wanted suddenly—intensely—to know where those women were. We could truly talk, I thought; they would still be able to hear both what I said and what I meant. It was Kierkegaard who'd said that if a friendship is true, it doesn't matter how much time has gone by, you just pick up where you left off. But how would I ever find them? Probably they had married and changed their names—we came before the time of casually keeping one's own; surely they were spread out in different cities, perhaps they were not even in this country. And I knew only too well of another disturbing possibility: One of them—or more—might have died. I leaned forward and back, forward and back, rocking myself in the ancient rhythm.

I took one more look at the sky, then stood to go back inside. Something in my knee hurt, doing this. Arthritis, already? So soon? Who would I tell my old-lady fears to now? Who would tell me I had lip-stick on my teeth, or that the story I was telling, I'd already told? Who would, sotto voce, suggest a mint and not have it embarrass me?

There was an old lady who lived on our block in Boston. She didn't come out except to get the mail, which she always retrieved as soon as it was delivered. Then she stood on the sidewalk and examined with great care everything she received, mostly junk mail and flyers, it seemed. "I'll bet she actually talks to phone solicitors," John said. He used to say hello to her, but she would only scurry back inside. I'd always thought of that woman's life as being so different from my own, alien, almost. Now it did not seem so strange what loneliness might do.

I went back into the house, folded the quilt, and lay it over the arm of the sofa. I looked around the living room, chaotic with unpacked boxes, but settled somehow, anyway, the rug in place, the furniture, too. John would have loved this house. "You," I whispered. **"John."** The specificity, as though it might help. As though it might bring him here in whatever form he chose: A step on the staircase. The wash of moonlight against the back of a chair. A touchless touch, a scent. I waited. I thought of Lydia Samuels and her eerie pronouncement: **He will come.** But he did not.

I turned out the lights and locked the front door. Then, as I was turning to go upstairs, I saw a small figure on the porch bend down and then run away. I opened the door again, mildly frightened, and saw a note on the top step, anchored by a rock. I brought it inside. In labored print, it read:

My name is Benny. In case you didn't know, I live next door. Welcome to our neighborhood! If you need any help done, you can hire me. It is only fifty cents (or more if you think I did a really good job). You can call me, and here is my number, get ready it is 555-0098. Or if you don't want to do that I can be found on the block after school and on weekends. When I am done, believe me you will say Wow, Everything is perfect!!!!

I'd seen a boy sitting on the porch of the house next door, earlier in the afternoon, watching me as I gathered leaves. It occurred to me now that he might have thought I was doing a pathetic version of raking, hence his entrepreneurial overture. He was a slight boy, with shaggy black hair, wearing glasses and a faded blue flannel shirt. About nine or ten years old, I'd guessed. I wondered what he was doing up now. I looked out the window at his house. Dark.

I went to the kitchen, opened one of the top drawers, and dropped the note in it. The drawer was otherwise empty, the surest sign that a house's inhabitants really have left. Soon it would become the junk drawer, full of the usual tangle of scrap paper and pens, coupons, rubber bands, random buttons, plastic silverware, and take-out menus. I used to also fill our old junk drawer with pictures torn out of magazines and newspapers, an odd habit of mine. "Why do you **keep** these?" John had once asked, in a rare fit of exasperation. "Why don't you either **do** something with them or throw them **away**?" "Leave them alone," I'd told him. "You are not the keeper of the kitchen drawers. I am the keeper of the kitchen drawers. You are the keeper of the workroom drawers and the garage drawers. I don't tell you to throw out bolts." "Bolts have a **purpose,**" he'd said. "So do my pictures," I'd told him. And when he'd said, "Oh? And what purpose is that?" I hadn't answered him. That was one of the last times I'd had the luxury of ignoring him—his diagnosis had not yet arrived and unpacked its terrible valise.

But a few days after John complained, I did remove the pictures. He'd been right—they were taking up too much room in the drawer. I pasted them into a small, suede-covered scrapbook, and when it became full, I started another. It became my habit to sit sometimes in the afternoon with a cup of tea, making up stories to fit the pictures. It was a different kind of writing, in a way; nothing I had to put to paper or turn over to a publisher or anyone else. It was imagination back to its purest and best form, unpolluted by thoughts of deadlines and reviews and sales figures and book tours. I liked the way the stories changed each time I flipped through the pages. I liked the way bits of dialogue would come into my head, strains of music, and I liked the way the pictures would sometimes expand in my mind so that rather than seeing just a yellow kitchen, I would see the living room next to it, then the street outside. And look, here came the woman whose kitchen it was, walking down the sidewalk with shopping bags knocking into her knees, smiling hello at a neighbor. Cheeks reddened by the wind. I had many of those scrapbooks by now, and I had unpacked them and stacked them by the chaise longue.

John never knew I did that with the pictures. I suppose everyone must have his or her own private pleasures. Surely he had his. Trout fishing, that was one—I never went with him when he did that. And oftentimes, in the evening, he took a walk without me and smoked a cigar. Sometimes he disappeared when he listened to opera with his headphones. He would close his eyes, his face full of longing, and I would envy the diva who moved him that way.

I sat at the kitchen table, hands folded in my lap. Overhead, the light hummed—something I'd not noticed in the daytime. Was that something I would need to get repaired? Whom did you call? An electrician? A handyman? A drop of water hung from the kitchen faucet, not quite heavy enough to fall. From the corner of my eye, I could see my face reflected in the window, and I could see the blackness beyond. This quiet was dense and annoying, just as too much noise was—I wanted to swat at it, to make it go away. I thought of putting on some music, but I didn't know where the stereo or the radio was and I was too tired to unpack any more.

But not tired enough to sleep. I'd need to be somnambulating before I went into the bedroom. Even in this new house, the bedroom was a dangerous place for memories—John, untucking his shirt, laying his watch on the dresser, then crossing the room toward me, his sweet intention in his smile. Here, on this first night, we would have held hands in the darkness, whispering excitedly about what part of our new town we would explore first. Always, we whispered, after the lights were out. Always, upon awakening in the morning, he smiled at me. "Welcome to Tuesday, Betta," he would say. He did that up until the end, when a pleasant routine had become grimly ironic. Welcome to Friday, Betta, and another day of hell. One kind of hell for you. Another, more breathtaking kind of hell for me. But welcome to it.

I got out a saucepan to heat water for tea—I hadn't found the kettle yet; I supposed it was in one of the few kitchen boxes I had yet to empty. I'd drink a mug of Sleepytime, and then, when I was sure I could no longer keep my eyes open, I'd go upstairs to lie down. In the morning, I could cross off another day. I put my hands to my lower back, stretched, allowed myself an **Oh, God.** "Healing hurts," someone at John's service had told me. "But hurting heals."

At 3 A.M., my eyes opened and I was wide-awake. I felt as though I hadn't slept at all, when in fact it had been four hours straight—not bad. I sat at the edge of the bed and looked around the room, made bright by moonlight coming in through the curtainless windows. It was a nice-sized room. Smaller than the bedroom we'd had before, but I appreciated the coziness, especially now. Tall wardrobe boxes stood like sentinels in the middle of the room, smaller cartons stacked up beside them. So much to do, in just this one room. I looked over at the dresser, thinking I didn't want it where I told the movers to put it after all—the opposite wall would have been better. But I didn't think I could move it by myself. Another mosquito bite of grief. I was beginning to learn that sometimes sorrow was a complex form of aggravation.

I didn't want to lie back down. Nor did I want to wander around what was still an unfamiliar house, no comfort stations yet established. The chenille-covered chaise longue was in the corner of the living room, but there was no glowing lamp beside it, no throw draped over it, no ticking clocks nearby or flowering orchid plants with their exotic, reaching stems. Instead, there were more boxes of things to be put away. And there was more silence, denser in the larger rooms, more alive, capable of replacing a hard-won calm with a pulsating panic.

I lay back down on my stomach in a position I'd learned in the single yoga class I'd taken last winter. I pointed one of my heels up, lengthened my leg, then did the same with my other leg. **S-t-r-e-t-c-h.** I remembered the merriment in the instructor's eyes when she'd asked the class, "Now! Have you all grown an inch or two?" She was an elegant-looking woman from Amsterdam with a charming accent. I'd wondered if she was like that all the time—yogacized—or if she had moments of pettiness and despair like the rest of us. Did she nearly float around her house on a cloud of enlightenment, or did she walk in with a pile of overdue bills, fling them on a table that needed dusting, and phone a friend to complain that all of her students were idiots? My inability to decide was what I turned into an excuse for dropping the class. What did **she** know? I asked myself, when what I was really asking was, Why should I wake up so **early** and go out into the **cold**?

Now, though, I tried to breathe the way she taught us that day. **When you breathe in this fashion, remember that it has a healing effect on each and every cell of the body.** I remember rolling my eyes when she said that, and at the same time wanting very much to believe it. Now, compliant out of class in a way that I could not be in it, I took a long breath in, made it longer, then longer still. **Think of a high waterfall; pull down, down, down. And now, let it go, let your breath rise up along your backbone in a continuous flow, and let it all, all, all out.**

I recalled the charged air in that yoga studio, the smell of sandalwood, the soothing periwinkle color of the walls, the way the dust motes glittered in the sun that streamed in from the high windows. I recalled too the luxury of seeing such calm and comfort and rejecting it on the grounds of not needing it. It was like seeing a platterful of food go by when your belly is full. At such times, it does not occur to you that you might someday be starving.

I would find another yoga class, and this time I would go. I would buy books on gardening so that, come spring, I would know how to care for my extraordinary backyard. I would honor John's request in a most deliberate way: I would try to find joy despite the necessary work of grieving, and I knew full well that **work** was exactly the right word to describe it. It was John's life that was over, not mine. I had to remember that recognizing the distinction was not disloyalty. I had to remember that I was still a young woman! Well, I was not an old woman.

I smoothed the top of the sheet over my blanket, folded my hands on top of my chest, and felt with relief the veil-like prelude to sleep, that falling away inside one's chest, the unsticking of self from self. And I felt a familiar hope, too: In dreams, I was sometimes with him still.

The doorbell awakened me, and I looked bleary-eyed at my watch. Ten-thirty. I went to the window to see if there was a delivery truck of some sort. The CDs I'd ordered, perhaps. One night in the motel I'd sat before my laptop and ordered thirty CDs from Amazon. I didn't even remember what they were.

But there was no truck out front. There was nothing. I put on my robe, went into the bathroom to quickly brush my hair and splash water on my face, then went downstairs to open the door. It was the boy from next door, standing there with a basket full of muffins.

"These are for you," he said. "From my mom. They're blueberry."

"Oh, well, thank you," I said. "Thank **her.**"

He pushed his glasses snug against the bridge of his nose and looked up at me through lenses that magnified his blue eyes in a way just short of comical. "I'm Benny Pacini. Did you get my note?"

"I did. I'm Betta Nolan."

"Betta?"

I smiled in spite of myself. "Yes. My mother couldn't choose between Betty and Anna. I do have some work for you, if you'd like to help me unpack boxes."

"I could help you tomorrow. I already have two jobs for today: walking dogs, and sweeping out a garage." He eyed my robe and pajamas. "Were you still sleeping?"

"I was, yes. I sleep late. Sometimes."

"Oh. Sorry."

"It's all right." I opened the door wider. "Would you like to come in?"

"Okay." He stepped just inside the door, shrugged off his jacket. "Do I have to take my shoes off?"

"No. No need. Why don't you come in the kitchen? I'll make some coffee, and maybe you'd like to have a muffin with me."

"They're just for you. I'm not allowed to have one."

"But if they're for me, I can decide what to do with them, right? And what I want to do is share them with you."

He shrugged in the exaggerated way of children, grimacing, shoulders practically reaching his earlobes. Then he followed me to the kitchen table, where he stood stiffly beside a chair. "At ease," I told him.

He stared at me. "Huh?"

"Have a **seat,**" I said.

He pulled out a chair and sat on the edge of it, his legs swinging, while I rummaged around a moving box, looking for coffee filters.

"Wow," Benny said, "you were on the **Mayflower?**"

I looked up at him. He pointed to the box. "Oh!" I said. "No. No, that's the name of the moving company I used." **Maybe,** I thought, **I should give in and color my gray.**

"Where did you come here from?"

"Boston."

"That's the capital of Massachusetts."

"That's right."

He looked around politely, his gaze not wandering beyond the confines of the kitchen. "I've never been in this house before. The lady who lived here was mean!"

"Yes, I met her."

"You did?"

"Uh-huh."

"A lot of people said she was a real witch. Grown-ups said that. Where did she go, anyway?"

"To a nursing home." I opened another box and began searching there: funnels, a colander, measuring cups, nesting bowls. "It's called the Rose McNair Home."

"We went there in second grade, at Christmastime. We had to sing 'O Holy Night' to them." He sang a few words of the song in a way so distracted and utterly unself-conscious I felt certain he wasn't aware of doing it. He was taking in his surroundings in a very concentrated way.

"Was it fun, singing to them?" I asked.

He snapped his attention back to me and contemplated the question like a politician hedging his bets. "No. They were mostly sleeping. I meant to ask you, do you have any kids?"

"I do not."

"Do you have a husband?"

Ah. I stood still for a moment, holding the small strainer I'd just picked up over my heart. Then I said, "He's dead."

Benny's legs stopped swinging. "He is?"

"Yes." I dug past pot holders, kitchen magnets, cheesecloth.

"Oh. I know how you feel 'cause my favorite grandpa died last month, two days after my tenth birthday, Grandpa Will."

"I'm sorry."

"Yeah. He knew magic tricks. One thing he could do was chop off his finger."

"My goodness!"

"Yup. And then he could heal it back."

"That's quite a trick." I reached the bottom of the second box without success. Where **were** those filters?

"He didn't really chop it off," Benny said. "But it sure looked like he did."

"Yes. I guess that was the trick part, that he made it look so real." I opened yet another box, lifted some kitchen towels, and uncovered a roll of paper towels. I could use one of those for a filter. Once, on a cold winter morning when we were out of both filters and paper towels, John had tried to use toilet paper. Then he'd used a strainer to try to separate the coffee grounds and disintegrating paper from the liquid. Then he'd tasted it. **Then** he'd gone to the store. And since the windchill was forty below, he'd bought lox and capers and beautiful bagels and gourmet cream cheese and roses and a type of wild rice we'd been wanting to try. That's the way he operated. Use errors to your advantage. "Your grandfather sounds like he was an interesting guy," I told Benny.

He sighed. "Sometimes I get mad that I can't ask him things anymore."

"Yes. I know what you mean." I lifted some boxes of tea. **There** were the filters! I brought them over to the coffeemaker and measured coffee, dumped in water, flicked the switch. "I feel that way, too."

"About your husband?"

"Yes." A satisfying aroma immediately filled the air, and I felt a reflexive lift in spirits. I'd once asked John, "Why do you think a simple ritual like coffee in the morning makes us so happy?" "Maybe because it's not simple," he'd said.

"What was your husband's name?"

"His name was John." I opened the refrigerator and took out a small carton of milk, brought it to the table, and sat down. "So."

"You don't have so much in your refrigerator, huh?" Benny said.

"No, I haven't been to the grocery store to stock up yet."

"Do you like Dr Pepper?"

"I think Dr Pepper's all right."

"It's my favorite. My mom always forgets to buy it."

"I'll get some for the next time you come to visit. How would that be?"

"Good." He smiled shyly, then said, "This guy in my class? Matt Lederman? He said I was gay."

"Did he."

"Gay is when you like boys if you're a boy."

"Right. Or girls if you're a girl."

"But I'm not that."

"It wouldn't be bad if you were."

"Well, I'm **not.**"

"Okay."

The coffeemaker beeped, and I got up to pour myself a cup. "Would you like some milk with your muffin?" I asked Benny.

"No, thanks." He peeled the wrapper from the sides of the muffin, put his hands behind his back, and bent down to take a bite. "This is how horses eat," he said around his mouthful.

I sat down opposite him. "You mean, no hands?"

"Right."

He took another bite and shut his eyes. "You can taste more with your eyes closed. Try it."

I closed my eyes for a moment and chewed. "You're absolutely right," I told him.

"People should always eat like this. But they just don't listen."

"Don't you think it would be hard to have a conversation when you were eating with someone if your eyes were closed all the time?"

"No, because you know why? You **hear** better with your eyes closed, too!" He cocked his head to the side, his eyes still squeezed shut and listening intently, as if proving his point to himself. But then he opened his eyes to ask, "Where do you work?"

"I don't have a job right now." Funny how, in saying this to him, I seemed to realize it for the first time myself.

He stared at me blankly. I suppose that these days, for a woman not to work doesn't compute. And so I said, "I used to write children's books."

His eyes lit up. "Like **Harry Potter?**"

"I wish!" I said. "But no. I wrote picture books, for younger children."

"What ones?"

I actually hated this question. The person on the airplane, on finding out what I did: "Well, have you published anything that I would know?" And then they never did know anything, and then would come the embarrassed silence, the returning to our respective reading matter. But I answered Benny. "Well, my favorite one was called **Grandma Sylvia's Pocketbook.**"

"What's it about?"

I took a second muffin. They were made from a mix, I was pretty sure, but they were very good. "It's about a grandmother who babysits every Friday night for her grandson, who really loves to look through her pocketbook."

"Why?"

"Because the things in there become other things. Like, one night, her compact becomes a little flying saucer."

"A real flying saucer?"

"A real one."

"Huh. What else did you write?"

"Oh, lots of books. The only one you might know is called **The People Who Lived Here Before Me.** That one sold a whole lot of copies."

He sat up straighter in his chair, astonished. "I have that book!" Now he was regarding me in a different way—with affectionate suspicion.

I smiled. "Do you?"

"Yeah! Where the kid lives in this real old house and he finds a marble in his closet and wonders who used to own it? And he finds out all this cool stuff about all the kids who ever lived there?"

I nodded. "That's the one."

He began to laugh, quietly at first but then in a high-pitched giggle, all but holding on to his stomach. "Remember about the **under**pants?"

"I do."

"I'm going to show my teacher that book and tell her you wrote it."

I felt embarrassed, suddenly, to be in my robe. I had an image of Benny's teacher, dressed in a clean white blouse and woolen skirt, looking down at me with eyebrows raised.

"Did your husband write books, too?"

"No, he was a child psychiatrist."

Benny nodded. "Stan Maken? This kid at my school? He goes to one of them. He's weird. We're not supposed to know, but everybody knows, because Stan **told** us. Wait! What time is it?"

I told him it must be almost eleven, and he said, "I gotta go!" He went into the hall where he'd dropped his coat. "I could come by tomorrow if you want, and help you unpack."

"That would be fine," I said. "Anytime."

He held up a finger. "One thing: Do I call you Mrs. Nolan or Betta?"

"Betta."

"I thought so," he said, and flew out the door.

I watched him from the window as he ran down the block, waving to another boy about his age who pedaled determinedly down the middle of the street, intent on business of his own. I remembered how, as a child, I used to dress every morning with great urgency, eager to meet the new day and all that it might present: a half-built house, a school of minnows, mastery over a one-handed cartwheel, money under chair cushions, even a sick thrill like the one I'd once had when I saw a naked baby doll shoved into the branches of a bush and covered with catsup to look like blood. I remember joining a circle of other children who were examining that doll, the way their faces were impassive, absent of horror. There is a natural quality of acceptance in young children, a blurring of distinction between bad and good; it is part of their great vulnerability. But it is also part of their great wisdom. A dog I once owned died with his eyes on the sky, panting and happy until the end. A friend once described the blackest parts of man's history as also beautiful, if only we could know true perspective.

Perhaps I didn't need another yoga class. Perhaps all around me were masters, both visible and unseen. Perhaps my "job" now was to learn what I needed to learn. John and I had often talked about how focused our culture was on distraction, about how ill suited we were to staying with things, following them through in a respectful and thorough way. There was a great discomfort with quiet, with stillness, at the same time that there was acknowledgment of how valuable these things could be. I once read an essay about a woman who spent an entire day simply looking at what she had, really seeing all the things she'd put in her house. I was as guilty as anyone else of buying books I never read, of rushing through days without ever looking up, of taking for granted things for which I should give thanks every day. Who appreciated their good health until they lost it? Who said grace? Who read to their children before bed without one eye on the clock, despairing of all they had to do before they themselves could sleep? Who engaged cashiers in grocery stores in conversations? Everyone seemed in a blind hurry, and there was no relief in sight. Technology rushed us ever forward, and simple civility—a certain kindness and care—got sacrificed. I was lucky not to have to take the first job that came along, lucky to be able to enter into a kind of purposeful inaction in order to refocus. I looked forward to it, in a sad kind of way. The price didn't seem worth the purchase.

I woke up the next morning full of a cheerfulness I was afraid to trust. I ate breakfast and
felt as though I were really tasting food for the
first time in a long time. I put on some Duke
Ellington to shower and dress by, and tried to ig-
nore the guilt simmering inside. To be feeling so
fine when my husband had so recently died! To
become aware of the relief I felt, frankly, that it
was finally all over!

On my walk to the center of town to go grocery shopping, I passed a group of young girls
dancing on their lawn—they were the sisters I'd
seen on the day I first looked at the house, who'd
been playing with the biting puppy. They held
their arms out, threw back their heads, stood on
tiptoe, and took mincing steps around and
around in a circle. I wanted to watch, but I didn't
want to make them self-conscious; I smiled and

kept going. John and I used to like to go to concerts and to the theater, but even more than that we liked going to amateur productions. A high school's version of **Oklahoma!** A Christmas concert at an elementary school, where all of the participants might march in with a lighted candle, their eyes wide and focused on their hands where the flames flickered—such danger! Such responsibility! One snowy evening we went to a dance recital at an all-girl school. One of the soloists was a fat girl whose girth strained piteously against her purple sequined outfit. She was flushed and untidy, her blond hair falling down from a bun decorated with plastic flowers, her eye makeup smeared so badly you could see it from the tenth row, where John and I sat. I was tense with hope that her dancing would be extraordinary—such things did happen—but it was not. Her style could most accurately be described as clomping. Perspiring, unsmiling, she soldiered grimly through something she'd obviously been forced to do. Most of the audience members regarded her with careful impassivity, but there were some whose smiles held back laughter and a few who'd exchanged glances full of a sanctioned kind of hostility—and these were not young people but adults. In the middle of the next number—tap dancing by an accomplished young woman whose father stood at the side of the front row to videotape her, and who received an enthusiastic round of applause easily lasting a full minute—John excused himself. He was gone for some time; I was sure someone had paged him for an emergency and he was out in the hall having a desperate conference. But when he came back in, he was carrying a bouquet wrapped in paper from the nearby florist. Six yellow roses, tied with a wide yellow ribbon. I knew who they were for.

After the program, when he presented them to the girl, he said, "These are to express my admiration." She was embarrassed and looked down to say thank you, and for a second I thought giving her flowers had been a terrible mistake, one of those things that, rather than correcting a bad situation, compounds it. But the girl held the flowers close to herself, and John had the good sense not to go on and on—rather he made a quick and elegant departure, and I saw that the girl smiled and raised her chin after we turned to leave. I took his hand and he said quietly, "Do you think we can adopt her?"

We had decided against adoption after trying for years to get pregnant; John had a low sperm count. By then, we'd grown used to our way of living. But John would have loved the presence of so many children in this neighborhood, just as I did.

It was a very nice shopping area that I could walk to: The town had a lot going for it, despite its small size. Among other things, there was a bookstore that felt like a bookstore and not a warehouse, and they had a wonderful selection of poetry. There was a movie theater where they popped their own corn. There was a clothing store for women, a few restaurants, a bakery, a stationery store, an antiques shop, a florist, two beauty parlors. Only one store was empty, a good sign for the town's prosperity. I stood before it for a while, imagining how it would look if it were mine. There were two display windows; I'd put a big armoire in one and fill it with beautiful and unusual things, and in the other I'd put a claw-foot bathtub surrounded by sumptuous products, a red cashmere robe draped over the edge. I grew excited, thinking about this, and started to write down the number to find out how much the rent would be. But then I noticed a small note saying the store rental included a two-bedroom apartment upstairs, no separate rental available. No wonder it was still vacant.

There was a train station at the corner, and I saw a double-decker commuter train. If I wanted to go to Chicago, I wouldn't have to drive; I could read or lean against a window and watch the scenery flash by, strobelike.

John would have liked it here so much. He would have appreciated having the antiques store especially; he had a wonderful eye. "Do you want a coffee?" he would have asked, outside the place I was now passing—he could almost never pass a coffee shop without going in. In honor of him, I decided, I'd go into Cuppa Java and have something sweet to bolster myself before I bought groceries and then went home to unpack both them and more boxes.

I ordered a coffee of the day and a lemon bar, then sat at a tiny table next to the window. Along with the smell of coffee in the air was the smell of newspaper, and the buttery aroma of things baking. I wanted to sit and watch people, to learn about who lived here, but it was difficult to concentrate on anything but the table next to me, where a young man and woman were having a quiet argument. "Why **should** it mean anything?" she said. "You fall in love with everyone!"

"No, I don't," he answered, his head down. He was shredding his napkin into long strips. Both he and the woman were wearing blue jeans and colored T-shirts with flannel shirts over them. Her long blond hair was twisted up and clipped carelessly to the top of her head, and the effect was lovely. Backpacks lay at their feet like dogs who'd been chastised for begging but refused to relinquish their posts entirely.

"You do!" she said. "And your loving someone doesn't mean anything! It doesn't mean anything about the person you supposedly love! I mean, tell me one reason why you love me!"

He looked up at her, his face full of longing.

He was remarkably good-looking: soft brown hair, huge blue eyes, a dimple in his chin. Cheek-bones a woman would kill for. "Because . . . you're **you**," he said. "You know?" He smiled, reached out to touch her hand.

She pulled it away impatiently. "That's exactly what I'm talking about," she said, her voice rising. "What does that **mean**? What does it say about me as an **individual**?"

It was all I could do not to lean over and say, "Sweetheart? Maybe this isn't the time or the place. Also, maybe if you'd stop being such a bitch he could tell you why you're so very special."

"I don't understand," the man told her, and she sighed loudly and looked away from him, directly at me. I turned quickly toward the window. There was a flyer for used furniture taped to the glass, an ad for a massage therapist, and one for someone looking for a roommate. Sunny back bedroom, the ad said. Nonsmoker. Three hundred dollars a month. None of the tabs with phone numbers had been torn off yet, but I saw from the date that it had just been posted today. What was it like when young people lived together these days? Did they write their names on their cartons of milk? Did they sit at kitchen tables and talk as my roommates and I did, or were they all hunkered down in front of their computers, lost in link land? It seemed to me that you couldn't look at one thing on a computer without enduring a barrage of suggestions for related topics, or pop-up advertising. For me, computers were like the kids in the classroom with their hands always raised, saying, **Oh! Oh! Oh! Oh!** On more than one occasion I had been known to have words with my computer for its infuriating interruptions. Once, as I sat in my chair deleting things and yelling, "No! No! **No!**" John walked into my office, saying, "Who are you **talking** to?"

Still, computers were good for some things. Perhaps my computer would help me find my roommates, those old soul mates. For so many years now, the conversations I'd had with women had been halting and false; I'd often snuck looks at my watch when we talked about the mostly superficial things we focused on. I knew it was my fault—I didn't make the effort to go deeper, to do what was required to achieve a true closeness. With my roommates, intimacy came by way of propinquity, and from the brutal honesty of youth. Now I longed to have that kind of friendship again. I needed to diligently pursue something I never should have abandoned in the first place.

"Fuck it!" the young woman said. She stood and slung her backpack over her shoulder. "I knew there was no point in trying to talk about this. What's the point? It's too late—I mean, I am gone. I told you, but you . . . Good luck, whatever. And don't call me!" She walked out of the coffee shop and moved quickly down the sidewalk.

I looked over at the young man and smiled sympathetically. Embarrassed, he smiled back. "Sorry," he said. "She's just . . . anyway. Sorry."

"No problem."

He took in a huge breath, raised his eyebrows. "Not my day, I guess." He grabbed his backpack and walked out, heading quickly down the block in the opposite direction. I felt bad for him; I wished I could have come up with something soothing to say. I watched him go, watched the wind lift his jacket and rush up underneath, wondered if he felt it. "This will be nothing in a few months," I wished I'd said. But he would not have believed me. I knew something about others predicting how long pain would last. Pebbles flung against a mountainside, that's what that was. Little bits of speculation thrown against an overwhelming fact.

In the grocery store I walked down the baking aisle, thinking I'd get some chocolate chips. It was Benny I was thinking of, but I was not opposed to having a bit of the dough myself—I preferred it to the cookies. I reached for flour, saw out of the corner of my eye a bottle of molasses, and it came to me what John meant by **gingerbread.** One night for dessert, I'd made gingerbread, complete with my mother's famous warm lemon sauce. When we'd eaten it, I'd told John that I wished I could have it for breakfast. "Have it, then," he'd said, and I'd offered reasons galore for not doing so—I was a big believer in sensible breakfasts. "Don't let your habits become handcuffs," he'd said, and I'd asked him if he'd gotten that out of some dumb self-help book. "No," he'd said. "It's my own dumb idea." Now I reached for the bottle of molasses and reminded myself to buy lemons, too.

It had gotten colder when I came back outside: dark clouds hung heavy in the sky. December had arrived without my quite knowing it. One reason was that the weather had been so mild, but the other reason was, I still wasn't really paying attention to what day it was. I walked home quickly, and my arms were aching by the time I climbed the front porch steps. My street was deserted now; no children outside—I saw no signs of activity at all, in fact. It came to me that serious winter weather would soon arrive, and with it temperatures so extreme a deserted street would be the norm and not the exception.

I carried the groceries into the kitchen, put away the items needing refrigeration, and left the rest. I needed to lie down. A sudden despair was rising up within me, and I wanted sleep's defense. "After it's all over," John had advised me, shortly after his diagnosis, "I want you to take really good care of yourself. Don't get too hungry, too tired, or too sad."

"Is that advice for widows?" I'd asked.

"For drunks, actually," he'd said. "They use it in AA. But it's good for widows, too." We'd laughed—laughed!—and I had felt proud of us, that laughter was still in us. And I had felt afraid, knowing that it was because nothing had made itself real yet.

I turned on a light, lay on the sofa, and closed my eyes. I felt a deep despair, a vague longing to go to sleep and not wake up. I knew it was self-indulgent and phony, really; if death appeared and said, "Ready?" I'd gasp and plead. What a change this was from my cheerful start to the day. But it was not surprising, really—so much of grieving was holding things at bay, resisting a great force bearing down. Every now and then it broke through. Nowhere to go then, but to tears or the nether land of sleep.

I slept briefly, and when I awakened I went into the kitchen and began putting groceries away with an intense focus that was close to rage. **There!** A small jar of peanut butter on the top shelf of the cupboard. **There!** Tinfoil in one of the long drawers. A loaf of bread . . . where would it go? I had yet to unearth the basket in which I kept bread. I turned around and around in a circle, saying out loud with mounting hysteria, "Where is it? Where is it? **Where?**"

The doorbell rang and I jumped as though I'd been caught stealing. I went to the door to find Benny, looking up at me with a half smile. "Surprise! I came to help you unpack—I got done early with my other jobs."

"Oh!" I said. "Good!"

"But I can come back."

"Why?"

He laughed nervously, looked over at his house, then back at me. "Because . . . are you crying?"

"No!" I put my hands to my face and felt the wetness there. "Well, not anymore. Come in. Guess what I got?"

"Dr Pepper," he said, striding in confidently and again dropping his coat in the hall. This time, though, I picked it up and hung it in the closet on what an efficient and rehab-minded part of my brain christened "Benny's hook." And then I confessed: It was the chocolate chips I'd wanted to tell him about; I'd forgotten to buy Dr Pepper.

He sighed. "That's okay. Everybody does. Want to get to work now?"

I nodded, then followed him into the living room. Such a small person to be such a savior.

At ten o'clock I took a bath, then came downstairs to make a cup of tea and sit in the chaise to contemplate my finished living room. An hour earlier, I'd paid Benny twenty dollars and felt like a thief. He'd been tireless: except for a dinner break with his mom, he worked straight through until nine o'clock, when he headed home for bed. We'd unpacked every box, and though not everything was put away, at least I finally knew where everything was. Surely a celebration was in order.

I moved to the stereo and put on a Thelonious Monk CD I had always loved and John had always hated. There were these things, these random compensations. I stood listening for a while, thinking that no other musician made music talk for me the way Monk did. No one else had such a transparent sense of humor. My roommates had loved him, too: we'd nearly worn out the grooves in our only album.

I started to go to the computer but went instead to the kitchen and picked up the phone. I was going to find those women. I was going to find them and suggest a reunion. I called directory assistance and asked for Providence, Rhode Island, the town we'd all lived in so many years ago. There was no listing for Maddy, nothing for Susanna. But there was a number for a Lorraine Keaton. I wrote it down with a soaring excitement I tried to temper—what were the chances, after all? There was no answer, and no machine. I supposed she could be online, whoever this Lorraine was. Or ignoring call-waiting, the new etiquette. I'd read for a while, then try again.

Forty-five minutes later the number still rang, unanswered. Fifteen minutes after that it was the same. I turned out the lights and brought the number upstairs with me and put it on the bedside stand. In the morning, then. She'd always slept late; I'd call early.

I lay in the dark, full of an odd kind of surety. I only had a phone number, but it felt like a major accomplishment. And I somehow felt positive it was Lorraine's. I wondered how she might look now. No doubt her hair had started graying, too. But I thought it must still be long, that would be her style. Long and wild. I wondered too if she could possibly have felt me thinking of her; if, when I called her, she'd felt some quick rush of **knowing.** Had she lifted her head from what she was doing to turn in the direction of me? Didn't we all occasionally feel such hair-raising beckonings? How to account for déjà vu, for the other supernatural ephemera to which all of us were exposed but, for the most part, refused to acknowledge?

As for me, I liked things that couldn't be explained. I liked outrageous statements of faith; defiant acts of belief that flew in the face of science and practicality. **Día de los Muertos,** for example: I loved the idea of bringing food and cigarettes to a grave site. The Japanese rite of sending out offerings on burning paper boats. The Irish custom of setting a place at the table for those who have gone on. I appreciated not only the intent behind such rituals but the form. In a curious mix of sacredness and absurdity, these things suggested—perhaps insisted—that the dead do not entirely leave us. Was it really only wishful thinking? Or was there old knowledge in our bones, a stubborn holding on to things ancient and true that, though they did not mold themselves to our current way of thinking, were nonetheless valid?

I resettled myself under the covers. Probably better not to think about such things now. In the morning I would make gingerbread, and on my most beautiful dish, I would set one piece aside. My little boat, anchored. Anchoring me.

I waited until Friday to try Lorraine again. Then, at half past seven in the morning, before I got out of bed, before I was fully awake, I dialed the number. No answer. I was becoming obsessed. But who cared? Who would know? It came to me how necessary the near presence of others was in keeping me civilized and sane; I could see how quickly I might become a woman gnawing a chicken leg over the kitchen sink for her dinner, a woman wandering around the rooms of her overly large house, talking aloud to no one. After my father died, I'd called my mother one night to see how she was doing. I'd asked what she'd had for dinner, and she'd said cereal. Straight out of the box. "Mom," I'd said. And she'd said, "I know," in a voice so thin and apologetic it broke my heart.

I hung up the phone, lay back, and pressed

my fingers against my temples—I had a bad headache, probably from a poor night's sleep. I'd awakened many times, suddenly very much frightened at being alone in this new place. The darkness had seemed alive, slithering about me like snakes, and turning on a light hadn't helped much—it seemed as though that only irritated the blackness, pushing it into corners, where it waited with ratcheted-up intentions.

It had never happened in this way before, that I had felt so afraid at night. When John had gone on business trips, I'd sometimes gotten a little frightened. But that was a woman feeling a little nervous because she was used to someone being around—a woman who listens overly hard to a normal rattling in the pipes; a woman who puts her head under the pillow to hide from lightning. Sitcom fear. What I felt last night was different.

At one point I'd had a dream in which it seemed as though I were wrestling with a smoky-faced, slit-eyed, terrifying presence. I'd awakened wide-eyed and struggling to breathe, and I'd not been able to swallow—it was as though someone's hands had been around my throat. I'd sat up quickly, so flushed, so hot, and then everything suddenly stopped—the terror seemed to crack open and fall away. There were my hands, clenched in my lap. There was the sound of my rapid breathing. There were the books stacked on my bedside table; there were the shadowy outlines of perfume bottles on my dresser. Eventually I'd fallen back into an uneasy sleep.

I splashed water on my face, put on my robe, and headed downstairs. Already my headache was receding. After I started the coffee, I went to the living room window to look out at the day. The temperature has risen again—what could have been snow became a downpour during the night, and now the sky was a redemptive blue, the pale pastel that often follows a rain. Birds sat in a convivial row on the nearby utility wire. Elongated drops of water hung beneath them, shimmying in the breeze. I watched the birds for a while, waiting for the invisible signal that would have them all lift off together, but it did not come. They sat content, enjoying their version of a coffee klatch.

Across the street, I saw a man dressed for work come out onto the porch for the newspaper, and I watched him hold his tie aside as he leaned down to pick it up. A memory of aftershave came to me, the smell of coffee and toast. And now the smell of John, that aphrodisiacal pocket between his neck and his shoulders. How long before memories of him would not intrude on almost every thought? How long did the real memorial service last?

Two doors down, a little girl came down the steps of her house. She hopped, her legs tightly together and her knees bent, making a game of her short descent. She was going to school, her backpack on, a pink lunch box in her hand. Farther down the block, a woman in a red plaid robe came out onto her porch to toss squares of bread to the squirrels gathered on her lawn. Her mouth moved; she was speaking to them, smiling. She tossed the last crumbs and stood for a moment with one hand on her hip, looking up to inspect the sky. Then she disappeared inside.

I watched to see who else might come out, but no one did; the only movement was of an airplane passing overhead. I watched it, imagining the people aboard straightening in their seats, looking down at where they would soon be arriving. From an airplane, the earth always looked so orderly, so gentle. So full of abundance and grace and purposeful intelligence. By day you could marvel at the precise patterns of the cultivated fields. At night, you could see clusters of lights, showing an obvious need for people to be near one another. Who would not be moved, looking down from such a distance, at the evidence of our great intentions?

I brought in the paper I'd ordered last week and went into the kitchen for coffee. I read the news and cut out a photograph I particularly liked: an old man on a city bus, sitting proudly erect and dressed in a three-piece suit. I would paste him into my scrapbook and imagine various destinations for him.

I stood to go to the cereal cabinet and was startled by the sight of Benny, his hair wetly combed, staring expectantly at me through the parted curtains.

I opened the door. "Did you knock? I'm sorry, I didn't hear you."

"I didn't knock. I didn't want to wake you up if you were sleeping."

"I was sitting right here at the table, reading the paper."

He looked at the torn-out picture I held in my hand. "What's that?"

I showed it to him. "You tell me."

He shrugged, then grinned. "**I** don't know!"

I looked at the picture again. "Well, where do you think he's going? Maybe . . . to see his girl-friend?"

Benny looked again, then said, "Nah. He's on the way to see the doctor. But it's good news—he's all better!"

I felt the cold now and pulled at the edges of my robe, tightening it across my chest. "So you were just standing there waiting? For how long?"

"I don't know."

"Well, come on in."

He glanced over at his house, where a car was backing out of the garage. "Uh-oh, too late, there's my mom. I have to go to school."

I came out onto the back porch and waved at Benny's mother. She was pretty, a young-looking woman, her hair tastefully streaked. "Good morning!" I said. "I'm Betta Nolan. Thanks for the muffins!"

She shaded her eyes against the sun. "You're welcome. I'm Carol Pacini. Has he been bugging you?"

"Not at all."

She turned the car radio down, reached inside her blouse to hike up a bra strap. "Well, if he ever bothers you, just send him home."

"He's a pleasure. Really."

"So are you able to come?"

I stared at her blankly.

"Didn't Benny ask you to come to dinner tonight?"

"I didn't have **time**!" Benny said.

"You've been there for ten minutes!"

"But she just now opened the door!"

"He didn't knock," I said, smiling.

She shook her head. "Get in the car, Benny." And then, to me, "We'd like to have you over to dinner. Seven-thirty?"

"Yes, thanks. I'll bring dessert."

Benny hopped into the car, and as it rolled past, he gave me the thumbs-up sign. I returned the gesture, though, truth to tell, I didn't know why.

The night before, I'd hung a calendar on the

kitchen wall next to the phone. Now, on the square for today, I wrote: **Dinner, 7:30.** Then: **Carol.** Beneath that, in small print: **Cranberry/blueberry pie.** As though I could not be depended upon to remember anything.

But I did remember the phone number I'd been trying, and I dialed it again now. When a woman's sleepy and highly irritated voice answered, I was so surprised I hung up. Then, gathering courage, I called right back.

"I'm going to kill you, whoever you are," the woman said.

"Lorraine?"

"Yeeessss?"

"It's . . . this is Betta Michaels."

Silence.

"I think maybe we used to be roommates. Back in—"

"Where are you?"

"**Is** this the Lorraine Keaton who—"

"Betta. Where **are** you?"

"Well, I was in Boston forever, but I just moved to a little town outside Chicago. Because my husband died and I . . . just moved here. I've been calling and calling you!"

"Your husband died?"

"Yeah."

"God. I'm sorry. Who did you marry? That guy you met right after you moved away?"

"Yes."

"Well, that doesn't surprise me. You guys seemed inseparable right away."

"Yes, we were. So anyway, I'm Betta Nolan, now. What about you? Are you married?"

She laughed, that old familiar sound. "Are you kidding? Only to the theater. I was in Canada on a visiting directorship, and when I go away I only use my cell phone for messages—that's why you couldn't reach me."

"Well, I . . . I'm so glad I found you! I was trying to call all of you—Maddy, Susanna . . ."

"We're still friends; we see each other all the time. They live in California, in Mill Valley, about six blocks from each other. I stayed here. You got lost. What's your address and phone number, give it to me."

After we'd exchanged information, she said, "Listen, I'm really late for an appointment. I'll call you back. What time is good for you?"

"Anytime. I'm just . . . I'm just . . ."

"Are you okay, Betta?"

Her at that kitchen table, leaning toward me, her strong heart-shaped face and clear eyes. "Betta? Are you okay? Just **tell** me."

"No."

"I'll call you back."

When I hung up, I pulled in a breath that seemed to break through a membrane and move down to where it had needed to be and could not, until now, go. I looked at the newspaper photo I was still holding, then went to tape it into the current suede scrapbook. It came to me to paste a penny beside the picture. Because . . . because the man on the bus was on his way to see old friends he'd recently rediscovered. In his pocket was a lucky penny, which he relied on in ways he would be embarrassed to admit to. Also in his pocket were the keys to his apartment in the retirement community where he lived. He was popular with the women for his waltzing skills, and he had a tiny garden in which he grew tomatoes and marigolds. Also in his pocket he carried butterscotch candies. And a wallet with the folding money neatly arranged in order of denomination, all the presidents' faces facing up. Rudolph was the old man's first name. I'd let Benny give him his last name. Rudolph was full of happiness; his heart was light with this unexpected gift that had come to him so late in life. Arthur and Douglas, there on the phone, after all these years, shouting to make themselves heard, but they were heard. He could hardly wait to see what his friends looked like now, though he knew he would also always see them as they were. Maybe they'd roll up their pant legs and try for some catfish. It would be harder, sitting on the bumpy riverbank now, but Rudolph thought they'd be able to do it. He thought they could.

After I ate breakfast—gingerbread with lemon sauce, **but!** properly seated at the kitchen table and therefore not disturbingly eccentric—I went upstairs, showered, and began to put linens away. I saw that they were getting worn; tomorrow I'd buy some new ones in a color that would coordinate better with my bathroom here. There was much to be said for the domestic high afforded by new towels and washcloths, folded and stacked in sybaritic readiness.

In the folds of one of the towels, I felt something. I lay the towel in my lap to open it carefully—I'd learned that the movers sometimes threw random things in places where they didn't belong. I'd found the key to wind the mantel clock in with my underwear; and Benny had found a spatula nestled amid throw pillows for the sofa. What was here was a camera, with an unfinished roll of film in it.

I sat still for a moment, my heart racing, wondering if it was pictures I took or that John did. Neither of us was ever very good about taking photos, and we were even worse about getting film developed promptly; I think we'd both enjoyed the element of surprise that came from looking at pictures months—or even years— after we'd taken them. No matter who took the photographs, there was every possibility that there were some of the two of us together, hands linked casually. Unknowing. There was every possibility that I'd find a photo of a healthy and smiling John that I'd never seen before. Another gift of him, when I'd thought the gifts were through.

I walked to town and dropped the film off at a one-hour place that was part of a camera store, then looked again into the empty windows of the store for rent. Probably I should call; I might be able to afford it even with the apartment, and then I could use that part for an office and storage. I shielded my eyes to peer inside. The place was dirty; there were large, flat pieces of wood resting against one of the back walls. How did one go about this, really? What was the first step? Did you have to hire an architect, or could you draw up your own plans? It was overwhelming, all you had to think about. I wasn't ready.

I shopped for the ingredients I needed to make the pie. After that, I went to Cuppa Java to wait the thirty minutes I had left. I was the only customer. The two employees, a young man and woman, stood in the back room talking in low, laughing voices. I ordered a cocoa, which was served in a mug that was to my way of thinking all wrong. A cocoa mug needed to be low and wide, easily able to accommodate the many marshmallows that should be floating around in there. In my store, I would have such mugs. I would have Dutch cocoa and long glass jars of vanilla beans. I would have chocolate-colored pajamas to go with the cocoa, brown flannel with red piping. To accompany this, I would have Joanne Harris's book **Chocolat** as well as Leah Cohen's most excellent **Glass, Paper, Beans,** because even though it talked about coffee, it also talked about mugs and therefore went with cocoa.

Enough! I read the **Chicago Tribune** someone had left behind and walked around reading descriptions of various kinds of coffee beans. Then I read again the signs posted on the window. The massage place was a little ways down the street, and the rates were much cheaper than in Boston; maybe I'd make an appointment. The last time I'd had a massage was shortly after John's diagnosis, and I'd wept with huge, racking sobs that embarrassed me. The masseuse was a very short and peaceful-looking woman who wore chopsticks to hold up her long hair, black and shiny as crows' feathers. She said, "It's **good** for you to cry, don't be shy, just let it out, let go." She told me I had an aura that glowed, she could see it, and she promised that great joy would soon come back to me. But I felt terrible; I cut the massage short, gave the woman a huge tip, and fled.

No one had torn off a tab with the phone number for the room for rent, and I saw that the amount had been lowered to $275. The word **furnished** had been inserted before **bedroom.**

I sat at a nearby table and looked at my watch again. I wondered if I'd be able to wait until I got home to look at the photos—probably it would be better if I did. The door to the coffee shop opened, and the young man I'd seen arguing with his girlfriend came in. He nodded at me, a bit embarrassed, and I nodded back. He ordered an espresso and then walked toward me, his hands in his pockets. "How you doing?" he asked, and I said, "I was about to ask the same of you."

"I'm good. **Really.**" He smiled, then looked behind me at the ad for a room. "No takers yet, huh?"

"No. I see they've lowered the rent, though."

"Yeah, we did. It's my house; my roommate and I are the ones looking. We've got a place a couple of blocks from here. We're kind of desperate because . . . well, one of the guys we started out with didn't work out. And now, the girl you saw me with? She moved out, too. You need a room?" He laughed.

"I'm tempted!" I said, and then, when he looked hopefully over at me, I said, "No, no, I'm just . . . well, I had a bad night. I just moved here, my husband just died, and I've never . . . I think I need a big dog. Or an alarm system. Or something." Too much information. Like a woman I once met in an airport bookstore. We were talking about one of the bestsellers when she suddenly said, "My husband just died. I'm carrying his sweater in my suitcase. I take it everywhere. I sleep with it." I had no idea what to say, and finally managed, "I'm sorry." She became flustered and said, "I don't know why I told you that." I said it was fine. But then we moved apart, unable, anymore, to talk about books or even to stand comfortably next to each other. I was newly married, the rings still a miracle on my hand.

I smiled brightly at the young man. "**Any**way, just . . . you know, a lot to get adjusted to!" I felt like a falsely cheerful host on a children's show: Can you say **mourning**?

"Yeah," he said, "I know how that can be." **No, you don't,** I thought. **You have no idea. We are geological ages apart.**

"**Espresso!**" the woman behind the counter said, and he went up for his drink. Then, coming back to me, he held out his hand. "I'm Matthew. O'Connor."

I told him my name and then shook his hand. There was a deep scratch on one of his knuckles. "Cat?" I asked, pointing to it.

He looked at it as though seeing it for the first time. "This? Nah. My roommate tried to put a bone down the garbage disposal, messed it all up. I must have cut myself fixing it."

"You're lucky you know how to do that!"

He blew on his espresso, then took a sip. "Pretty easy."

"Easy for you, maybe. My husband was very handy; I don't know how to do anything. If I can't repair it with duct tape, I'm out of luck. I don't even know how to hang pictures properly."

"You live near here?"

I nodded.

He took a napkin from the dispenser and wrote down a phone number. "If you ever want some help, just call me—this is my cell phone. I'm pretty good, and God knows I could use some cash at the moment. I'll charge you fifteen dollars an hour to fix almost anything. If that's not too much."

"No, that's not too much at all." I put the napkin in my pocket, looked at my watch. "I've got to go—I'll see you again, I'm sure."

"Okay." He sat down and pulled a book out of his backpack. Just before I was out the door, he said, "Excuse me? I just wanted to tell you, you can call anytime, even late at night. I'm always up. So . . ." The top of his ears turned red. Last puppy in the cage. I nearly hired him on the spot to carry my purse. Instead, I said, "I'll definitely call you."

On the way to get the pictures, I felt for the presence of the napkin in my pocket. Neighbors who seemed nice. A good-priced handyman—

apparently available twenty-four hours a day. Lorraine. Into my looming empty basket, I laid these gifts. There was the sun, shining through the bare limbs of the trees, making it warmer than I'd thought. I wondered if Matthew could do carpentry. In my mind's eye, we lifted up the pieces of wood resting in the corner of the store and began crafting a perfume bar, where you could use essential oils to create your own scent.

Though I had decided to wait until I got home to look at the photos, I found it impossible to do so. I paid for the film, then tore eagerly at the envelope to look at the first offering before I was even out of the store. But the shot was only one I had taken of laundry. Laundry hanging in Paris, I remembered, so the film was over two years old. There were bedclothes, lingerie, colorful little bits of children's clothing. I remembered telling John when I took that picture that I would love to have a big fat coffee-table book of laundry on the line. I loved looking at laundry on the line. There was a kind of romance to it, a comfort, I'd said. And then I'd told him to move so that he wouldn't block anything.

"Something wrong, ma'am?" the man behind the counter asked. "Are the pictures okay?"

I smiled at him and said yes, then I shoved the pictures into my purse and walked quickly toward home. I told myself that surely a picture of John was in here somewhere. I also told myself I would look at a picture a week, and that way they'd last longer. But the real reason I was going to delay looking was that I was afraid. I was afraid of finding one of John and reopening a tender, healing place; and I was equally afraid of not finding one, of coming face-to-face with the fact that the last picture I'd seen of him was indeed the last.

When I got home, I checked for a message from Lorraine—nothing. I picked up the phone and listened for a dial tone, just as I used to when I was impatient for a boyfriend to call. I tried her number and got her voice mail—not her, but a mechanized voice saying that the party at this number was not in. If I cared to leave a message . . . I hung up.

I made the pie and put it in the oven to bake, put in a load of wash, and ironed a few blouses. There were still things to unpack, but instead I sat at the kitchen table and dreamed. I thought of how my store could have shelves of heavy pasta platters from Tuscany, roosters from Paris for the kitchen, antique keys from who knew where strung from long lengths of satin ribbon, drawing paper and charcoal pencils, verbena soap and antique buttons. I felt myself being pulled more and more strongly in this direction, with no practical sense at all of how it could come to be. And little courage to do it, if truth be told. But was I not here, after all, in an entirely new place, entirely on a whim? Could you not in fact dream some things into being? As much as I wanted to honor the past, to take the time necessary to fully grieve what I had lost, I wanted to lift the lid off the future.

It was what John would want me to do, wasn't it? I tried to think of him sitting across from me here, thought of how he might advise me, but instead saw him at an outdoor café in Paris where we ate lunch one cloudy afternoon. It had been cold; the tables had been deserted. But it was a pretty place—we'd liked the deep red color of the chairs contrasted with the creaminess of the marble tabletops and the white cut-lace café curtain. Behind the curtain there'd been a young man looking out the window lost in thought, a cigarette in his hand. He had one of those timeless faces, one that you might see in paintings from hundreds of years ago. He would have fit as a muscular angel at the top of the Sistine Chapel or as a white-stockinged, ruffled-shirted lord in blue velvet breeches—he had tangled curls on his head, full lips, a patrician nose. Above him, scallop-shaped ceiling lamps glowed golden, like a practical benediction. I remembered that John had wanted to take his picture, but just as he'd lifted the camera, the man had moved away. **"C'est la vie,"** we'd said together, then laughed.

Before we ordered, it had started to rain—the kind of spitting, misty rain you feel foolish putting your umbrella up against. But we'd stayed at our table, determined to eat outside anyway, and an agitated waiter came to take our order—he wore a white apron tied over a belly so round he appeared pregnant. The pencil he used to write our order was stubby and chewed-on, and looked to have been sharpened by a knife. We liked this; we agreed that it added a kind of authenticity. We ordered cheese, fruit, bread, and wine—so predictable, our waiter seemed to think—but we enjoyed it, marveled as we always did at the texture and the taste of even the plainest of foods in France. I asked for butter at one point—I wanted more bread, but buttered—and when I asked shyly for **du beurre,** the waiter scowled and asked, **"Pourquoi faire?"** I sat silent, unsure of how to answer, and John came to my defense, saying in emphatic English, "She would like to **eat** it, if it's not too much trouble." John did not often suffer rudeness, even if it was built into the contract, as it often seemed to be in Paris.

We'd gone shopping afterward. I bought two small plates for us to have breakfast on: they featured roosters, and were in the Gallic colors of yellow and blue. Just this morning I'd put them away in their new place. John had bought himself a vintage watch at an antiques store, and for me, a fiery opal bracelet; after he put it on me, he turned my hand over and put his lips to my wrist.

The mantel clock struck five, startling me from my reverie. Outside, night was beginning to suggest itself. I moved to the kitchen window and watched the movement of clouds across the sky, then the lazy revolutions of a falling maple seed just outside the glass. It looked like a tiny pair of discarded angel wings, browned with age. It turned around and around all the way down, as though looking to find something of which it might ask an essential question. And then it landed without sound onto an earth that would take its time in transforming it. John and I used to talk about that sometimes, transformation—about what would become of him after he died; we shared that bravest and most sorrowful of intimacies. Mostly, though, I would say that we talked in silence. In the language of lying in the dark and moving one's hand to the other's hip for a specific kind of anchoring. That's how we talked most. Even before.

The buzzer on the stove sounded. I took the pie out and put it on a cooling rack, closed my eyes, and leaned in to smell. Then I headed upstairs to find something to wear tonight. I would bathe, rest, dress, and go to search out the company of others, bearing the gift of fruit in pastry. What did we do here but pull ourselves along in this fashion? Never mind our various life circumstances, what I believed was that we had all been flung into the water without having been taught to swim. We ate, we slept, we formed our kaleidoscopic relationships and marched ever forward. We licked chocolate from our fingers. We arranged flowers in vases. We inspected our backsides when we tried on new clothes. We gave ourselves over to art. We elected officials and complained. We stood up for home runs. We marked life passages in ceremonies we attended with impatience and pride. We reached out for new love when what we had died, confessing our unworthiness, confessing our great need. We felt at times that perhaps we really were visitors from another planet. We occasionally wondered if it was true that each of us was making everything up. But this was a wobbly saucer; this was thinking we could not endure; we went back to our elegant denial of unbreachable isolation, to refusing the lesson of being born alone and dying that way, too. We went back to loving, to eating, to sleeping, to marching and marching and marching along.

I was almost out the door when the phone rang. **Lorraine,** I thought, and rushed to answer it. But it was not Lorraine. It was Ed Selwin. "Remember me?" he said.

"Yes," I said. "I do."

He laughed. "Yeah, I was the guy sold you the yogurt."

"Right."

"Well, if you remember that, you might also remember I asked if you'd like to be on my radio show?"

"Uh-huh," I said. "How did you get my number, Ed?"

"Oh, I ran into Delores Henckley. She comes in all the time, she's a fool for that vanilla-chocolate twist. That's what **she** says, that she's a fool. We got to talking and she told me she'd sold Lydia Samuels's house to a woman from Massachusetts. So you moved here, just like I predicted, remember?"

"You know, Ed, you caught me at a really bad time; I'm just on the way out, and I'm late already."

"Doesn't take long to give a guy a yes or a no, does it? We can work out the details later."

"Fine," I said, thinking, **I can always get out of this later.**

"That's the spirit!" he said. "I'll call you tomorrow, we'll find a day. Now I can't promise for sure, but it could air as soon as next week."

C arol Pacini was a single mother. After Benny went to bed, she and I cleaned up the kitchen together. There is something about shared labor that makes people more easily open up, and while she washed the non-dishwasher items and I wiped them, she told me her story. She married at nineteen because she got her cheerleader self pregnant by the star quarterback, who she quickly came to realize had not much going for him but football. "He was sweet," she said, "and real nice-looking. But did you ever dive off the edge of something and hit the bottom **way** too soon?" She was divorced before Benny was born, and now here she was. Her father had given her the down payment for the house, and she was struggling to keep it— she worked full-time at an insurance company and occasionally supplemented her income by working as a cocktail waitress in a club the next town over. There was a natural kindness to her, and a practical strength I very much admired. "Benny told me about your husband," she said. "I'm really sorry. I just wanted to tell you, if there's anything you need . . . I mean, even if you get nervous being alone at night and want to borrow Zeke." She was referring to her huge black dog, now lying on his back in a corner of the kitchen. "He'll sleep with anyone," she said.

"I might take you up on that," I said, and told her about the nightmare I'd had. I was nervous doing this—when a relationship is so new, every-thing one says has disproportionate weight and staying power. But it felt good to unburden my-self by telling her the whole story, unedited.

"That's a terrible dream," Carol said. "You probably had it because of evil residue left by the old bitch who lived there before you."

I laughed.

"I'm serious!" Carol said. "She was awful, I couldn't stand her, but she was sort of weirdly powerful. Believe me, I was always very nice to her! Why don't you go ahead and take Zeke home with you tonight? See how you like having a dog."

I looked over at him, snoring now in a light, ruffled way. "I always wanted a dog," I said. "But my husband had allergies."

"Try him out," Carol said. "If you like having

him, we'll share him." She yawned, then apologized.

"I should go," I said. "Thanks for dinner. And maybe . . . can I really take Zeke?" His tail thumped at the mention of his name, though he did not rouse himself.

"Absolutely," Carol said. "Hey, Zeke, want to go out?" He leaped up as though he'd been shocked. One ear was turned over on itself. He came to drop his muzzle in her lap, rolled his eyes upward, martyrlike, and she scratched behind his ears. "He does have a way about him, doesn't he?"

On Carol's advice, I walked Zeke to the curb before I went in. He took a long, contemplative pee, then trotted off toward home. Short of his own house, I pulled him into mine. I took his leash off and he sniffed eagerly around my kitchen, his tail wagging slowly in a way that I thought meant he was happy, but very busy. I filled a bowl with water and put it in the corner. Already I felt better, having him there. I crouched down and called him to me, showed him his water. He took a quick drink, then wandered away to check out the other rooms.

The message light was blinking. Surely this had to be Lorraine. And it was. "I'm at the airport," she said. "United, flight five twenty-four. It arrives in Chicago at ten forty-nine. Where are you? . . . Okay, I'll take a cab to your place." I should have known when she asked for my address that this might happen.

I looked at my watch. Ten-thirty. I stood still for a long moment, then went upstairs to put linens on the bed in the guest room. An extra blanket—Lorraine always used to complain of cold. She used to paint her toenails in ten different colors. She kept all her clothes balled up in one dresser drawer, ate peanut-butter-and-pickle sandwiches, sat at the edge of her bed and played her guitar for hours, and at such times she was unreachable. She almost never went to class—she held all but one of her humanities professors in contempt—yet her grade point average was just under 4.0. She drank double scotches when she went on dates or at any other time she wasn't paying, and she put them down as smoothly as if they were water. Her penmanship was beautiful—very artistic, and she favored peacock blue ink in fountain pens. I remember once watching her make out a check for her share of the rent, and later trying to imitate her style when I wrote out my own check. We each paid $32.50 a month, and it was always hard to come up with the money. Once, after I'd paid the rent, I had one dollar to last me two weeks. I spent it on a rose, which I later left on a rock at a park as a public offering, and then I ate Cheerios until the next payday. Another time, I'd given blood to get money for groceries, and after I walked home with my heavy bag, I passed out in the middle of the kitchen floor. I revived in time to save the ice cream from melting. So many memories were coming to me, one on top of the other. Maybe it would be good to have Lorraine here; there'd be no sudden spasms of sadness or fear. In addition to the memories we would surely uncover and hold up like treasures from a trunk, there was no doubt in my mind that Lorraine still had a way of taking up all the room in a room.

I dialed her number, just to make sure she was really gone. No answer. Then I called to see if her flight was going to be on time. Ten minutes early. I stationed myself at the window, rigid with anticipation.

Her hair was as long and wild as I'd imagined, though not gray. Instead, it was dyed the same blue-black she'd always had, Archie's Veronica's color. After a perfunctory and, at least on my part, rather nervous embrace, we stood on the porch in the cold night air, looking at each other and laughing. Zeke stood behind us at the open door, apparently having appointed himself master of the house.

"This is so strange," I finally said. "In the wonderful sense of the word."

"But aren't you glad I came?"

"Yes. Now come in."

She put her suitcase at the bottom of the stairs and took off her coat—my God, what a figure she still had! She was wearing skin-tight black pants, a red V-neck sweater—a nice cashmere, it looked like—and many gold bangle bracelets. No gut. No thighs. No arm flab, from what I could tell, but at some point I'd make her let me see. I supposed she worked out at some Teutonic gym—she was never one to shy from physical challenges. Rather, she was one to create them. Oftentimes, after we had all been studying for what she deemed too long a time, she would put herself into some weird pose and say, "Hey girls. Can you do this?" "~~Fuck~~ you," Susanna would say, not even looking, and Maddy would almost always get down on the floor and assume the position with ease. As for me, I would decide it was time for refreshments and offer marshmallows on toothpicks. Peanut butter on tablespoons. A Snickers, cut into fourths, with a slight advantage given the cook.

I poured us glasses of wine, and Lorraine and I settled down on opposite ends of the sofa. In the better light, I could see minor signs of aging, but they did not detract from an intimidating beauty. If anything, she looked even better than she had all those years ago.

"You look great," I said, shaking my head. "How much work have you had done?"

"None," she said, and I felt a sorrowful astonishment until she said, "Oh come on, are you kidding? I had my first face-lift at thirty-five. Susanna and I did it together, but I came out way better than she did."

I smiled. "And Maddy?"

"Oh, hell, Maddy is Mother Earth. The only work she'll have done is on her house. And then she's right out there with whoever comes, making sure they're doing it right. Some guy fixing her sewer pipe got so mad at her for interfering he threatened to sue her." She cocked her head. "You look good, Betta."

"No, I don't."

"Still gracious about taking compliments. You look good, I said!"

I rolled my eyes. "Thank you."

"So, Betta. What brought you here? I mean, I never featured you as a small-town midwesterner." She looked around the room as though she herself had suddenly been dropped here.

I told her how my move had come about, then added, "I have to tell you, in some ways, I feel like I've come to where I always should have been. I really like it here. I don't even miss Boston."

"No surprise there."

"What do you mean?"

She tossed her hair back, took a drink of wine. "Well, you left **us** all behind, no problem."

"Not really. I never did leave any of you behind. John and I were so besotted we just . . . we let ourselves be everything to each other. It was wrong, really."

"I'll say! A girl needs her friends, especially at our age."

"So. Here we are." I held up my glass.

Lorraine toasted me back, then shifted her position, lengthening her legs and wiggling her toes, now painted a uniform red. "So what will you do here?"

"I don't know yet, really. I've got some ideas. I could always go back to writing, but I don't really want to. I want to do something different."

"You could teach."

"I could." I started to tell her about the store but decided against it. It seemed silly, now, a girly pipe dream. "I've got time. I'll just take some time. It was all pretty recent that he . . . you know, that all this happened."

Lorraine looked over at me, a softness in her eyes. "Do you want to talk about it?"

"What, John?"

"Yeah."

"Oh, well, Lorraine . . . He was . . . you would have loved him. He was a gentle intellect, such a sensitive and wonderfully evolved man. He—" I swallowed, took in a breath. "You know, maybe this isn't a good time. Yet." Ever so slightly, my throat tightened. I pushed my hair back from my face, smiled brightly, gulped some wine.

"That's fine," Lorraine said. "We'll talk about whatever you want, whenever you want." She lifted up her hair, let it hang over the top of a pillow. "So what kind of dog is Zeke?"

"I don't know. He's not mine. I borrowed him from next door."

"How come?"

I would spare her the details of the frightening dream I'd had. I knew Lorraine as an instant problem solver—she was more like a man than a woman in that respect. She wouldn't shiver empathetically and reach out to touch my arm. She'd hold a séance, call some ghost buster, race upstairs to the bedroom, and invite the challenger to do battle with her. She was like a colleague of John's, who when he was diagnosed with cancer stood naked in front of his mirror weeping and yelling, "Come out where I can **see** you!" I didn't want to have Lorraine try to solve my nighttime terrors— that would just make them more real. And so I said, "I just like dogs." And then, "Hey! Remember when we invited that guy to dinner and he showed up with a **gun**?"

Lorraine nodded. "We wouldn't let him in."

"Right. And he sat on the back steps spouting his terrible poetry—**loudly**—for what seemed like hours. Remember? It was written on a legal pad? And he just kept reading and reading?"

"Actually, I remember thinking some of it was pretty good. Who was that guy, anyway?"

"His name was initials . . ."

"R.M.," Lorraine said. "It was R.M. Maddy said it stood for 'Real Maniac.' Which I guess he was."

"Right. Maddy never did like it when you and I dragged strangers home with us, but most of them were good. Remember that guy who worked nights cleaning floors in the grocery store? Who picked us up hitchhiking? And the next day he brought us stolen steaks for dinner? They were porterhouse! Susanna slept with him after dinner to say thank you."

"He brought us coffee, too, remember?" Lorraine said. "When coffee had gotten so expensive? And a whole bunch of butter. We hadn't had butter for so **long.**"

I leaned my head back against the sofa cushion, suddenly dizzy with fatigue. I wanted to look at my watch, but I didn't want Lorraine to see me doing it. "What do they do, Susanna and Maddy?"

"Susanna's a divorced divorce attorney—talk to **her** about marriage. She's got a gorgeous grown daughter who's also an attorney—something environmental. Maddy became a nurse-practitioner and married a doctor. They have three sons. The last one just left home."

"After we were all so sure Susanna would be an actress! And then **you** turn out to be in theater! What got you into it?"

"When was I ever not onstage? I figured I might as well get paid for it. And then I figured I might as well direct, since I'm so good at bossing people around."

I yawned, covered my mouth. "Sorry."

Lorraine squinted at her watch. "Two-forty! Want to go to sleep?"

I nodded gratefully, then followed her upstairs, admiring the dancer's carriage she still had. In the hall I pointed out the linen closet and the bathroom. Then I embraced her again. "Thank you for coming."

"No big deal. Frequent-flyer miles." But then she pulled away from me and smiled. "You're welcome." She kissed my forehead and started for her bedroom. Zeke followed her. It was ever thus. I never wanted to introduce her to my boyfriends; they'd all stand transfixed while she ignored them; then they'd turn reluctantly to me, their consolation prize.

I turned out my bedside lamp and considered the mix of emotions inside me. I wasn't sure it was right to abandon myself to lighthearted banter, to allow someone to interfere with my being able to behave in whatever way I chose, whenever I wanted. What if I wanted to enjoy a memory or a good cry? I wasn't weaned from that yet; I wasn't finished being with him in the only way I had left.

But how long would she stay, after all? One day? Two? And what harm could there be in revisiting another time and place, one that existed before John, and was therefore free of memories that could trigger another sad implosion? Being with Lorraine was a pleasure, after all, and in that respect was only honoring another promise I had made to John.

I closed my eyes and let myself go back all those years, to that tiny little apartment in a falling-down house that probably no longer even existed. There were high, narrow windows there, warped floors. We had a room-sized braided rug that someone found for five dollars at a garage sale, and it smelled like raw potatoes. We had tall kitchen cupboards with the paint blistered and peeling; we kept red licorice in a jar on the kitchen radiator. There were at least eight tubes of mascara in one of the kitchen drawers, cakes of eyeliner, a couple of sets of false eyelashes, lipsticks in every color, including white. We had miniskirts that came up to the middle of our thighs, bell-bottom jeans, maxi-coats. We wore feathers and rhinestones in our hair. We had a turquoise-colored dial phone that chimed instead of ringing. The bathroom overflowed with boxes of tampons and plastic discs of birth control pills. I turned onto my other side, pulled a pillow close against my stomach. **Stop. Go to sleep.**

I awakened before Lorraine and took Zeke for a walk around the block before I returned him. When I came back, Lorraine had gotten up and made coffee. We sat at the table together to drink it. "I know this woman," Lorraine said. "Her husband died suddenly at age fifty—a brain aneurysm that nobody knew about—and she was completely helpless. When I went to see her a couple of weeks after his funeral, she was sitting at the kitchen table in her bathrobe, crying. She said, 'I don't even know where the **stamps** are.' You're not like that, are you?"

"Well, **no,**" I said. "I have my moments, but mostly I feel like I'm doing pretty well. I mean, come on; I moved here by myself. Isn't that brave?"

Lorraine shrugged. "Might be. Or it might be

because you were afraid to stay in your house and deal with everything you needed to."

"**I** think it's brave. But the truth is, I really don't know much about living an independent life. John did all the tax stuff, paid all the bills, fixed everything that broke." I sighed.

"You can hire people to do anything, you know," Lorraine said. "Don't be afraid to hire people if you can afford to. I pay somebody to clean my condo, to pick up my dry cleaning, to do my taxes, to help me with my computer. To satisfy me sexually."

I laughed.

"Never mind, that's next," she said, grimly.

"Didn't you **ever** think of getting married?" I asked.

"Nope."

"Why not?"

"Look around. Not much to recommend it."

"**Some** of us are lucky in love."

She crossed her legs, leaned back in her chair. "So tell me what it was like. Tell me a normal day, tell me what that was like."

"Well, it's . . . I don't know, it's like working with a net. When John and I had just gotten married, the people in the apartment next to us were newlyweds, too. She went and got her hair cut one day, and it was a total disaster, I mean she looked **awful.** She called me over to see what they'd done to her, and I just put my hand over my mouth. So she was sitting on her sofa crying, and then all of a sudden she looked up and said, 'God. I'm so glad that I'm **married.**'"

"No," Lorraine said. "I mean, tell me the specifics of a normal day. Tell me, **When the alarm went off, we . . .** like that."

I leaned in close to her. "Okay. When the alarm went off—" I stopped, smiled a wobbly smile, then leaned back and quickly pressed my fingers to the corners of my eyes.

Lorraine reached over to touch my hand. "That's all right. I'm sorry. I'm sorry I asked you that. Don't tell me. Don't say any more."

The phone rang and I leaped up gratefully to answer it. It was Ed Selwin, saying, "Good **mor**nin'! Now, tell me I didn't wake you up!"

"No," I said, "you didn't. I'm just sitting here having coffee with my best friend from a long time ago. It's a surprise visit, and we have a lot to catch up on—in not much time, I'm afraid." I pointed to the phone and rolled my eyes at Lorraine. I was sure she could hear him—he was yelling into the phone as though he were on the shore and I on the ship.

"Well, I won't keep you. Just calling to let you know we can go ahead and tape tomorrow at six-thirty. And seeing as how you have your friend there . . ." He laughed, a whooping sound. Lorraine looked questioningly at me. I held up my finger—**I'll tell you later.** Ed went on. "This is how it comes to me, sometimes, you know? Just like that." He lowered his voice. "Now. Suppose we do a show about you called 'Old Friends and New'? Right? You can have your friend on to be 'old,' and I'll get Delores Henckley to come on to be 'new.' She hasn't been on since she first started in the real estate business—we did a show we called 'Bright Buyers and Savvy Sellers'— well, actually, I called it that, that was my idea, with all due modesty. So! What do you say?"

"Well, Ed, that's a really nice idea, but—"

"Your friend's right there, idn't she?"

"Yes, she is."

"Well, go ahead and ask her! I'll wait."

"All right." Good. I knew what Lorraine would say about getting up at six to appear on a radio show with a listening audience of the host's mother. I held my hand—lightly—over the mouthpiece of the phone. "Lorraine? Want to be on a radio show?"

"What?"

I spoke slowly and deliberately. "This is the host, Ed Selwin, asking if we'd come and do a seg-ment for his local show. It's taped in a studio over the drugstore. It's called **Talk of the Town,** and this show would be 'Old Friends and New.'"

She smiled. I began to worry that her refusal

would contain something not only nasty but obscene, but what she said, loudly enough for Ed to hear, was "Why, **certainly.**"

"**Lorraine!**" I whispered.

"I'd **love** to!" she said—again, loudly.

"We would need to be at the studio at six-thirty," I said. "In the morning." I felt as though my eyes would soon bore holes into her.

"Oh, no **problem!**"

I took my hand off the mouthpiece. "Ed?"

"No need to say a word; I heard everything! So I'll see you bright and early tomorrow. Now, some people like to not eat until after the show on account of nerves. I been saying that since Sally Rethers lost her breakfast right on the air— we had to get a brand-new microphone, and they don't come cheap! So I always like to tell people: You are the best judge of your own insides, but be aware of the stomach effect of high nerves. Now, we do have donuts at the station that the bakery gives us—they're day-old, but I'll tell you what, you would never know it. And you are welcome to those donuts either before or after. Okay, well, I said I wouldn't take up much time, and I won't—I'll give Delores a call now. Thanks a lot!"

I hung up the phone, turned to Lorraine, and echoed Ed's last words. She smiled and smiled, stirring more sugar into her coffee, with her pinkie held up high and her lips pooched in that smart-ass way I now remembered so well.

L orraine was remarkably cheerful at six on Sunday morning. As opposed to me, who, despite a cold shower, was still half asleep. I drove slowly toward Main Street, irritated by what we were about to do.

"I can't wait to meet him," Lorraine said. "Can't you go faster? I don't want all the donuts to be gone."

"Ha, ha," I said.

"I mean it! I love day-old donuts. Oh, I hope they have the plain kind with chocolate frosting, don't you love those? They actually improve with age. If we're really lucky, they'll be real moldy, and then it will be like we're eating Maytag blue cheese, you know, all veiny and—"

"Lorraine," I said.

She grew mercifully quiet except for an occasional **"Mmmmm!"** to which I did not respond;

I remembered that when she got this way, negative attention only encouraged her. With any luck, we could do a quick "interview" and be on our way to Chicago—we were going to tour some of the city before I took her to the airport. We'd meant to go yesterday but instead spent all day lolling around, catching up, changing out of our pajamas only when we'd gone out to dinner. I'd learned that Lorraine was as tired of directing as I was of writing. Both of us were poised for something new. I'd finally told her about my idea and she thought it was wonderful. We'd stood outside the empty store after dinner, peering in. "Put some head scarves and sunglasses in there," she'd said. "And some huge jars of body creams that **work.** And journals that lie flat. And that Italian olive oil that comes in the beautiful bottles. And chandelier earrings that don't make your lobes drop down too far. And spa towels wrapped in really good silk ribbon that you can recycle." I'd asked if she wanted to be a buyer, and she'd said absolutely.

I parked directly in front of the drugstore. There was one other car there, Delores's Cadillac. I felt a sudden rush of gratitude for her being there—both because she would make the interview easier to endure and because it was an opportunity to see her again. A few times, I'd wanted to call, but hadn't.

"Oh, boy," Lorraine said, unhooking her seat belt.

"Never mind," I said. "Stop it."

"Do you think Lydia Samuels will be there?" Lorraine asked. I'd told her about my meeting with Lydia at the nursing home. I thought Lorraine was probably intrigued by the idea of someone bolder than she.

"No, she will definitely not be there."

"Let's go get her. She's a new friend!"

"Settle down," I said, and felt an urge to laugh. It was nerves, I realized; often my response to feeling nervous was to laugh. I undid my seat belt and opened the car door. "Come on. Let's get this over with."

"Wait." Lorraine pulled down the visor and checked herself in the mirror. "Do I look all right? Oh, and after we fall in love and consummate our marriage, do you think he's okay being on top? I don't like to be on top anymore—my face falls."

I looked at my watch. We were ten minutes early. "Let's take a little walk," I said. "I don't want to get there early."

"Are you **nervous**?" Lorraine asked.

"No."

"You're nervous!" she said, and I took her arm and began walking purposefully down the sidewalk.

"Everything you need is here, see?" I said. "Isn't this a sweet little town?"

"I can't believe you're nervous!" Lorraine said. "Come on, Betta, this isn't the **Today** show."

That was for sure. When we opened the door beside the drugstore, it led to a tiny foyer with bent mailboxes and a narrow flight of stairs covered in yellowing linoleum and wide metal strips. A hand-lettered piece of paper saying WMRZ SUITE 221 was taped to the wall, with an arrow pointing up.

"I'm sure glad they put that arrow there," Lorraine said.

Down a long, dingy hallway we found the door open to the reception area of the station. There were four mismatched chairs against the wall, two on either side of a table holding a massive lamp with a ruffled shade and a stack of weary-looking magazines. Across the room, a coffeemaker sat on top of a dresser découpaged with yellow pansies. The promised donuts were arranged on a paper plate, LIFE BEGINS AT 60! napkins fanned out beside them. Two black-and-white photographs of older, beaming men hung on the wall, exuberantly autographed: **Lenny and Tiny Shulerman, Shulerman's Autos.**

Delores sat in one of the threadbare chairs, reading **Reader's Digest.** She put down the magazine and smiled at me. "Well, there you are. And your **old** friend, too." She stood and shook hands with Lorraine. "Hello, I'm the **young** friend, Delores Henckley."

Lorraine smiled; I could see she liked Delores on sight. They began talking about how each had met me, and I headed to the bathroom, which was identified by two gold peeling-off silhouettes of a man's head and a woman's, a slash drawn between the heads with Magic Marker.

I splashed water on my face and took in a breath. I could not for the life of me get rid of the butterflies in my stomach. Maybe I was just hungry.

I came back out and surveyed the donuts, then selected a plain cake one. "I wouldn't do that if I were you," Delores said.

"How bad?" I asked.

"Do you like hockey pucks?"

I put the donut back and went to sit beside her.

"How's the house working out?" Delores asked.

"Fine," I said. "I'd love for you to come by sometime and see it."

"When?"

I laughed. "How about if I make us dinner sometime?"

"When?"

"Wednesday?"

"I'll bring baked-potato soup." She looked over at Lorraine. "Will you be there, too?"

"No," Lorraine said. "I'm flying back tonight. But next time."

I heard Ed's voice, and then he stuck his head out from a smaller room. "Showtime!" Seeing Lorraine, he stopped smiling. I introduced them, and we filed past, Lorraine making a point of brushing herself suggestively against Ed. "Oh, now," he said, laughing, then abruptly stopped.

He seated himself at a desk with a microphone and tapped against it, frowning. Then he smiled brightly and said, "Hello, all you fans and neighbors! You're here with me, Ed Selwin, on another **Talk of the Town.** Today our show is about old friends and new, and my main guest is Ms. Betta Nolan. Say howdy, Betta."

". . . Howdy," I said.

Ed adopted a Bob Eubanks style to say, "She's a newcomer living by herself over in Lydia Samuels's old place, but don't think she's alone, because guess what? She is joined here by old friends and new. The new one is none other than Delores Henckley, our town's real estate wizard. Delores, say good morning and give our listeners your phone number!"

He handed the microphone to Delores with a flourish. "Hi," she said. "Ed's right. I can help you with buying and selling. Henckley Real Estate, 555-8893. I'm in the yellow pages if you forget, and if you're like me, you've forgotten already." She handed the microphone back to Ed.

"Well, I'll tell you one thing we don't forget, and that's old friends. Let's have a word from our sponsor, and we'll be right back to tell you more."

Ed turned the microphone off, leaned back, and smiled. "We don't play the real commercial now, don't worry. We just have to leave room for it. We're going to get right back to the show now. But with that teaser, they'll all be eager to hear what comes next." He cleared his throat and turned the microphone back on. "We're back. And sitting right here close enough to pinch is our new town resident's OLD FRIEND, Lorraine Keaton! Now, I've got to tell you the truth, Lorraine is one easy-on-the-eyes woman!" He laughed. "I know that dudn't have much to do with anything, but I'm telling you, she is one fine female specimen, no offense intended and I'm sure none taken. Whooee, make a man tongue-tied, even me! But . . . good morning, Lorraine." He thrust the microphone toward her, and Lorraine wrapped her hand around Ed's, then pulled her hair back to lean over the microphone and say in a sultry voice, "Good morning, Ed Selwin."

Ed swallowed. "Well! You can't beat that!"

"Oh, I don't know," Lorraine said. She leaned back in her chair and crossed her legs. Smiled and licked her lips. Now I knew why I'd been nervous.

"Now, how long have you known our new resident . . . uh . . . Betty Nolan?"

"I have known your new resident Betta Nolan for . . ." She looked over at me, then said, "Thirty-five years!"

"Uh-huh," Ed said. "Well, **you** sure don't look your age!"

"I know it," she said, and Delores snorted, laughing.

"And how did you meet Betta?" Ed asked Lorraine.

"In college. We were roommates. It was real crowded in our apartment, and sometimes Betta and I slept together."

Ed stared at her for an overly long moment, then turned to me.

"Okay! Betta, I wonder if I could ask what you do for a living."

I took the microphone with great relief. "I used to write children's books. But now I'm . . . well, I guess I'm reevaluating, thinking of what else I might like to do." I took in a breath, then said, "I might open a store here, for women."

"Seems to me every store's for women!" Ed said.

"Well, this would be different."

"Gotta make a living, huh?" Ed said. "Get a real job."

"Oh, writing was a real job."

"Well, you don't hardly get paid for writing

children's books, do you?" He looked at Lorraine, winked.

"I got paid," I said.

Ed looked back at me, puzzled.

"I was published," I said.

"**Oh!** I see!" He leaned over toward Lorraine. "Now, did you ever see this coming? Were the creative roots there in Betta's old life, waiting to spring forth into the tree of books? Lorraine Keaton?" His tongue investigated his cheek, and he raised his eyebrows once, twice.

"Oh, my," Lorraine said, and covered her mouth as though the question was so provocative she needed to think for a moment to come up with an answer worthy enough. But I knew what was really going on. I knew she was trying not to laugh. Delores, her head resting on her hand, was half asleep.

I snuck a look at my watch and let out a tiny sigh.

Lorraine's flight wasn't until seven that night, but we left immediately for Chicago—we wanted to take advantage of the light. On the way, we discussed—again—Ed Selwin and his radio show. "You know," Lorraine said, "a guy like that, I mean, I just wanted to pick him up by his scrawny neck and smother him in my boobs."

"Yeah. I believe he might have picked up a little bit on that."

But in the end Ed had actually been more skilled than I'd imagined he could be. He asked questions about writing that were notable for not including "Where do you get your ideas?" or "Did you always want to be a writer?" or "How long does it take you to write a book?" or "So, what's your book about?" or the increasingly popular "Is there anything you wish I'd asked you that I did not?"

After we talked about writing, Ed had asked all of us to talk about what made for friendships, about what drew people together. He may have been an odd and lonely man asking questions fueled by his own alienation, but what resulted was a remarkably refreshing interview. Chauncey Gardiner takes to the airwaves. What did we all have in common, he wanted to know. What were our differences? What were our respective ideas of a good time? How vulnerable must one make oneself to enjoy a really true friendship? Though the way Ed phrased it, again looking pointedly at Lorraine, was "Do you have to knock down the warriors at your gate to let the good Trojan horses in?"

The result of the interview was that we all came to know one another in a truly legitimate and enjoyable way. At one point, Lorraine suggested we call and put Lydia Samuels on the air, and Ed had seriously considered the notion until he realized we were out of time.

"So, are you really serious about the store?" Lorraine asked.

"Oh, I don't know," I said. "I keep fantasizing about it. But what would I do with that apartment upstairs? I thought about using it as an office and for storage, but it's really too much space for that. I don't want to pay for something I'd never use."

"I've got an idea," Lorraine said. "Why don't you make a women's getaway? Decorate it wonderfully—excessively, you know? Make it a place where women friends could come together and not be in a hotel. In an apartment, they could cook together if they wanted to. They'd be more comfortable than in a hotel. You could put in movies and books that appeal to women."

"There's not much to do here, though."

She looked at me. "Except for dinner, did we even leave the house yesterday?"

"Okay, you're right. It's a thought."

Lorraine sat silent for a moment, then said, "A whole wall rack full of hair products in the bathrooms. Full-sized bottles."

"Good cheese, good wine, good bread in the kitchen to welcome them. Beautiful dishes."

"Costumes," Lorraine said.

I laughed. "What for?"

"Fun," she said.

"I'll think about it," I said. "I really will."

"There! There! **There!**" Lorraine sat up straight and pointed to the exit I needed to take. Lorraine and I both had well-deserved reputations for being terrible at directions. Once, when we'd taken a trip out of town, I'd said, "So we're supposed to exit at Green Street. It's coming up in about a mile. We take a left."

"Okay," Lorraine said, signaling for the right lane.

"Lorraine!" I said. **"Left!"** She gave me a look. **"What?"** I said, and waved the directions at her. "It says you take a left at Green Street!"

"You don't take a left from the **high**way," Lorraine said. "Jesus. You're worse than I am."

John used to say, when we were lost, "Which way do you think we should go?" And then, after I'd told him, he'd confidently proceed in the opposite direction.

Now I pulled off the freeway onto Michigan Avenue and drove as slowly as I could. "Look at this! I didn't know Chicago was so beautiful. Did you?"

She took off her sunglasses and leaned forward to see better. And then we were both quiet, admiring the breathtaking expanse of the lake and the stunning architecture across from it—building after building after building. "The University of Chicago's here," Lorraine said.

"Where?"

"Well, not **here,** here. It's in Hyde Park. I think that's south of here." She knew more about the city than I, yet I felt like a child the day after Christmas, sitting knee to knee with my best friend and opening the lid of a box to show her what **I** got. "The streets are so clean!" Lorraine said.

"I know," I answered, as though I were vaguely responsible.

We went up Michigan Avenue, then north on Lake Shore Drive, then came back south and wove in and out of the downtown streets. Back again on Michigan, Lorraine yelled, "The Art Institute!" and I veered toward a nearby parking garage even before she said, "Let's go!" The statues of lions on either side of the entrance wore gigantic wreaths around their necks; the people going into the museum looked open and friendly, more relaxed about the shoulders than the East Coast people I was used to. A little over forty miles away, the sunlight poured through the windows of my beautiful house. It waited for me, its art glass and wooden floors, its wide windowsills and its porches, its winter garden, bare but for the suggestion of all to come. I wondered about the house's well-being in my absence as a parent might wonder about her child's.

Lorraine and I agreed to split up, and I wandered around for a long time, paying less attention to things in the museum than to the fact of it. Some mornings when I read the newspaper, I wanted to weep or pound my fists on the table in frustration. Some mornings I actually did one or the other. But museums offered up the other side of humanity: the glory and the grace.

Before the Chagall windows, I sat down on one of the long benches and stared, then remembered that **Chagall windows** had been on one of the slips of paper in the Chinese chest. John and I must have seen something about them once, and on that small piece of paper he'd been urging me to do precisely this: sit before these tall blue panes. The air around me was cool and quiet and to my mind fragrant—a mix of stone and paper and something not quite incense but close to it. I felt as though I were in a spontaneously created church, truer for its being non-denominational.

After a long while, I looked at my watch. Five more minutes until I had to meet Lorraine at the entrance to the gift shop. I rose with regret, then remembered: I could easily come back here. I wouldn't even have to drive. It seemed so odd to me. It reminded me that I had not yet fully stepped into my life here—part of me still lingered at John's side, staring both at him and at the future without him, waiting to see if he were going to change his mind and come with me after all.

When we walked down the museum steps and

out toward Michigan Avenue, the sun was starting to set and everything was colored rosy gold. Lorraine looked around and sighed happily. "I'm not sure how to say this," she said. "But did you ever notice how after you look at art for a long time you come out onto the street and see only art?"

"Yes," I said. "I know exactly what you mean."

We were mostly quiet on the way to the airport—talked out, I imagined, which we certainly deserved to be. But just before Lorraine got out of the car, she said, "Remember **Night of the Iguana**?"

"Yes."

"That's what we did, so long ago. That's why this was so easy. Okay. I hate goodbyes, and I'm not going to say it. Call me." She climbed out of the car. Before she slammed the door, she turned to shout, "Soon!"

I drove away, my hands light on the wheel. What Lorraine had referred to was a line in the movie that we had always loved, about people building nests in one another's hearts.

The telephone light was flashing when I got home. Two messages. The first was a man, clearing his throat and then saying, "Yes. My name is Tom Bartlett. This isn't a sales call. You don't know me, but I heard you on the radio this morning and uh . . . well, you said you wrote children's books and I wondered if you, you know, ever taught or anything like that or if you . . ." He laughed. "Guess I'm going on here. A bit. You know what? If you wouldn't mind calling me, I'm at 555-7501. I hope you don't mind my having called you—Ed Selwin gave me the number. Thank you."

I replayed the message and wrote down his number. Nice voice, low and easy. The second message was from Susanna. "Oh, my **GOD!**" she began, and I pulled up a chair to listen to the rest. Lorraine had just called her from the airport, Susanna couldn't believe this, she couldn't **believe** this, she would be home tonight, all night, call her, call anytime even if it was in the middle of the night, in fact she liked to be called in the middle of the night. I dialed the number.

"Susanna?"

"Yes!"

I smiled. "How are you?"

"More like, how are **you**? Oh, sweetie, I'm so, so sorry. About your husband. He died."

"Yes."

"I'm so sorry."

"Thank you. So you spoke with Lorraine."

"Yes, and I am so glad we **found** you! We've looked for you, you know, every now and then. We all went to Barcelona, years ago, and we tried to find you to come with us then. That was when we were in our thirties, infants. My **God,** it was over twenty **years** ago! When can we get together?"

"Um . . ." I wasn't sure, suddenly. I needed a breath, a respectful visitation to a place I'd been ignoring. It had been good—it had been a relief—to be so purposefully away from the reality of what had brought me here. But in an odd way, I missed my sorrow.

But then Susanna said, "No rush. We'll wait. But when you're ready, we'll all come there together. Oh, sweetheart, we'll have such a good time. Maybe it's a function of age, maybe it's the scary political climate, but more and more we're talking about how necessary it is to tell people you love them, how important it is to keep in touch. And you meant a lot to us. We all used to fit so well together! And the three of us have had such a good time over all these years. Did Lorraine tell you about the concerts?"

"No."

"Well, we go to them at least once a year, we go to all the Stones concerts—Mick is just **cadaverous,** worse than in photos. We saw Leonard Cohen, who depressed the hell out of us, and we saw Joni—what a great jazz vocalist she is now, isn't she? She's **aged** so much—although what she said about happiness being the best face-lift? Is that not our girl? Is that not just the most beautiful, soulful, wise thing? Of course, it's not true.

Oh, well, we're all ancient now, except Lorraine, of course, who is eternally beautiful, mostly due to her biweekly visits to the plastic surgeon. Our next trip will probably be to the arthritis spa—do you have it yet, arthritis? I do, and my **fingers** in the morning! That over-the-counter thing helps, chondroitin. And it's natural. Oh God. Listen to me. Did you ever imagine talking about such things? I'm telling you, though, Maddy and I are suddenly **beset** with these health worries. Chest pains, memory loss. Maddy called the other day and said, 'Okay. Today it's not only Alzheimer's, it's that I'm **riddled** with cancer. Six months, tops.'" She started to laugh, then stopped abruptly. "Oh, Betta. I'm so sorry. I just meant—"

"I know what you mean. Before John got sick, we did the same thing. I remember him once . . . well. We did the same thing." I sighed, quietly, thinking of John once turning away from the bathroom mirror and a mole he'd just found on his chest to say, "I'll be right back. I'm just going to run over to the lawyer's and put my affairs in order." And I'd said, "Closed casket or open?"

"I guess I'm a little nervous," Susanna said. "I'm just going **on.**"

"It's okay."

An awkward silence, and then I said, "We will find a time to get together, Suse. I'll call you. I'll call everybody—we'll set a date."

"Good. Did Lorraine give you Maddy's number?"

"No."

"Well, that's Lorraine for you. She's in first place and everyone else is in last. If I didn't love her so much, I'd . . . love her anyway. Here's the number."

After I hung up the phone, I moved to the kitchen table and sat quietly for a while, thinking about calling Maddy. Not yet. Then I thought about calling back the man who'd left the message, but decided against that, too. Outside, it had begun to snow: tiny flakes that made it look like the earth was being salted. Tomorrow I would need to buy a new shovel—the one John had used was too heavy for me. He'd appreciated hard manual labor, saying he liked to do work that was outside his head, for a change. I liked reading a good novel while he cleared the walks, popping up every now and then to look out the window and see how he was progressing. That was my contribution. Of course, I had reciprocated—bringing him dinner on a tray when the Sox were playing an important game. Sewing on buttons for him. Finding things he insisted weren't there when they were actually right before him. I wasn't sure Lorraine and others like her—ones who were so despairing of marriage, ones who were so sure their expectations could never be met—understood that it was these small moments of caretaking that meant the most, that forged the real relationship. The way one pulled the blankets over the sleeping other, the way one prepared a snack for oneself but made enough to share. Such moments made for the team of two, which made for one's sword and shield.

I took a long, hot bath, turned down the bed linens, sprayed them with lavender water, plumped my pillows just so, and put Erik Satie's **After the Rain** on the CD player. Then I sat at the edge of the bed, wondering about the advisability of what I was about to do. Finally, from the top drawer of my nightstand, I pulled out the package of photographs and slid out the picture on top.

Disappointingly, it was not of John; but it was John who'd taken it—as soon as I saw the image, I remembered vividly that mild spring day we'd spent in a small town in France. Soon after we left the hotel, my back had begun hurting from carrying my overstuffed purse, and John had taken it from me and slung it over his shoulder, never mind its floral motif, he was man enough to not worry about that. This he did without a word, of course, in spite of the fact that he had warned me against carrying so many things. We'd had a lunch of fish and salad and little red potatoes drenched in butter and glorified with parsley, and it had been delicious. Before bed that night, we'd tuned the radio to a classical station, flung open the tall shuttered doors that led to the balcony of our hotel, and lain together looking out at the stars, talking about how, when you were in a foreign country, the stars seemed foreign, too. Yes, there was the Big Dipper, but it was the French Big Dipper. **Le Dipper Français,** John called it. And something else, this quick flash of memory: I remembered standing naked before the minibar, looking for chocolate for a late-night dessert, and triumphantly pulling out a candy bar. **"Sneekairs!"** John had said.

But that afternoon John had taken a picture of two men standing together at the railing of a stone bridge. They were dressed alike and casually: tan pants, knit shirts, light jackets, and porkpie hats. One had his hands clasped before him; the other held on to the rail of the bridge with one hand and with the other held a red heart-shaped balloon on a short string. The men were perhaps in their mid-sixties and not what you would call attractive. But they'd stood with a heart-shaped balloon, and I believed they were looking for love.

What, I wondered, would I do, when I felt ready to look for love again? Stand outside with my own red balloon? Would I begin to **date**—ludicrous word, at my age—and go through the excruciating process of sharing personal histories? It was exhausting to even think about: **I was born in, I was an only child, I worked as, I voted for,** blah blah blah. A newly divorced friend of mine named Peggy had told me about calling an upscale dating service. She had asked about how the service worked, and the woman who'd answered the phone told her with immoderate good cheer that it was a fail-safe operation: The agency, after taking your thousand (!) dollars, put your picture and bio in a book and made a little video of you. The men chose what women they wanted to meet, and the women chose what men. Unless you chose each other, you didn't meet. Then the woman had said to Peggy, "So! Now that I've told you about us, let's talk about **you.** How old are you?" "I'm fifty," Peggy had said, and there was silence on the line. Then the agency woman had rushed to fill it, saying, "Okay, well, I just have to tell you that most of our clients are in their thirties. But new people call every day, just as **you** did!" Peggy had hung up, stared out the window for a while, and gone to the library, where she checked out an armful of fat novels and a book called **How to Fix Everything**—no irony intended. "I'm better off anyway," she'd said. "Can you imagine the indignity of breaking **up** at this age?"

I knew it wasn't completely hopeless; I knew people met and fell in love in later years. But as to what a decent relationship might progress to, how could I ever sleep with someone else? Yet I didn't want that part of my life to be over. Bad enough to never have had children. What if I never again had a sex partner? Soon after we'd first met, John had told me, "You're a hot-blooded woman, Betta." I'd answered, "Yes. That's for you, you hot-blooded man." What if I never again enjoyed that particular pleasure?

Maybe it wouldn't be so terrible. Maybe I would simply grow used to it. There were other things I could still do to add spice to my life. Travel, for one—John and I had never gotten to Greece. Or to China. Or Africa. Or Alaska. I took a pen and paper from the drawer—perhaps it would be good to make a list of ideas for things to do, and cross them off as I did them. It would keep me focused and looking forward to the future; it would lessen my anxiety. In times of despair, it would be good to have a whole list of possibilities I might refer to.

I leaned against the pillows and rested the pad of paper on my knees. I tapped the pen against my teeth, thinking. And thinking. Finally, I put the pen and paper away. The things that brought me the most comfort now were too small to list. Raspberries in cream. Sparrows with cocked heads. Shadows of bare limbs making for sidewalk filigrees. Roses past their prime with their petals loose about them. The shouts of children at play in the neighborhood, Ginger Rogers on the black-and-white screen. But trips? No. Without John, no. For now, only raspberries, only cream. Only books waiting at the bedside. Only the worn flannel of my favorite pajamas. Everything else was just too big. I recalled a message I'd seen on an online widow support group, emphasizing that there was no true timetable—people had to honor their own needs and their own methods. One woman had written in saying she felt fine after three weeks, was something wrong with her? Another said it had been three years and still she felt immobilized by pain.

I turned out the light, slid down flat under the covers, and closed my eyes. It was Sunday night, the part of the week that used to make John melancholy. Well, as melancholy as he got, which was not really melancholy at all. People who didn't know him well wouldn't have been able to see the difference in him, but I could. It manifested as a kind of distractedness—his mind was being pulled toward the patients he would see the next day. He had to leave behind Sunday before it was through, and this always made him a little sad. His hands stayed too much in his pockets; his head hung lower than usual. His smile was close-mouthed, and anytime he embraced me, on those days, he'd make a tiny, side-to-side rocking motion he did not otherwise make, a movement of consolation meant for both of us. Goodbye to the lovely leisure of the newspaper in bed on Sunday morning, of home-made scones and coffee served on TV trays as we watched the political shows with their blustering and defensive guests, they with their sweating, bald heads, their unironic thick-rimmed black eyeglasses.

When evening came, we went out for dinner, always sushi on Sunday nights, and always he made a toast to what he called our continuing honeymoon. He was such a sweet romantic. His notes on scraps of paper left on the kitchen table. His washing my back in the tub, kissing my fore-head on completion, and then saying, "There's more where that came from. Come and let me dry you." Surprise necklaces under the pillow, the warm grasp of his hand over mine every time we went to the movies. So long married, and yet the touch of his fingers pushing my hair back from the side of my face could still arouse me. And always he brought me flowers, sometimes huge bouquets from the fancy shop on Boylston Street that had me reapportioning the stems into several vases, other times a single peony snapped from the corner bush in our own front yard but presented with such flair—a bow at the waist, a sweeping motion of his pianist's hand, a kiss to my own. "My lady," he would say, and I would say, "Oh, stop," hoping he never would. And he never did. It occurred to me that perhaps one of the reasons I kept thinking about opening my store was that I could give to other women what John had given to me.

I thought for a moment about looking at the rest of the pictures but decided against it. There was hope in the waiting. And even though I'd not yet found a picture of John, I'd found memories to enjoy. I wanted them to last.

I turned on the light again, then headed downstairs to the Chinese chest. Perhaps I would find something there. The living room was lit beautifully by a gibbous moon, and I slid the drawer open in that milky glow, thinking its natural magic would help me find something that would make sense to me, that would give me the only nearness to him I could now enjoy. I reached in and pulled out a slip: **Amber.** I thought hard, to no avail. The stone? The color? Was it the name of a painting, a song, a person, even a small town we'd been to? Nothing came to me. I pulled out another paper: **Yolks only.** Yolks only? What could this possibly mean? What—the fact that I preferred the yolk to the white? Did **yolks** have another meaning altogether? Was it the punch line of a joke? Or had he meant **folks**? But that word would not suggest anything, either. I tried one more: **Pepper mill.** Oh, John. Oh, Betta. Standing in her living room in her nightgown, digging through a drawer, looking for her husband.

I carried the last slip of paper upstairs and laid it on the pillow next to me. It made no more sense than any of the others I'd looked at tonight. But it was the ink from his black fountain pen on that slip of paper, and he had written it when the blood ran warm in his hand, when images registered and reversed on the back of his retina, when the elegant exchange of oxygen occurred in the alveoli of his lungs, when he was alive.

I turned out the light again. Satie's wandering and melancholy notes filled the room, and I gave myself over fully to the music, just as I used to years ago. Absent anyone else's company, I felt no silent commentary interfering with my enjoyment, worried not at all about the volume. There was that. I had always loved Satie as much for his charming eccentricities as for his music. The way he kept two pianos, one on top of the other, in his studio apartment. The way he collected umbrellas and bought twelve gray velvet suits at the same time. The whimsical instructions he included on his scores: "Light as an egg." "Here comes the lantern." And one that seems particularly apropos now: "Work it out yourself."

When I was in eighth grade, I had an art teacher I particularly liked. She was a pretty, reckless blonde who wore huge hoop earrings and laughed loudly all the time, and she made all of us excited about art because of the obvious if erroneous assumption that if we loved art, we'd be like her. Once, when I was trying to sketch something, she came over to help me. She put her hand over mine, and together we began creating a lovely image. Then she said, "Okay, you finish it now." But I couldn't finish what we had begun—it didn't work. Instead, I ended up drawing something altogether different. "Oh, my goodness," she'd said when she saw the finished drawing. "You did something else! Wonderful!" But I was disappointed. I knew that if her hand had stayed on mine, out of our combined imaginations would have come something neither of us would have done alone. And that it would have been so much better than what I went on to fashion alone. But what was I to do? There was a full forty minutes left to the class. I had to fill the time.

I turned onto my side and sighed deeply, pulled the blankets up higher. This room stayed stubbornly cold, even when the rest of the house was warm. As I punched at my pillow to reshape it, my fingers brushed across my lips, making for a rich tingle. Such a gnawing hunger inside for the simple pleasure of touch, such an edgy despair that came from the lack of it. Tomorrow I would call the man who'd left a message. He might be someone I would like to get to know. I swallowed hard against a sudden montage of imagined humiliations, then decided I'd do no such thing.

In the kitchen the next morning, I looked out the window, blinked my eyes against the brightness, and moaned. It was snowing—large flakes that looked like shredded lace. But I was immune to the beauty: there were three or four inches on the ground already. I didn't feel able to shovel it. I didn't feel able to do much of anything. Once again, I'd had terrible, frightening dreams, and this time when I'd awakened, I'd heard a man's voice, ominous and low, seeming to come directly from a corner of the room. I'd sat up, terrified, but when I'd turned the light on, nothing was there, of course. But I hadn't been able to go back to sleep.

I pulled out Matthew's number and dialed it. I would ask if I could hire him to shovel—if not to rent me his room to sleep in at night. The phone rang several times, and then there was

Matthew's voice mail, hopeful-sounding. No doubt he was waiting for his girlfriend to come to her senses. I started to leave a message but decided against it. Who knew when he would call back? I needed to get the sidewalk and porch steps cleared as soon as possible. I'd eat a quick breakfast and get over to the hardware store for the widest, lightest shovel I could find.

I took a long time at the store—it was soothing to be in a place full of things that could help you repair or rebuild or maintain. There was the smell of coffee in the air, coming from the back room; and two men in paint-splattered clothes talked and laughed at the checkout counter where they waited for keys to be made. I looked at the plastic bins of nails and screws and washers and hinges, the wide variety of lightbulbs, halogen to pink-tinted, then moved over to the housewares section to view the basic pots and pans, the blue-and-white-speckled coffee percolator, the gargantuan bottles of Windex and Formula 409. If a high-end fashion store was a singing siren, a hardware store was your practical Uncle Walter, wearing bib overalls and carrying a hammer, asking you in a hearty, sausage-and-egg voice to point him in the direction of what needed to be done. After I'd finished examining drill bits and wrenches, pliers and ball-peen hammers, and many other things I had no idea how to use, I selected a huge blue plastic shovel, light enough to carry home but heavy enough to get the job done, I hoped.

It took an hour for me to shovel—it was heavy snow and I had to do it twice, because by the time I finished the first time, another inch had fallen. I looked up at the sky—still dark and cloudy, the snow seeming to fall even faster. I supposed I needed to load up on some groceries, too. I rested the shovel against the front porch, then headed resolutely back to town. I needed to check the newspaper or listen to the radio—what were we in for, anyway?

Apparently something bad. Lines at the grocery store were long. People were stocking up on toilet paper, on milk and bread and eggs, on cans of soup and boxes of pasta. Several people had turkeys in their basket. "How bad is it supposed to **be**?" I asked the cashier, and she rolled her eyes. "Oh, not that bad. They can predict half an inch for the first snowfall and people will do this. It happens every year, I swear. Come January, they can predict three feet and nobody raises an eyebrow."

I looked around at all the full carts, then at my little basket. "Maybe I should get more."

"Do you have to drive far to get here?"

I laughed. "I can walk."

The cashier laughed, too. She was a pleasant-looking woman, curly brown hair streaked with gray. An open smile. She wore many pins on her smock, mostly jokey ones but also a larger one with a picture of two young children, beneath which was written, GO AHEAD: MAKE MY DAY. ASK ME ABOUT MY GRANDCHILDREN.

"This is just the usual mass hysteria," she said. "People scare people." She looked at her watch. "Good. Quitting time." She put her CLOSED sign at the end of my groceries, apologized to the irate customer who was forced to go to another check-out lane. Then, after she rang me up, she untied her apron and said, "Think I'll go home and snuggle under a blanket with my hubby—watch a movie and eat popcorn for dinner."

"Sounds great," I said, and concentrated on the lemons resting at the top of my grocery bag. I didn't want to look at her face and see how happy she was. I didn't want to begrudge her her simple pleasure. When I walked home, I thought about the last snowstorm John and I had endured. It was a surprise nor'easter that ended up dumping more than twenty inches of snow on us. The minute I heard the forecast, I called John at work and told him to come home, but he didn't leave his office until two hours later. By then, the roads were a mess—there'd been accidents on top of accidents. I waited for more than three hours for him to arrive, at first calling his cell phone every twenty minutes or so to make sure he was all right. Finally he told me to stop calling, that he'd see me when he saw me. This enraged me—the traffic reports were so bad, and I thought that somehow my checking in with him would ensure his safety. When he walked in the door, snow like a caul over his head and shoulders from his short walk from the car, I was weak in the knees with relief, but then I coolly ignored him until morning. I'd wanted to punish him for being short with me when my only sin was concern. I should have watched a movie with him. Under a blanket. Eating popcorn for dinner. I should have uncorked the most expensive bottle of champagne we had and flung my arms around him. I hoped we never had to realize all the opportunities we missed in this life.

At home, I rubbed the cavity of the chicken with a paste made of garlic and kosher salt and stuffed it with punctured lemons. I put it into the oven along with quartered red potatoes tossed with olive oil and rosemary and plenty of salt and pepper. I shoveled yet again, and when I came back inside, delicious smells were filling the house. So tired my muscles burned, I carried **The New Book of Middle Eastern Food** into the living room. One of my favorite things to do was to read about cooking while smelling something cooking. I was grateful to have the pleasure so unambivalently back. I turned on a lamp against the gathering darkness, stretched out on the sofa, and started with the acknowledgments.

"I never knew anyone who actually **read** cookbooks," John had once told me. I'd been engrossed in **Beat This!,** my all-time favorite cookbook, which, in truth, I had already read cover to cover. "Lots of people read cookbooks," I'd answered testily—I'd been at a good part and didn't want to be interrupted. **"Why?"** he'd asked. I'd looked over at his book, something about the North Pole, and said, "Why do you read that?" "For pleasure," he'd said. "For escape. For edification. For thrills." I'd held up my cookbook, raised my eyebrows. "Okay," he'd said.

But it was more than that. It was something harder to articulate. How are poets able to unzip what they see around them, calling forth a truer essence from behind a common fact? Why, reading a verse about a pear, do you see past the fruit in so transcendent a way? There are circumstances under which food is not just food—Jane Hirshfield, in her poem "Pillow," calls a provolone sandwich just that. But this is always true about food, as it is always true about a thousand aspects of daily life that we do not, cannot, fully appreciate—there is only so much room inside, and we are a busy species. It takes the poets to make for a divine displacement. The poets and death. Before, cookbooks were interesting to me, comforting. Now they served as testimony to my own kind of faith.

The introduction to this cookbook talked about how the author heard the voices of the people who gave her the recipes every time she made them. I understood that. I still heard my grandmother's tremulous but authoritative voice every time I baked her pistachio cake. I saw her, too, sitting at my mother's kitchen table, her still wonderfully thick white hair up in a glorious French twist, her light blue eyes direct and intelligent. In these visions, she wore a small-print housedress, safety-pinned at the top for a little extra modesty, though her legs were always spread wide apart. I saw her nylons knotted at the knee, her maroon corduroy slippers with the heels run-down disgracefully—but God forbid you try to replace them!

I turned to the list of recipes. Meatballs with eggplant sauce. Phyllo triangles with spinach-and-cheese filling. Sweet couscous; apricots stuffed with cream. I looked at pictures of blue plates holding red stuffed tomatoes, of brown pottery bowls holding thick yellow egg-and-lemon soup, of a large platter holding a whole fish in hot saffron and ginger-tomato sauce. Just as I was so hungry I was starting to get a headache, the timer went off and I went into the kitchen to fix myself a plate.

It was still snowing. I went closer to the window to watch the flakes falling, lazily now. Such a contrast: their delicate form versus the damage they could do. I saw Benny and two friends out in his backyard hurling snowballs at each other. "DIE!" I heard one of the friends say, and I pulled my cardigan closer about me and moved away.

It took me five minutes to eat dinner. Five minutes. Another minute to wash my dishes. Then I leaned against the kitchen counter, arms crossed, contemplating what to do next. I thought again about calling the man who'd left a message, but I was weary, and talking to a stranger would require something I now felt incapable of. I could go to bed but would probably only have another frightening dream.

I'd try Matthew again. And in addition to hiring him to shovel my walk for the season, I'd ask him to repaint my bedroom walls a soothing shade of blue. Who knew? It might help. This time, when I dialed the number, someone answered immediately.

"Yes." It was a man's voice, an impatient edge to it.

"Matthew?"

"No."

"Well, is he there?"

"Yes, he is here."

"May I **speak** with him?" **Jesus.**

The sound of someone getting up. And then, "Matthew! A call for you!" An accent. Spanish?

A distant response, and then the man said, "I know. But it's no her, you have on some other woman!" A pause, and then, "How do I'm supposed to know? I'm not your reception."

"Relax, Jovani," I heard, and then, "Hello?"

"Hi!" I said. "This is Betta Nolan. The woman from Cuppa Java?"

"Oh! Yeah!"

"I'm sorry if I'm calling at a bad time."

"No problem. Jovani's just . . . no problem."

"I was wondering if you'd be able to do a couple of jobs for me. Snow shoveling? For the season?"

"Sure."

"And then another job. Painting. Just one room."

"Yeah, okay."

"You've painted before?"

"Sure!"

"All right, so how soon do you think you could get the room painted?"

"Depends on the size. Depends on what shape the walls are in. I'd have to see it, then I could tell you. How soon do you need it done?"

"As soon as possible."

"Well, where do you live? I'll come and look tonight if you want, figure out how much paint you need."

"Tonight?" I looked out the window. Snow was still falling.

"Yeah," Matthew said. "It would be good if I could come tonight."

"But are the roads all right?"

"Yeah, the plow's been by. And anyway, you're close, aren't you?"

I told him my address, and he said, "All right. Fifteen minutes, tops."

It was a reflex, I supposed, that had me go to the mirror and inspect myself, then smear on some lipstick. I wondered when that reflex would finally go away. Once I passed an old lady waiting for a bus, and she had on so much makeup she literally looked like a clown—eyebrows drawn as severe black carets, rouge in comical circles. I remember saying to John, "If my makeup ever starts looking like that, you have to tell me right away." "I will," he'd said.

The phone rang. It was Matthew, saying, "My car won't start. Piece of junk. But if you want to come and get me . . ."

"Hold on." I went to look out the front window. Matthew was right; the plow had been by recently. I came back to the phone and said, "Okay, I'll come. Just tell me how to get there."

He gave me directions to his house, only a few miles away, and I started to put the chicken, barely touched, in the refrigerator. But then I left it out. He was a kid with money problems. He might like some free food. As natural as the instinct to primp for a man was my urge to feed one. A chicken sandwich, I was thinking, and a nice salad. I'd bought potato chips and Milano cookies at the grocery store.

I laid the table before I left and felt a rush of happiness at the prospect of caring for someone again. I once dropped in on a woman to deliver something, and she'd been preparing lunch for her husband. The table was set, and on her husband's paper napkin she'd drawn a heart with an arrow through it. When I saw it, she got embarrassed. But I told her I thought it was lovely. And I did. I also thought it was brave. The world was full of cynicism and judgment and what I believed was a knee-jerk recoiling against sentimentality. What had happened to us that we sneered at expressions of love and devoured stories of alienation and rage? Give me the hearts drawn on napkins, the men who walked on the street side of the sidewalk, the woman I met at a party who told me she always turned on Johnny Mathis to clean her bathroom. Give me the nurse who said, "You know, people think I'm such a good person to do what I do. But they don't understand that I get back far more than I give—it feels really good to take care of someone. It really does lift you up. When I go to work, I'm going to church."

I used to fantasize a lot about the son John and I could never have. **Ma,** he'd always be saying, laughing. That's how I'd always seen us: him as an older teenager, sitting in the kitchen with me, his feet so big. A handsome boy, goofing around with me. **Ma!** Lightly thwacking me with a dishcloth.

In these fantasies, the sun was always shining. Bright spring sunshine. The sun was shining and we were in the kitchen and the floor was a black-and-white-checked pattern I have never had and the windows were dressed with sheer fabric curtains I would never choose. The kitchen seemed to create itself of its own will, as did my fantasy son: he with his curly blond hair and wide shoulders, wearing gray sweatpants and a T-shirt and unlaced sneakers. He'd had a hoarse laugh and a mole at the side of his mouth. But now I would sit in a kitchen with a flesh-and-blood boy who looked nothing like that and who certainly was not my son. And yet.

I put on my coat and gloves, went out to my car, started it, and rubbed my hands together for warmth. Then, as I put the car into reverse, I noticed that I was almost out of gas. And that suddenly seemed insurmountable. I knew the exhaustion I'd been holding at bay was skewing my perception. But it didn't help to know why I felt like crying. I sat in the driveway, my hands over my face. And then I heard a small tapping at the window. Benny, a snowball in his hands, exaggeratedly mouthing something. I rolled down the window, forced a smile. "Hi," I said. "You guys are having fun, huh?" I offered a weak wave to the two other boys behind him. They looked at each other, then waved back.

"Are you okay?" Benny leaned his head in the car and took a quick look around, like a miniature state trooper.

"Yeah. I'm just going somewhere."

"Because it **looked** like you were crying."

"I felt like it for a second. But I'm all right now. I'm fine."

"Okay." He stood there, making sure.

"What do you do after school, Benny?"

He shrugged. "**I** don't know. Homework."

"Why don't you come over sometime? We'll make some cookies. Do you like to bake?"

"Well, mostly I only like to eat cookies."

"Me too. When you come, we'll bake cookies and then we'll eat them. What kind do you want?"

"Snickerdoodles, which I am the **only one** in my house who likes them."

"Great suggestion. Stand back now; I'm going to pull out."

"Okay." He moved back a few feet.

Before I turned the corner, I checked my rearview. Still standing there. For his vigilance and care, his cookies would be made with Vietnamese cinnamon.

"Come in, come in," Matthew said when I rang the doorbell. "Don't mind . . . don't mind anything. We haven't got the place too fixed up yet." He was wearing a baggy red sweater and blue jeans, a baseball cap, thick gray socks. Behind him, stretched out on a battered maroon sofa, I saw his roommate, a thin, dark-haired man wearing dress slacks and an untucked white shirt who smiled at me and then returned to watching a blaring television, some kind of game show. In addition to the sofa, the living room held two mismatched kitchen chairs and a board-and-brick bookcase. No rug. No curtains or blinds. A ripped poster of Avril Lavigne on the wall. One floor lamp, no shade.

"I just have to get my boots on," Matthew said. "You can wait in the living room with Jovani if you'd like." I looked over at the roommate, who was frowning, concentrating on the television. "Or," Matthew said, "I can show you the room for rent, see if you're interested." Hastily, he added, "Just kidding."

"I would like to look at it," I said. Besides, anything would be better than sitting in a room with some mindless television show on. I once heard two women at a restaurant talking about television. One liked it; the other hated it. The one who liked it said she kept it on for background noise; otherwise, it was too quiet. The other one said, "Buy a parakeet."

The room for rent was actually charming—dormers added character and coziness without making the room too small. There was a dresser and a twin bed, and an old wooden kitchen table to serve as a desk, complete with study lamp. The wallpaper was a clean blue-and-white stripe, and the floors were golden oak—recently refinished, judging by their condition. "Funny you're having trouble renting this," I told Matthew. "It's a really nice room."

"It's the time of year," he said, standing at the doorway and looking in as though he himself were considering renting it. "If it were August or early September, we'd be all set."

I nodded, thinking of how I'd decorate the place. How I'd move the bed to be between the dormers, how I'd add a chenille bedspread, a vintage flowered rug, a bedside table and lamp. "Want to see my room?" Matthew asked. "It's awesome."

Well, it was **large,** anyway. There was a bare mattress against one wall with a blanket tossed over it. No pillow. There were several plastic crates stacked up and serving as a chest of drawers of sorts, with clothes neatly folded inside them. CDs were piled high next to a portable player. There were a few photographs Scotch-taped to the wall, including one of Matthew and the young woman I saw him with in the coffee shop. I walked over to look at that photograph, and out of the corner of my eye I saw Matthew stiffen. "I've got to get rid of that."

I turned and smiled at him. "No, you don't."

"I just forgot about it. I really don't want it anymore."

"After a while, you might want it. Put it away somewhere. When you're an old guy, you can show your grandchildren all the beautiful girl-friends you used to have."

He laughed, his head down. "They haven't all been beautiful. One was real ugly. Annie Dupres, she was the one I actually liked best. Cool woman. Marathon runner and a medical student. She was in the Peace Corps; she went to Africa and taught English. Real dedicated type. And she could cook, oh man, she made such good stuff. I still feel bad about messing that one up."

"What happened?"

He pointed to the picture. "She did. Melanie." He said her name like he was spitting out a piece of foil he'd just found in his sandwich. "I met her at a party Annie and I went to. And I just . . . have you ever heard the expression, 'let the little head do the thinking for the big one'?"

I nodded, felt my face coloring.

"I'm sorry," he said quickly. "That was gross. I didn't—"

"It's fine," I said. "I don't know why I'm embarrassed. I've heard that expression a million times." I didn't want to add that I'd also used it.

He stared at the photo a moment longer, then pulled it off the wall and threw it into one of his crates. "Anyway." He stood with his hands in his pockets, looking down at Melanie's disarming smile. I thought I knew something about the way his stomach felt, missing her so. His tattered heart.

"Shall we go?" I asked gently.

On the way out, he pulled a light jacket from a hall closet jammed with coats, scarves, gloves, athletic equipment, books and papers and backpacks. I had to stop myself from asking if he'd be warm enough. No one wants to mother more vigilantly than a woman who is childless and wishes she wasn't.

"Cold in here!" Matthew said when he stepped into my bedroom.

"It is, isn't it?"

"Maybe it's haunted."

I started to unburden myself but quickly decided against it. And was glad, because he walked over to a corner, looked down, and said, "Here's your problem, right here. You gotta open your

vent." He tugged at a lever. "There you go. Now you'll be warm."

I walked over to the small grate I hadn't seen until now, put my hand down, and felt the rush of warm air. "Well, that was pretty simple. I feel like an idiot."

"It's only easy if someone's told you where to look," he said. He looked around the room and ran his hands along one wall. "The walls are in good shape. The paper will come down pretty easily, too. I could get a friend to help and do everything in maybe eight hours—that would be with primer and two coats of paint. So it would cost you sixteen hours of labor plus materials."

"Deal," I said. And then, "Would you . . . are you hungry?"

He looked off into space for a moment, his hand to his stomach. "Yeah. I guess I didn't eat dinner."

"Come on," I said, heading downstairs. "I've got leftovers. Do you like chicken sandwiches?"

"Sure."

"Milanos?"

"Of course!"

"Would you like a salad, too?"

"Okay."

In the kitchen I flipped on the overhead light. "Would you say that you're pretty easy to please?"

He sat at the table, tipping his chair back on two legs. "I don't know. Yeah, I guess."

I made up a half sandwich for myself, so that he wouldn't feel odd, eating alone. But it tasted so good, I made another half. Then I ate one Milano, two Milanos, three; and licked with pleasure the small smears of chocolate from the ends of my fingers. John used to say that it was uncivilized to eat alone. I always thought that was pressing the point, exaggerating unnecessarily the minor discomfort one feels in such a situation. But in this as in many other things, he was right. I now had intimate knowledge of how the deterioration could progress. First: Why sit down at a table? Then: Why use a plate? Why bother with silverware? Finally: Why eat at all?

Matthew ate the last potato chip, then said, "I hope this isn't rude, but—"

"Would you like another sandwich?"

He smiled.

By the time I drove Matthew home, the storm had suddenly worsened; my windshield wipers could barely keep up, and I was careful to leave plenty of space between me and other drivers after one car ahead of me fishtailed wildly. By the time we reached his house, visibility had been reduced to almost nothing—I turned in to his driveway only because he said, "It should be about here." Then I turned off the ignition and sat still for a moment, collecting myself.

"I don't think you should drive home," Matthew said.

"I think I can make it," I said.

"It's pretty bad. You could stay here. I mean, you saw the room. You could stay if you want."

"Thanks, but I'll be fine."

He shrugged. "Okay. So go look at some samples and tell me what color blue to buy—I'll get the paint from this place that gives me a discount. I'll have your room done by the end of next week." He opened the car door, then immediately shut it—the angle of furiously falling snow was such that it blew in forcefully. "You **sure** you want to drive home?"

No. "Yes, uh-huh."

"I feel like I ought to say, 'Well, you can't,' but . . ."

"You're too little?" I said, laughing.

"Well, no. I mean, I just thought it would be disrespectful or something." He pulled his jacket tighter about himself, shivered. "Maybe you could . . . I don't know, maybe you could call me when you get home?"

I stared at him, smiling.

"I mean, you don't . . . if anything happened to you, there'd be nobody . . ."

I stopped smiling, looked down. **Right.**

"Oh, man, I'm sorry. I only meant—"

"It's all right. I'll call if you want. It was nice of you to suggest it."

"Okay. So, you know the number. Be careful!" He climbed out of the car, slammed the door, and waved. I waved back, then put both hands tightly on the wheel and started pulling out of the driveway. It was hard to see anything but a white mass. Well, probably no one else would be idiotic enough to be out on the road; there'd be no one to hit. Of course, there would be other things to hit—lampposts, for instance. And what if someone was walking in the street and I didn't see them in time to stop? I sat thinking for a moment, then turned on the radio and heard the tail end of the announcer saying that again, unless it's absolutely mandatory, **stay off the roads.** I turned off the radio, backed up a few more feet, then put the car into park. I looked up at Matthew's house. Why take a chance? What was I trying to prove?

I pulled forward again, turned off the engine with great relief, and ran up to his door. It opened before I knocked. "Good," he said. "Want a beer?"

In the morning, there was a Dutch Master quality to the light coming through the window. The wooden table and chairs glowed golden; the blue in the wallpaper was deeper, more vibrant. I heard the muffled sounds of children playing outside, then the reassuring scrape of a snowplow. I looked at my watch—nine-thirty! For the first time since John's death, I'd slept all night. I sat up at the side of the bed, stretched. I'd slept in my shirt, and it was thoroughly wrinkled, but no matter, my sweater would cover it. Matthew had offered to let me use some pajamas, and then Jovani, not to be outdone, offered his own—silk! From Milan!—but I'd declined both offers, reassuring them that I'd be fine. I'd seen them exchange looks and had wondered what they were thinking. **She's not going to sleep nude, is she? Eew.**

We'd stayed up late, watching movies and taking turns going to the window to announce that the snow was still falling. Matthew had the **Godfather** trilogy, and we'd watched two of the movies and ate nachos courtesy of Matthew, who apparently had an extraordinary love of jalapeños. "Why you are always put it so many?" Jovani had asked, and Matthew had said, "Aw, here we go again. Just pick them off!"

"And then what?" Jovani had said. "An ugly little pile, make me sick. What I don't eat, I don't want to see it."

"Deal with it," Matthew had said.

In between films, Jovani had bemoaned his difficulties finding a job—he'd arrived in this country from Brazil early in the spring and still had done nothing but low-paying temp work. Matthew had suggested one of his problems was that he wore sneakers to interviews. "I keep telling you, you have to dress up a little," he'd said. "You can't wear sneakers to a job interview!"

"Listen, Matthew," Jovani had said. "I have twenty-nine years. I know exactly how to put on my feet."

I'd smiled at this, and when Jovani noticed, I'd pointed with a nacho to the television screen, where Diane Keaton was screaming after bullets were fired into Al Pacino's and her bedroom. "What?" Jovani had said. "You think to see this is funny? This is not funny."

"I know," I'd said.

"One thing in Americans is always violent," he'd said, sniffing. "I am tired in my mind of it."

I got up and went to the bedroom window to look outside. The sky was a cloudless blue, and the sun was out; the road was for the most part clear. But the driveway was blocked by what the plow had pushed aside—a good couple of feet of snow.

I heard a knock at the door and then Matthew said, "Coffee's ready."

"Thank you!" I quickly dressed and went to the door to listen—I was embarrassed to be seen before washing up. I heard no sounds, so I cracked the door, peered down the hallway, and went into the bathroom. It looked worse in the daytime: towels flung everywhere, the uncapped toothpaste, the water glass splattered with white, and the toilet seat emphatically up and not ex- actly ready for a starring role in a Ty D Bol com- mercial. I spread toothpaste onto my finger and brushed as well as I could, then splashed water on my face and dried it with my shirt. I combed my hair with my fingers and wiped at the dark smudges of leftover eyeliner beneath my eyes, then stood back to have a look. It seemed to me that every woman past a certain age who looked closely at herself in a mirror had the same reac- tion: **Oh, well.**

In a grocery store, I'd once heard a woman who

looked to be in her eighties say to her companion, "Every day I think I'm back in my thirties, and then every morning I get up and look in the mirror." Her companion, a woman at least as old as she, leaned over to grab her friend's wrist and confide with a Parkinsonian tremble, "You know, I always say this; I still feel like a girl inside." I'd looked at their bowed backs, their tight perms, the single-sized cans of baked beans in their carts, thinking, **Me too.** It seemed impossible that I was so far away from standing sleepily before my dresser drawer, pulling out white cotton underpants and a T-shirt, then dressing quickly and racing out the door without so much as a key to weigh me down.

I went back to the bedroom, folded my blankets, placed them neatly at the foot of the bed, then went downstairs to the kitchen. Matthew sat at the small metal table in sweatpants and a flannel shirt, reading from one of his textbooks. His feet were bare, his hair uncombed, a shadow of a beard on his face.

There were three lawn chairs around the table, the folding, woven-plastic-strip variety, missing a fair number of strips. On one counter were a coffeemaker and a toaster oven; otherwise, it was bare. A threadbare rug whose design featured a sleeping cat was in front of the sink. But the sun shone through the windows, and the room held a stubborn cheerfulness.

"Thanks so much for letting me stay here last night," I said.

"No problem. It was fun, actually." He clasped his hands behind his head and smiled.

"Do you have class today?"

"Way later. Have a seat. It's my turn to give you a meal."

I sat gingerly on one of the chairs. Once, a man who worked with John came to dinner at our house. He sat on one of the kitchen chairs—they were beautiful antiques—and it broke, spilling him onto the floor. He rose up quickly, embarrassed, and began to weep. "I'm so sorry," he said, at the same time that I was asking if he was all right. Then he began to laugh, saying, "Obviously, I've got some things going **on** in my life." I always liked that man, because I saw him as someone like John, someone unafraid to tell the truth about what he was feeling. Perhaps it was the incident of the broken chair that forced him into a kind of intimacy he might not otherwise have shown. I saw it as a happy accident, if that were the case. But I didn't want to fall out of this lawn chair, and so I sat very still and tried to support some of my weight on my legs.

Matthew went to the cupboard, pulled down a mug featuring the fading head of an Irish setter, filled it with coffee, and put it before me.

"Do you like setters?" I asked.

"What do you mean?"

I pointed to the dog on the mug.

"Oh. No."

"Would you have any cream?" I asked.

He shook his head. "Sorry. And we don't have sugar, either. Do you take sugar?"

"No, I don't. But . . . how about milk, would you have a little milk?"

"No, I guess not."

"Powdered milk?"

He scratched at his neck, frowning.

"Never mind," I said. "This is fine." I took a sip.

"I hope you like strong coffee." Matthew poured himself another cup.

"Yes, I do," I said, although this tasted not so much like strong coffee as like dirt.

"So, um . . . would you like your Pop-Tart now?"

"Oh! A **Pop**-Tart."

"That's all we've got. Unless . . . I could make you nachos."

"A Pop-Tart would be fine. Thank you."

He pulled a box from the otherwise nearly empty cupboard, then looked inside. "Uh-oh. Empty. Aw, man, I'm sorry."

"It's fine," I said. "I'm not hungry anyway. So! Have you heard anything about the weather for today?"

"Yeah." He sat across from me. "The snow should all melt; the temperature's going way up."

"Where's Jovani?"

"He went to fill out an application somewhere. In sneakers, of course."

I took another sip of the coffee, then looked at my watch. "Oh, look at that, I've got to get going!" I dumped the coffee discreetly into the sink, then added the mug to a high pile of dirty dishes. When I was in college, one of the boys who lived next door with four other guys once came to get me. "It's my turn to do dishes," he'd said, "and I don't know how. Will you help me?"

"You know how to do dishes!" I'd said, and he'd widened his eyes and held up his hand— **I swear.**

"Oh, all right, I'll help you," I'd said, envisioning some scene from a romantic comedy. Bubbles on the end of the girl's nose; the guy wipes them off and gives her a little kiss. Not that I wanted a kiss from Jerry Kessler, whose idea of high culture was a belching contest where one took **turns.**

Jerry's kitchen sink was overflowing with dishes caked with what looked like take-out food— pizza, mostly—and the counter was covered, too. Mold grew everywhere. If it hadn't been so nauseating, it would have been fascinating.

"No way," I'd said, and turned to leave.

"I'll fix Lorraine's car," he'd said, desperation thinning his voice. "The timing is way off." I'd turned back and said icily, "Well, isn't that nice. Get Lorraine to help you then."

"Like she would!" he'd said. "Come on, I'll give you a doobie and **Sgt. Pepper.** I just bought it—I haven't even played it yet, I swear."

"Where's your stupid dish soap?" I'd asked, rolling up my sleeves.

"I don't know," he'd said. "Where would it be?"

Now Matthew stood and pushed his lawn chair up to the rickety table. Something about the misplaced elegance made me smile—he might have had a white linen towel draped over one arm. "Let me get some boots on and I'll shovel you out," he said.

"I'll do it," I said. "You've done enough."

"What have I done? Really. I mean, all I did is let you sleep here. Big deal. It's like coffee, you know, when people have dinner at somebody's house and the host says, 'Anyone want coffee?' and the guests all say, 'I'll have a cup, but only if you're making it anyway.' Like it's a big deal to make coffee."

"I know," I said. "It's true."

"Did it **used** to be a big deal to make coffee?"

"You mean . . . like in the olden days? When I roamed among the dinosaurs?"

"**No.** I just meant . . . you know."

"We've had coffeemakers since I can remember," I said. "I mean, they used to be percolators, but—"

"Sorry I said that."

"It's okay. We just . . . **have** had coffeemakers since I can remember. I guess it used to be a big deal. You had to grind the beans, let the water boil . . . Well. Anytime you're ready. I've got to go home and take my Geritol."

He looked at me, puzzled.

"Never mind," I said.

Outside, the sun reflected hard off the new snow. I dug in my purse for sunglasses, then stood watching Matthew work. At one point, I insisted on a turn, but he shook his head. "I'll have you right out of here," he said.

When he finished, he opened the car door with a flourish and waved me in. I started the engine and looked up at him. "Thank you."

"You're welcome."

"You're such a nice kid. Who taught you your wonderful manners?"

"My mom. Though she never liked the way I ate."

"Oh?"

"Yeah. Too fast. She liked you to sit up straight and take your time. She—" He looked away for a long moment, then back at me. "She died when I was fourteen."

"I'm sorry."

"Yeah. I really miss her. Especially sometimes."

"Yes. I know." I fastened my seat belt, adjusted my rearview.

"This friend of mine said that when his mom died, he felt like he'd been dropped onto a mirror planet. Like everything was still familiar, only kind of backwards. He said he felt completely disoriented."

"I understand that, too."

"For me, it didn't feel like I was in a different place. It was the same place. Just way lonelier. Like a big chunk had been cut out of the best part."

"Right."

Matthew looked at me, deliberating. Then he said, "Hey, Betta? What are you going to do tonight?"

I pointed to myself, an old habit I would apparently never break. "Me?"

"Yeah."

I thought for a moment, then said, "I don't know."

"Want me to take you to a really cool restaurant that nobody knows about?"

I laughed.

"No, I need something to do. And I'm not ready to go back to . . . I don't know, dating." He put his hands in his pockets, shrugged.

"I know what you mean," I said. "I'll go. But only if you let me pay."

"No deal. Dutch treat."

"All right. How's seven o'clock?"

"Good. I'll come and get you."

"What about your piece-of-junk car?"

"I'll have it running by then. I'll fix it this afternoon."

"Is there anything you can't fix?"

He grinned. "Nope."

I started backing out of the driveway and saw his mouth moving. I rolled down my window.

"Don't forget to pick out your paint color," he said. "And find brushes and a couple of good rollers that you like; I **might** let you help."

"Okay, Tom."

He stared at me blankly.

"Tom Sawyer?"

He looked worried. "No, it's . . . Matthew O'Connor."

"I meant Tom Sawyer like the character in the book."

"The book."

"The Adventures of Tom Sawyer."

"Yeah, but what's the name of the book?"

There was a message on the machine when I got home. Lorraine, saying, **Hey, Betta. I was thinking about some things you could do. To feel better. You've got the time and the resources, right? I mean, you really do have time and resources. I was thinking, there must be fifty ways to grieve your lover, ha ha. You know that song, right?**

Wait. Is that funny? It was meant to be funny. But I'll bet it's not.

Okay, I hate when I do this. Disregard this message. It was meant to be funny. I hate that I said that. It's . . . you know when someone's in the hospital with something really serious and you think, Well, all those other people are weeping and moaning and being all serious and sensitive, I'll just offer some comic relief? Did you ever feel that way?

Betta? You're not standing there and listening to this, are you? Like, in horror? Betta? Oh, Jesus, delete, delete, delete. I just have never learned certain social graces, okay? I didn't mean to be insensitive. I'm sorry.

Good God, how long does your machine let people talk? Okay, I'm going. Call me. Or I'll call you. Though you can rest assured that if you're not there, I—

At last, the beep cut her off.

Lorraine was right—she didn't have many social graces. Her policy was to act first, think later—if at all. But such carelessness, such selfishness, seemed to be license of the glamorous. The really good-looking people I knew all capitalized on and benefited from their genetics in one way or another. In their defense, I believed some of this was forced on them by people eager to ingratiate themselves with such superior specimens. Still, there was something about Lorraine

that made most people like her. I myself had re-
sponded immediately to her honesty and direct-
ness. I called her number and got her machine.
"Hello," I said. "I'm calling from Acme Charm
School to tell you we're running a special in your
neighborhood. Call back for details."

I showered, looked in the yellow pages for a
paint store, then called for directions. "I'm new
here," I said, by way of explanation, and the man
who answered said, "Well, **welcome,**" so warmly
it brought tears to my eyes. When I opened the
door to go out again, there was a package on the
porch. The return address showed it was from
Maddy, and I brought it to the kitchen table and
opened it eagerly. On top was a letter.

Dear Betta,

Oh, sweetheart. I'm so sorry about your husband. I wish I'd known him, but I know you—
I **do** feel like I still know you—and so he must
have been wonderful. I'm sure you've been
through hell and aren't finished yet with the
particular and very personal sorrow you must
endure. But I want you to know I'm thrilled
that we have connected again. I can't wait to see
you, but Lorraine told me you need time, and
I'm happy to give you that. You take all the time
you need. Do everything good and bad you feel
like doing. But I wanted to at least write to you
and to send you a few things. These are just for

fun. And for love. Call me if you want. Otherwise, I'll wait for our grand reunion.

I wonder what you look like. I'm so fat now.
But I stopped caring about three months ago—
it's so nice to step up to a bakery case and
not immediately self-flagellate. Call me anytime. Come visit anytime. I'll send you a ticket,
I'll come to you, I'll do anything you want. We
all will.

I look upon this as the most profound of gifts,
that we have found you again. Maybe Lorraine
told you, but we have come to depend on each
other even more than we used to. Welcome
back to our little constellation. We've always
saved a place for you.

Love,
Maddy

P.S. Susanna is fat, too. Only Lorraine isn't.
And maybe you, are you still skinny? Remember
when we lay out on the roof of our house in our
underwear and our stomachs were all FLAT? I
can't really remember. I think I made it up.

XXXXXXOOOOOO

There were four wrapped packages beneath the
letter. I picked up the first one, the smallest, and
opened it. It was a bar of wonderfully scented
soap, cushioned on a thick white washcloth. The
second was silk long johns. The third was a tin of
toffee, the smell of which nearly lifted me right

out of my chair. And the fourth, a large package, held a thirties-style dressing gown, a beautiful apricot color, with ostrich feathers at the ends of the sleeves. I smiled at it, thinking it lacked only cha-cha shoes. And then, when I lifted the gown out of the box, there they were. Little backless heels, dyed to match. If I ever opened What a Woman Wants, Maddy could be in charge of the whimsey department.

I reread the letter, sat back in the chair, took another long drink of coffee. And noticed a specific and breathtaking absence. At the moment, nothing hurt. What I felt was only hope, that internal sunrise. The image of John's face came into my head, and I felt only my great luck at having had him for as long as I did. I'd learned enough about grieving to know that other ways of feeling would come back soon enough. But it seemed to me that this was the way we all lived: full to the brim with gratitude and joy one day, wrecked on the rocks the next. Finding the balance between the two was the art and the salvation.

On the way to get paint, I drove to the empty storefront. I'd lost the number, and I had promised myself that today I really would call it. I'd make an appointment and take a good look at the place. But the store was no longer for rent. The sign was down, and brown paper had been put up so that you couldn't see in. I sat idling for a long time, trying to put things into perspective. Because although this was only a space that I had been interested in and could no longer rent, what it felt like was another death. I tried to remind myself of my great fortune at not having to work at all. At being able to take plenty of time before I decided on anything definite. But I did not feel fortunate. I felt bitter. And I felt foolish for not following through on an impulse I'd known full well was a good one.

I arrived home in the late afternoon, walked in the door to a ringing phone, and dropped my packages to answer. It was a man, saying, "Oh, hi! Ms. Nolan, this is Tom Bartlett. I'm just trying you back. I called the other day; I don't know if you got the message."

"I did," I said. "I just . . . I haven't gotten a chance to call you back yet." I looked with sudden longing at all the things I needed to put away. And I wanted to cook something to have ready for Matthew to take home so that those boys would have something to eat in the house. "Actually, this isn't the best time, either."

"Okay. I'm sorry to disturb you. Thanks anyway."

His voice was so kind I felt ashamed of myself. "Well, wait," I said. "I have a few minutes. Maybe we can just . . . you wanted to talk to someone about writing, is that it?"

"In all candor, I called in the heat of the moment. I heard you on the radio and thought, Well, why not? I've always been interested in writing, but I've never tried it. But now that I'm retired, I'm going to take the plunge. I thought if I could just take a few moments of your time, I'd get some idea of how to get started."

"Well, there are many books on the subject," I said.

"Are there?"

A true innocent! I'd expected him to say the

usual: "Yes, and I've read a lot, but there are just some things I'd like to talk to **you** about."

How bad could it be? A grandfatherly type, trying to finally scratch an itch. An image came to me: blue eyes, thick white hair, a cardigan sweater with leather buttons. I could talk to him. I could tell him about the value of writing for oneself, or of passing on his life story to his grandchildren, if nothing else. "I'll tell you what," I said. "How about if we meet at Cuppa Java, on Main Street?"

"That would be wonderful. What time would be good for you?"

"Sunday? About eleven?"

"Perfect. And shall I bring . . . well, how much will this cost?"

I laughed. "Nothing."

"Oh. Well, thanks very much. I'll look forward to seeing you. I'm tall, and . . . I'll wear a red sweater."

"I will too," I said, smiling. The old cutie. I always liked being around old guys. Their chivalry. Old Spice cologne. Their suspenders and tie shoes. The way their experience showed and the way their opinions seemed well considered. The way their hands still seemed so strong. I hung up the phone and started putting the groceries away. Next I'd make Jovani and Matthew a spinach lasagna. And a chocolate cake that would make them both my slaves. Buttermilk and **good** coffee in the batter, cream cheese frosting, strawberry fans for the top.

After Matthew dropped me off from our dinner, I came into the front entry and hung up my coat, then walked over to the sofa and sat numbly staring straight ahead. I felt terrible. Some of it was because of Matthew's sweetness, his vulnerability, and the way he continued to endure abuse from Melanie. She'd called on our way to the restaurant, and he'd agreed to build her some bookcases in her new place right after she told him all about her new boyfriend. He'd asked if he could delay painting my bedroom for a while.

"Of course," I'd said, "but are you sure you want to do this?" He'd stared straight ahead, then nodded. "Yeah. She can be rough. But I want to do this for her because I want to see her again. I guess it's dumb, but I . . . ." He'd sighed. "I still love her. It sucks. I think about her all the time.

I can't get interested in anyone else. She's not all bad—I mean, I know I made some mistakes. I'd really like another chance. I guess I could make some changes or something. I could make some changes."

But mostly my sorrow was for myself. For one thing, I'd felt so odd sitting across a restaurant table from a man who was not my husband. I kept seeing the way John used to put on his half-glasses to study the menu, the elegant and discreet way he signaled for the check, the way he helped me on and off with my coat, the steadiness of his affection. In our house, he loved me. At a restaurant, he loved me. While I slept, while I worked, even when we argued, he loved me. It was a second heartbeat, as vital in its own way as the first. Now there was only a sticky Formica table and a young man across from me in harsh light bobbing his knee and asking who was Huey Newton after I happened to mention him. (And then, after I'd answered, who were the Black **Pan**thers?)

For the first time, I'd felt old. It hadn't been only because of Matthew's **Save the Tiger** questions; it hadn't been the way that, in the presence of the other young couples there, the fact that I could be his mother was accentuated. It wasn't the background music that Matthew hummed along with that I'd never heard. It was that tonight I'd felt the sudden collapse of a kind of internal support wall that heretofore had offered me a certain protection, a wall built and maintained by my husband, I now realized. No one could ever be for me what John had been because he had known me **when,** and that had kept me away from the true reality of my years. I'd joked about bifocals, about memory loss, about the losing battle with gravity. But I hadn't really felt my age until now. Was I ready for the rocker? No. But was I as young as I'd thought? No.

Sitting at that table and smiling falsely, my mouth had gone dry. I'd seen that I was in for many more grim discoveries, psychological land mines. I'd known when I met John that he was uniquely suited to me in hundreds of ways. But there'd been the knowing in his life, and there was the knowing after his death.

The restaurant, optimistically called Lucky's, was a small, storefront place, the owner from some eastern European country. He spoke almost no English. Matthew went there often—the food was cheap, the servings large, the décor charming, in its way. Personal, at least, with black-and-white family photographs on the wall. Near the cash register was an absurd little grouping of porcelain dogs and cats. But the meat had been tough, the vegetables watered-down, the laminated menus fingerprinted with grease in a way less funky than disgusting. One hopes to discover something in restaurants like this: Waiters full of character and charm. Fabulous food at rock-bottom prices. Neither of these had been there. The food had been awful, and the staff silent and sad beneath a veneer of pleasantness.

Or maybe it was just me.

John had talked, soon after he was diagnosed, about a sense of separateness, of seeing through cancer glasses, thus having distorted vision. He was not **among** the rest of us anymore, he'd said; he felt irrevocably apart.

I felt apart now, too, looking at the world through widow glasses. The mantel clock chimed ten. I stood up and moved to look out the window, wrapped my arms around myself, and noticed, dully, that I'd lost more weight. I thought, **It's true that when someone you love dies, part of you dies, too. And then must be reborn.** And many people were reborn, they suffered through their pain and emerged victorious: their love for the lost one revered but put away, their lives now open to a separate course. Others never did quite recover. I'd made a promise— many promises—to John to be among those who not only survived but thrived.

I was trying, in what I supposed were haphazard ways. Move to a new town; befriend the child next door; eat dinner with a tortured young man afloat in the restless sea of his own young life; entertain the notion of creating my own business, in my own way. Reestablish contact with the girlfriends of yesteryear.

What luck that I had found them again. I had been thinking of having them all here, inviting them for next weekend. I had envisioned us sprawled out in the living room, talking, talking, talking, without fear of censure, without embarrassment of need. Now I didn't know if I was up to it.

I went to the Chinese chest and pulled out a slip of paper: **Iron grates.** I had no idea. Quickly, I pulled another: **Japanese tea ceremony.** Again, I had no idea.

I went upstairs to my bedroom, got the packet of photos from my nightstand drawer, and pulled one out. It was of a courtyard in Portugal where there was a statue of a man whose mustache seemed intent on flying off his face. I remembered John taking that shot, remembered, too, that we'd just had lunch and he'd gotten a stain on his sweater, an unusual occurrence for such a fastidious man. The picture showed two old women dressed in black, sitting and talking, kerchiefs on their heads. One stared directly at the camera, her black-stockinged legs wide apart; the other sat in profile with her hands clasped in her lap, her knees together. I remembered that it was only after the picture was taken that the women smiled; one had had no teeth. Behind the women were buildings with walls the colors of apricot and burnt sienna and sage green. There were lace curtains at the window of one apartment, and draped over one of its wrought-iron balconies were white shirts, drying in the sun. Above that, a clothesline stretched from one window to another, full of more laundry, which probably was the reason John had taken the photograph; a gift to me and my odd predilection.

I remembered that after the shot was taken, those two women had asked John if he would like them to take a picture of us. Oh, no, we'd both said. We'd explained how neither of us liked to be photographed. Oh, no. What need did we have of photos when we had each other?

I dumped the rest of the pictures out on the bed. Façades of churches, a group of pigeons at the feet of a smiling old man, a lovely sunset. Not one of John. But here was one taken in Venice, and I remembered it distinctly. It might be good to revisit that particular memory.

The photo was of a gondola we'd ridden in. John hadn't wanted to go for a gondola ride. He said he would feel like an idiot. I said, John. We're in Venice. **Everybody** who comes to Venice rides in a gondola. Precisely, he said. I stood blinking at him. Finally I said, SO? So you can't do something just because other people do? Since when? Do you sit alone at the opera? Did you invent fishing? This is different, John said.

It's too much a display. And it's pedestrian, really; we can find something much better to do. Yes, I said, let's go and find something none of the idiotic **tourists** do. We'd jousted back and forth, I far more angry than John—he was actually amused—and I think it was that air of superiority, Ricky smirking at Lucy, that made me so furious. When the gondolier pulled up to the pier where we were arguing and asked if we wanted a ride, John said, "Why, yes, we were just talking about that!" and he jumped into the boat and offered his hand to me. What was I to do? I had no idea where I was; I spoke no Italian; and John had the room key with the hotel name and address. I vowed never again to travel without my own key.

I remembered seething, sitting in that gondola with my arms crossed tightly over my chest as we glided along. Some better part of me had wanted to shrug off my vile mood and point to the many things that delighted me, to share with John what my friend Marianne had said about Venice: that it was like an aging beauty queen in need of some serious dental work. Instead, I took in the sights frozen-faced, and John eventually positioned himself so that he would not have to see me. And that poor gondolier, clueless as to what our problem was, wanting only for us to attend to his weak tenor and the charm of his navigation. I would have none of it. At the end of the ride, we tipped him extravagantly—each of us—apparently agreeing at least on this point: Someone so ill treated ought to get some kind of reward at the end of his ordeal. The irony, of course, was that John had ended up enjoying the ride and I'd hated it. When we disembarked, he'd snapped the photo in a move of ironic sentimentality that had only made me more angry. The red velvet seats festooned with gold plastic flowers! That evening had not ended well. We'd gone to bed angry and had slept as far from each other as possible.

I sat still, the photograph in my hand. The memory had not helped so much after all. It had not reminded me that life was not perfect with John. Instead, it had made me long for him with a deep and specific desire; I could feel it from my hips all the way up into the back of my throat. I would never stop longing for him. I would never be happy without him. I was the kind of person who needed to share something in order to fully experience it myself. But I had lost my partner, and I would never find a relationship even close to what I had. What was the point in pushing myself through the rest of my days?

I slid off the bed and onto the floor and put my hands over my face. "Please," I said. "Oh, **please.**"

I felt suddenly that something had come into the room with me, a presence, and I held stone still. I looked at the chair in the corner of the room, and there he was.

"John?" I put my hand to my chest, clenched at my sweater. "Are you here?"

He was smiling. His legs were crossed; he sat relaxed and looking over at me.

I began to cry. He uncrossed his legs and leaned forward, resting his arms on his knees, and there was such radiant love on his face, my pain disappeared. I felt pleasantly hypnotized, caught between worlds. "Are you hungry?" I asked. "You must be starving."

His face, looking back at me.

"I don't know why I said that."

I started to get up, and he shook his head no. I patted the floor. "Can you come here, then?" He stayed still. "Then I'm coming over there."

He disappeared.

I stared at the chair and listened to myself breathing. Then I reached for the phone and called Lorraine. When she answered, I started bawling.

"Betta?"

"Lorraine. I think I'm going crazy." More bawling.

"Go ahead and cry," she said. "It's all right." I continued to weep, and after a while, she said, "Okay, hold on. Let me get a cigarette."

When she returned, I told her what I had seen.

"Don't ever tell anyone I told you this," I said between hiccoughing sobs. "But what should I **do**?"

"I don't find what happened so unusual, Betta. You're in a very vulnerable and strange place right now. And anyway, these things happen all the time—I've had hallucinations!"

I wiped at my eyes. "Yeah, but you used to take drugs all the time. This wasn't a hallucination. He was really here!"

"No, honey, he wasn't."

I sat still, staring at the chair he'd been in. Then I said, "Could you come back here, and bring Maddy and Susanna? Will you bring them here?"

"Yes, actually, we were just talking about that."

"Lorraine, I'm . . . I feel scared."

"I know you do. Talk to me. I'm right here."

"Maybe . . . I shouldn't have moved. Maybe I shouldn't have lived after he died—I don't think I have the strength of character to do this." I began to cry again. "I don't want to **do** it anymore, and I'm so far from **done**! Oh, I shouldn't have even met him! Or I shouldn't have loved him so much. Or I shouldn't have **relied** on him so much. See, Lorraine, you don't know. You don't know. I shouldn't have thought I could recover so quickly. **'What an adorable town! What a pleasure to be here! I'm so strong, look at my new life, just falling into shape!'** No! I came out here and bought the house in this blind rush of confidence. But now I can't seem to . . . I lost that store, Lorraine. Somebody else rented it."

"Well, you can find another one. I'll come back and help you. Just sit tight and I promise I'll help you find another place."

"It was supposed to be John and me together, not just me! Not just me! I can't stay here; I'm going to have to move back to Boston, and now I've sold my **house**!"

I held the phone so hard it dug into my hand. I sobbed, making loud, ragged sounds that seemed to be their own, primitive selves, that astonished me with their utter authenticity. When I finally finished, I said miserably, "I don't know. I don't think I meant everything I just said. I don't even **know** what I just said."

I heard Lorraine blowing out a long column of smoke. Then she said, "I should think we could all be there by next Friday night, and stay for the weekend."

"Okay," I said. "Good."

"We'll get ourselves there, you just stock the cupboards. Okay?"

"Okay." I hung up the phone and took in a deep breath, looked again at the chair, which seemed to look back almost defensively.

Well. Nothing like a good cry to reverse your spirits. I went downstairs and put the teakettle on, then put **Lyle Lovett and His Large Band** on the stereo. I stood thinking about John, real as life, sitting in a chair in the corner of my bed-room. I didn't really believe these things hap-pened "all the time," as Lorraine had said. I turned the flame off under the kettle and walked back upstairs. In the hall just outside my bed-room, I hesitated, then walked in and sat at the side of the bed. Staring straight ahead, I slid off onto the floor and put my hands over my face. "Please," I said, and snuck a glance at the chair. Nothing. **"Please."** I squeezed my eyes shut and listened. Nothing.

When the doorbell rang, I turned quickly toward the sound, thinking, **John?** But it was Benny.

"Can I come over?" he asked. "My mom was supposed to be home at nine, but she's not back yet."

"Of course," I said. "Where is she?"

"Work," he said, shrugging off his jacket. "Sometimes she works late."

He had no sooner positioned himself before the television in the guest room when the door-bell rang again. It was Carol, embarrassed and apologetic, holding the note Benny had left her. "I'm so sorry," she said. "Is he here?"

"Upstairs," I said. "Come on in."

She stepped over the threshold, came no far-ther. "I was . . ." She took in a breath, then whis-pered, "Okay. I went to a motel with a man I work with. I turned off my cell, just while we were . . . anyway, we both fell asleep and I . . . God, I'm so embarrassed! What must you think of me?"

"Mom?" Benny called from upstairs. Then he clattered down. "Hi, Mom. Where were you?"

"Honey, I'm so sorry I'm late. It will never happen again. You run home; I'll be right there. I just want to talk to Betta."

Benny thanked me and left; Carol stared at the floor.

"Don't feel bad," I said.

She looked up at me, her eyes shining with tears. "I just . . . I need to be with a man sometimes, and I don't want to bring them home. And babysitters have gotten so expensive. This has never happened."

"Tell you what," I said. "Why don't you give me Benny one night a week?"

"I can't pay you. Right now, things are just so—"

"You don't have to pay me. Really. I'd love to do it."

"I don't know what to say."

"Wednesdays?"

She shrugged, then quickly hugged me. "Okay. Thanks."

I watched her run over to her house, which was not so very different from my own. Two lonely women, doing what they had to to get by.

I turned out the porch lights and it suddenly

came to me. **Japanese tea ceremony:** a way of honoring oneself by putting another's needs first, the joy that could be found in intimate service. A conversation we'd had one night on the way home from a movie. I remembered how that night he'd put toothpaste on my brush before his own, then bowed. I'd smiled, but I'd understood too that such small gifts were one seed that blossomed in two hearts.

Sunday morning I slept late and then took myself out for breakfast to Sutton's Pancake House, two blocks from the coffee shop. It looked good; it was a place I'd been meaning to try. I ate strawberry crêpes in the loud, bacon-scented restaurant and watched the people around me: a sleepy young couple dressed in sweatpants and flannel shirts reading the newspaper; a family of four dressed starchily for church; a young girl sitting on her knees, "eating **Mickey** Mouse! eating **Mickey** Mouse! eating **Mickey** Mouse!"; a group of six old ladies all wearing hats who laughed loudly and often. Over in the corner, a disheveled man muttered angrily while he ripped a piece of paper into small bits and sprinkled it over his uneaten eggs and bacon. And by the window, a man about my age in a nice leather jacket was nursing a cup of coffee and looking frequently at his watch. I wondered who he was waiting for. I checked his ring finger: nothing. I laid odds that if he were waiting for a woman, it would be someone thirty-five or under. But I couldn't wait to find out.

When I got up to pay, he did, too. We smiled at each other, and then I paid and walked rapidly toward the coffee shop. As I turned to go in, I saw him again, a short distance behind me. I remembered a woman once telling about meeting her husband this way. "I thought he was following me," she'd said. "I thought he was a psychopath."

I smiled hesitantly, held the door, and yes, he was coming in, too. We nodded at each other, took our tables, and when he took off his jacket I saw that he was wearing a red sweater. I swallowed, removed my own coat, and stared pointedly in another direction.

The man stood and came to my table. "Betta Nolan?"

I looked up at him. "Tom Bartlett."

"We meet again," he said. "Hello."

I cleared my throat. "Hello," I said.

He pointed to the chair. "May I?"

"Of course. But should we . . . did you want to order something first?"

"How about **Mickey** Mouse pancakes?"

"I know," I said, smiling.

"What would you like?" he asked.

"Tea, please. Any kind of herbal." I reached for my wallet.

"I've got it. Be right back."

I stared at the jacket he'd left hanging over the back of the chair, blew some air quietly out of my cheeks. Balding a bit, but still.

Hours later, I pulled a shortcake out of the oven and told Tom it would take a while to cool. "Why don't we go into the living room?" I said.

He followed me to the couch and sat beside me. "I never thought a ten-minute meeting would turn into"—he looked at his watch—"a seven-hour one!"

"Me either." I hadn't realized how much I'd missed talking to a man. Disparate things had poured out of me, as unstoppable as a waterfall. But he had seemed not to mind. He had the ability to listen, and he was a wonderful conversationalist. He had been married for fourteen years; his wife died seven years ago, no children. He hadn't really dated much, hadn't met anyone he was interested in. But he had just taken an early retirement from a computer consulting service and was ready to start making some changes in his life. His call to me about writing had been the opening salvo—though truth be told, we hadn't talked about writing much at all.

We'd walked around town, gone to a movie, had a drink at a small bar connected to an Italian restaurant, and then I'd invited him home for a quick dinner. I'd made chicken breasts in a wine sauce with mushrooms, pasta, a huge salad, and then decided we needed a blackberry shortcake.

"You know, Betta," he said, "it was an unusually brave thing you did, moving here. But I'm glad you did."

"Okay. I mean, me too." I laughed. "You know, I think I had way too much wine with dinner!"

He smiled. "That's all right." Seen from the proper angles, he really was a handsome man, quite fit, blue-eyed. This close, I could see the starlike design in his irises. "It's all right, isn't it?"

For a long time I said nothing, and then I leaned forward and closed my eyes. He kissed me and my stomach flipped. I pulled back, successfully converting my desire into annoyance. "You know what?" I said.

Tom nodded. "I understand. I really do." He looked at his watch. "Listen, I'd love to have dessert, but the truth is, I'm stuffed."

"Another time," I said, and walked him stiffly to the door.

"I'll see you," he said, and I smiled, said nothing. I watched him walk down the sidewalk, his gait quick and purposeful, his breath rising up in the night air. I wanted him to be a toy man that I could bring upstairs with me, then store on a high shelf in the closet. But he was alive and complicated. He came with his own parts that had their own demands. I did not know him. He was a stranger who had breathed in too much air in my house. I kind of hated him.

I leaned against the door and closed my eyes, full of confusion and a piercing regret. What? **What?** I was sorry. I was wrong and mean-spirited. I wished he'd come back. I wished I hadn't met him. I didn't want to want anyone. I wanted to want only John; I wanted for that not to be hopeless.

I slammed my fist against the door, once, twice, three times, turned out the lights, and went to bed without washing, without brushing my teeth, without putting on pajamas. I lay naked under the covers staring at the ceiling, then moved my hand slowly downward. Inside was undeniable need mixed with bowed-head humiliation. Inside was a weary kind of vacancy. I thought of strippers with their flat eyes, prostitutes leaning against cars. Sex that couldn't come close to satisfying any real desire.

Three A.M. A man's voice. That voice again. I sat up in bed, pulled my covers around me. "Come out!" I said. "I can see you!" Of course I could not. And of course if I could see a man hiding in my room, the last thing I would do is invite him to come out. I turned on the light, reached for the phone, and dialed Matthew's number. He answered immediately.

"It's Betta," I said. "Are you still awake?"

"Yeah! Uh-huh . . . what's up?"

"You're not up. I'm sorry I woke you, but can I come over there? Can I rent your room? Just to sleep in at night?"

"Well . . . yeah. But I'd feel bad charging you."

"It's no problem. I just need another place to sleep for a while. I'm having a lot of trouble sleeping here. Maybe I could just rent the room for a month or so."

"Sure, Betta."

"Okay, so . . . I'll just come over."

"You mean . . . now?"

"Yeah. Is that okay?"

"Well, **yeah,** I mean . . . yeah!" He yawned. "It'll be fun."

"Yes. It'll be fun." I hung up and sat still for a long moment, willing my muscles to unfreeze and start working. Then I dressed and went to gather blankets and pillows, towels and wash-cloths, a change of clothes for the morning.

The streets were empty of traffic, and I drove through a red light, almost wanting a cop to pull me over. I wouldn't have minded the presence of an authoritative figure about now. I still felt frightened, my back was stiff with it, and I wiped away tears of frustration. When would that voice stop?

When I arrived at Matthew's and he opened the door, I lunged at him, hugging him. "Whoa!" he said. "What happened?"

"I keep **hearing** things," I said. "I keep hearing a voice in my bedroom. I can't be there. I can't sleep."

A light came on in the upstairs hall, and Jovani came to peer over the stair railing. He was wrapped in a ratty maroon blanket, and his hair stuck straight up in the back. "Hi," he said, squinting.

"I'm renting the room," I said.

"Oh. Good. Good night."

"Good night." I turned to Matthew. "I'm sorry I woke you up. You must be exhausted. Me too! So I'll just—"

"Wait just a minute, okay?" he said. "I've . . . got someone here."

"Oh!" I lowered my voice. "Melanie?" He wouldn't look at me. "That's okay," I said. I started up the stairs. "I'll be quiet."

"Well . . . hold on. See, she's sleeping in your room."

I stopped, turned to him. "Oh, Matthew. You should have told me."

"Well, she's . . . I mean, she's staying with **me,** but . . . I don't know, she always leaves. But anyway, I'll tell her to come back to my bed."

"No, I'll go home." I'd sleep in my guest room, on my sofa. What was I thinking, to come here?

"Don't leave," Matthew said. "I'd love to have you rent the room, it would really help, it would be great. I just didn't tell Melanie yet. I'm sorry, I fell right back asleep again after you called. But really, it's no problem. Let me just go get her out of there. It'll be no problem at all."

He headed up while I waited on the stairs. I heard him knock softly on the door, and call her name. He said something in a low voice, and then I heard her yelling, "NO! NO WAY!!!"

"Melanie," he said.

"NO! Now get out, I'm **sleeping!**"

"Shut up, Melanie!" Jovani said.

"Fuck you, Jovani! Loser! And get **out,** Matthew!"

I started for the front door. Matthew came quickly down the stairs, saying, "Betta? Don't go. I'll sleep on the sofa. You can have my bed."

"It's okay." I went outside, threw my suitcase into the backseat, and drove home. When I arrived, I went into my bedroom and stood there. Nothing. I left the lights on, pulled back the bedclothes, and climbed in. I closed my eyes and listened carefully: nothing. I turned out the light and listened again. A car going by, my alarm clock ticking. I took off my coat and boots, then lay back down. Some nights lasted weeks.

D elores had had to break the first lunch date
we'd planned. "Doctor's appointment too
close to the time," she'd explained. "You know,
they can keep us waiting so long we need to
change the age on our chart by the time we get
seen. But if we're so much as five minutes late,
they want to see us in small-claims court."

But now on this sunny Friday afternoon Delores and I were at a small Italian place near her
office. I'd told her my friends were coming late
this afternoon for the weekend.

"I wish my best friends could come and visit
me," Delores said. "Unfortunately, we'd have to
exhume two of them."

"I'm sorry," I said.

"Oh, well. Death, the major design flaw. What
can you do?"

I picked up a sugar packet and stared at it. "Delores? When did you start dating again after your husband died?"

"Oh, it took me a year." Then she added quickly, "Don't you do that! That was just a waste of time. I thought I **had** to wait a year. The truth is, I was ready long before that. Just didn't want to tell anybody."

"How soon were you ready?"

She put her cup down, leaned over toward me. "Okay. I have never told anyone this. There was a guy at my husband's funeral . . ."

"No."

She held up her hand. "I didn't do anything. I just thought about it. I'll tell you what, I wish somebody would come up with a dating service for people over fifty. It's hell when you're over fifty. The last blind date I had took me out to a nice restaurant, but after dinner he popped his upper denture out and laid it beside his plate, it was bothering him. Then he said oh did I mind. I had a good mind to rip off my new underwire bra, which was killing me, and throw it in the bread basket. 'Cept the old coot probably would have eaten it—he couldn't see worth a damn!" She took out her compact and powdered her face. There was something lovely and old-fashioned in it; I liked watching. "Ready to go?" she asked.

"I wanted to ask you something else," I said, then hesitated. I looked at her friendly face, her wide eyes.

"Go ahead," she said.

"Okay, this is . . . I can't tell you how silly I feel asking this question. But did you ever have night terrors after your husband died?"

She laughed. "Did I! Honey, I moved in with Marion O'Donahue for a month, and even there, I slept with the lights on. Do you know her? Glamour Daze, the hair place? Anyway, she lived by herself and had an extra room. I'd tried staying alone, and I lasted a whole three days. I was scared to death being alone."

"Well, I've . . . been hearing things," I said.

"Uh-oh. What kind of things?"

"Voices. A man's voice. Not all the time, but sometimes. At night."

She leaned back in her chair and sighed. "Well, I am sorry. Lydia told me she'd left a radio there up in the attic. But I told her I'd found no such thing. The truth is, I couldn't climb all the stairs there, as you recall—I didn't go into the attic or the basement. I'll bet you anything it's turned on and you just don't hear it in the day."

"I hope that's true. If it is, I'll feel very foolish. And very relieved!"

Delores looked at her watch. "Let's go see. I'll go with you. If it's there, I'll bring it to her.

But I've got to hustle—I've got two clients this afternoon. I guess Ed Selwin's show gave my business a jump start—I've had more calls than I can handle lately. I don't like it one bit."

I pulled down the ladder to the attic, then climbed up. I supposed it was an omission of sorts that I'd never been up there, but I'd never needed to be. I had enough room for storage in the basement, and I'd never liked climbing ladders into attics: going up was one thing, but coming down was difficult. What if I fell? I was alone now; I had to think about such things.

The attic smelled of dust and old fabric, and even with the light turned on, it was dark. But in a far corner, I saw it—an old brown radio. It was on top of a box, next to a chair stationed by the one window. And as I walked closer, I heard it. It was half tuned in—only the low sound of static now. What had Lydia done up here? Sat alone, listening to the radio? Why, when she had the whole house, did she isolate herself further in this way? I turned the radio off, unplugged it, and carried it down to Delores. "So you're going to bring it to her now?" I asked.

Delores looked at her watch and sighed.

"I'll do it," I said, taking the radio back.

"You don't have to do that!"

"It's no problem," I said. I'd see if there was anything in the box the radio sat on—Lydia might want that, too.

I walked Delores out to the car and waved as she drove away. Mystery solved—I wouldn't be hearing that voice anymore. But I was going to rent Matthew's room anyway—I'd made that decision the moment I found the radio. I really wanted to stay there once in a while. I'd get to fulfill my Snow White fantasy, and they'd get some much needed income.

I climbed back up the ladder and opened the box the radio had been sitting on. Letters. Two high stacks of them. I opened the one on top, dated December 2, 1942, and written in blue ink on tissue-thin stationery:

My own Lydia,

Say, you should have seen the fellows fighting over those things you sent! I shared some of the hard candy and the fudge, and I'll pass on the paperback books after I read them. But the salami is mine alone, and of course the scarf you knit, too. Thank you sweetheart, but you shouldn't have spent so much money—I know how hard you work.

You cannot imagine what it is like here, how far away I am from you and our life in New York. Farther than miles. It truly is a kind of hell, all smoke and redness, and full of things I

could never describe to you, nor would I anyway—I have, after all, vowed to love and protect
you and I mean that. Oddly, there are times of
extreme boredom here, and it is then that I rel-
ish thinking of you, of what you see and do
every day. I imagine you in your classes, your
quick mind, what a fine teacher you will be!
(And what a privilege it was to teach you!) I
think of your proud independence in your very
gait, your hats and gloves, the high sweetness of
your voice. I miss talking to you so; we do not
enjoy any women's voices here.

Sweetheart, I must tell you I seem to have lost
a good thirty to forty percent of my hearing—
from the guns, the doc said. I hope you won't
mind so much. Sadder to say, I have now lost
all five of the five friends who came here with
me—Lester was killed yesterday, not thirty feet
from me. What was good about his horrific
death is that it was instant. I will miss him, that
short boy who loved telling tall tales. And you
know he had a keen appreciation of you—
he often told me how much he admired your
forthrightness. Stubbornness, you mean, I once
joked, and he became quite serious and said no,
it was a valuable thing to have a partner whose
words you could always trust.

When I come back to New York, I want to get
married right away. I know we said we'd wait a
little while, but Lydia, it took so long for us to

find each other and I, as you, truly believe we are the only ones for each other. Anyway, if I've learned anything from this war, it's that people must not delay doing anything good.

So often, I think about the day before I left, our clothes in a tangle under the apple tree, how golden the light was against your body, how you, too, tasted of apple. I wonder, should I tell you something else? I will, but you must promise to never mention it again after we are at last—at long last!—reunited. I would be very much humiliated to have you bring it up again, face-to-face. But here, where even day is night, I feel a need to say everything to you, it is my consolation and my greatest joy. So I will tell you, Lydia, that every night before sleep I make a fist in a certain way and I pretend that two of my fingers are your mouth. And I kiss it, imagining

My eyes filled and I stopped reading. **We are the only ones for each other;** I knew exactly how that felt. I let the letter close along its softened folds and slipped it back into the envelope. I checked the postmark of a few more letters, all of them in order and dated before this one; this had been the last. I ran my fingers over the fine script on the outside. **Miss Lydia Samuels.** The woman she used to be.

I put the letter back on top of the pile and

closed the box. I looked at my watch, took in a deep breath. Next week, when I could take the time I wanted to, I would bring it to her—right now, I had to get ready for my friends. I looked out the little window onto the street below and saw children playing, a woman walking a dog, cars passing, the white clouds against the blue sky. I saw my true age and circumstances; my great, great luck.

When I came home from shopping, I filled the house with roses—a bouquet for every room. I put out fancy wines: white, red, Merlot, Syrah. I'd also bought cold cuts and cheeses, fancy spreads, five pounds of mixed chocolates, beautiful breads, and I'd gotten Patricia Locke bracelets for all of us—Locke was a Chicago designer whose work was sparkling and beautiful and celebratory—what could be more fitting?

When the doorbell rang, I stood still for a moment, then opened it wide. There they were. It was stunning, really, how little it had taken to create such a grand moment. We stood on the porch, squealing and embracing, and then they came inside. A mix of perfumes. Nice-looking coats and purses thrown onto the sofa, luggage piled in a heap in the middle of the living room floor. We were all of us talking at once, and we moved as a group to the kitchen and took our places as though we had been there last night. I had imagined showing them to their rooms, giving a little tour of the house and the town, then suggesting we go into Chicago for a show or dinner. **What could I have been thinking?** I wondered.

Three hours later we were still at the table, on our third bottle of wine. Lorraine was dressed entirely in black: slim pants and a cashmere turtleneck sweater, her hair piled on top of her head and anchored with a silver barrette. Susanna, her straight and still-thick chin-length hair dyed a beautiful auburn, wore jeans, a low-cut turquoise sweater, and three necklaces: a single pearl, coral beads, and a long rope of crystal. Also two silver bangle bracelets and a large oval turquoise ring. Maddy was in a long brown skirt and a flannel shirt over which she wore a wide brown belt. She had not dyed her long hair: it was streaked with gray, like mine, but permed.

We were talking about what failure really meant, because I'd brought up the idea of my store, and had told them all my fears about failing, the biggest one being that I would squander all my money and then have to worry about how to make a living. If I did nothing, I'd be able to live comfortably for the rest of my life.

"But it would be boring!" Lorraine said. "You have to keep taking risks or you die inside!"

"Well, there are many ways of taking risks," Maddy said. "You don't have to open a store to take a risk."

"Yeah, but listen to her idea," Lorraine said. "This isn't just a **store** store." She looked over at me. "Tell them!"

I shrugged. "Oh, it's just . . . I wanted to have a store that would be all different stuff that women love. Beautiful things, but unusual, too. Like antique birdcages with orchids growing in them. Designer jewelry, handmade paper journals. Vintage linens . . ."

"Aprons?" Maddy asked. "I love aprons. Could you have some bib aprons?"

I saw that my friends were all genuinely enthusiastic, and I began warming to the idea all over again. "I'll have bib aprons," I said, "and I'll sew a good-luck charm inside them so everything you make when you wear them will come out perfectly. But you know, I want more than things. I want a place where women can just come and hang around. Maybe we could have readings."

"Tarot card readings," Susanna said. "Voice recitals. Performance pieces. Use little kids, like the old backyard plays kids used to do. The blanket curtains, some dog playing a part. My dog, Pepsi, used to always be a wounded soldier. We put catsup on his head and then wrapped toilet paper around it. I'll be a partner with you; I'll go in. This is a good idea, Betta!"

"I'll go in, too," Maddy said. "I want to help buy things. I want to be in charge of polka dots. I love polka dots. I'd put in polka-dotted plates. And socks. And dog beds. Okay?"

"I already told her I'm in, too," Lorraine said.

"Okay, okay," I said, laughing.

"It won't fail," Susanna said. "You'll just have to be willing to put the time in."

I leaned back in my chair and nodded. "I'll think about it."

"If you decide yes," Susanna said, "I want you to have one thing in there for me. Little legal contracts that your customers have to sign, saying if they buy something for themselves, they'll use it! Not store it away because it's 'too good.'"

"Who's hungry?" I asked, because I was. Also, I wanted to stop talking about something I wasn't really quite ready for yet.

Maddy looked at her watch. "Let's go get lobster."

"I don't know of any place to get that here," I said.

Susanna started for the phone. "Then let's order out. You do have pizza here?"

"Of course!" I said.

"Well, I mean, it's so **little,**" Susanna said. "I wish you wouldn't have mentioned lobster,

Maddy. Now I want lobster. These small towns are cute, but . . ."

I suddenly felt my throat tighten. John and I at Bay State Lobster, picking out our dinner. Later, him sucking the meat from the tiny lobster legs, laughing and saying I was crazy not to. A napkin tucked into the throat of his shirt.

"Oh, **God,**" Susanna said, "did I offend you? I didn't mean to offend you. Wait, did I?"

"No, I just . . . still rocky."

Maddy got out of her chair and knelt beside me, took my hands into her own. I stared straight ahead and then into her warm brown eyes. Lorraine and Susanna sat silent. After a moment, I smiled and said, "Okay. Pizza."

Lorraine said, "While we're waiting for it, let's watch a movie. I brought **Strangers in Good Company.** It's made by a woman, and the cast is all women and it's fabulous. You need to stock it in your store, Betta."

When I turned off the television, there was a collective sigh of appreciation. "'**I'm** not gonna die; I'm gonna catch some **fish**!'" Susanna said, in perfect imitation of one of the characters in the movie. She was always like that, able to imitate almost anyone, able to enter fully into whatever emotions were required for any scene, even if it was only something she'd witnessed at the drugstore and then come home to act out for us in our tiny living room. She could move her body like a ninety-four-year-old or a toddler; her face had its own extensive vocabulary. I'd seen her star in so many productions in college, and inevitably I'd heard the people behind me whisper about how **good** she was, who **was** that? And then she became a lawyer. Now I said, "Susanna, why did you not pursue acting? You were always so good!"

"I was, wasn't I, darling?"

"No, but you really were!"

She shrugged. "The truth? It was too hard."

"Being a lawyer can't be easy."

She laughed. "Compared to acting, it is! But who ends up doing what they thought they'd do anyway? I wonder about that all the time. Although I have to tell you, once I was getting a manicure and I was watching this woman do my nails, she was about forty-five, and I was feeling so bad for her, her crappy polyester blouse. And I said, 'Hey, Denise? What did you want to be when you were a little girl?' And she looked up from sort of dreamily filing my nails and said, 'I wanted to do nails. My aunt Chichi used to come over every Friday to babysit us, and she'd bring this little overnight bag just **full** of nail polish and she'd let me do her nails. Red, pink, sparkly silver. I just always loved doing nails. Did my little friends in elementary school, did my high school friends. It's peaceful; you make people happy—I'm telling you, I volunteer one day a month at a women's shelter and one day a month at a nursing home, and I am Miss Popularity! And this job, you go home at the end of the day and you're **done,** you know? You can just enjoy your family, read a good book, watch TV.' Then she said, 'Why do you ask?' and I said something like, 'Oh, just wondering,' because I wasn't going to tell her I'm the elitist asshole that I am, thinking nobody wanted to do work like hers. So then she said to me, 'What did **you** want to be?' and I said, 'An actress,' and she got this really sad look on her face and very quietly and sincerely said, 'I'm sorry.' I said, 'That's okay,' and then I spent the rest of the time just looking at the little picture of her family that she keeps on her station, looking at how happy they looked and feeling like an idiot. I thought, This woman is one everyone famous does everything **for.** You know?"

"I wanted to be a priest," Lorraine said, and quietly, nearly respectfully, belched.

"What?" Susanna said, and Maddy said, "You did not; you weren't even Catholic."

"I know, but I wanted to be a priest."

"Why?" asked Maddy.

"Because they were the only ones who could touch the host. Remember when only priests could touch the host? I wanted to touch it, too."

"What did you want to be, Maddy?" I asked.

"I'm being it," she said.

"Even when you were little, you wanted to be a nurse?"

"Yeah. I went around the neighborhood, saving things. Baby birds fallen from the nest, a kid who scraped his knee. I still like being a nurse, too."

I yawned hugely, and Lorraine said, "Betta wants to sleep. But what did you used to want to do?"

"Be married," I said.

Lorraine snorted.

"Really," I said. "And have a bedroom where all it was, was bed. Like, you'd open the door and it would be wall-to-wall mattress. And a refrigerator built into the wall." I thought for a moment, then said, "I didn't think I'd end up **here.**"

Later, after we had all gone to bed, I heard my bedroom door open. Softly, Maddy called my name.

"I'm awake," I told her, and she crossed the room and climbed into bed with me. She shook the bed settling in, making exaggerated movements. It made me laugh.

"Hi," she said, her nose right up to mine.

I smiled at her in the moonlight.

"Are you okay, honey? You were crying pretty hard during the movie."

"Not as hard as Susanna!" I said.

"Well, for God's sake. What did you expect? Forever the drama queen. I love being around her because she gives you permission to let it all out. No matter what you do, it won't be as much as she. Everything she does has to be a big production. Remember when she used to bring her boyfriends home? Remember how **loud**?" She began making rhythmic grunting sounds.

"I remember." We giggled together quietly.

"Lorraine was crying, too," I said. "I was pretty surprised."

"She's having a lot of trouble," Maddy said. "She hardly gets work anymore, and she's slipping in other ways that . . . well. She'll tell you about it, I'm sure. She probably hasn't yet because your plate is pretty full. How are you doing, Betta? Really."

I sighed. "I don't know. It depends on the day. Depends on the hour of the day. I feel like I'm walking around carrying a really full—overly full—bowl of water. When I don't look at it, nothing spills."

She reached over and turned on the bedside lamp. "Is this okay? The light?"

I nodded.

She lay on her side again, her face close to

mine. "I just want to tell you . . . I think it's bad for you to have too much free time."

"I need time, Maddy. This is a big deal, what's happened. I need time to understand all that it means."

"Yes, but you need some structure, don't you think? Your store idea is good. We're all willing to be partners. Why don't you go ahead and—"

"Oh, I don't know if I really want to do that. I think I do and then I think I don't. It makes me really nervous to think about really doing it. Sometimes things feel so . . . unreal right now. Flighty. I think I just need to grieve. I'm entitled to a year of grief, according to the etiquette."

"How about a year of pleasures, instead?"

"Right," I said.

"I mean it. So many people who lose someone think that they need to behave in a prescribed way. Of course you're hurting! But what if you determined to find one thing every day that you—"

"I know. Count your blessings. Remind yourself every night of every good thing that happened to you that day."

"No. I'm not talking about things that happen to you. I'm talking about things you make happen. I'm talking about purposefully doing one thing that brings you happiness every single day, in a very conscious way. It builds up the arsenal, Betta. It tips the balance."

"A whole **year,**" I said. "When I can hardly commit to eating lunch tomorrow!"

"You're taking it too literally," Maddy said. "Don't think of it as calendar days to cross off, or as an assignment with a beginning and an end. Think of it more fluidly—as a philosophy that you exercise daily. And the days turn into years. And the years turn into a lifetime."

I nodded. "I think what you're saying is what John was trying to tell me, too. But you don't know what a confusing time this is!"

"I do know. I lost someone, too."

"Who?" I asked.

"My eleven-year-old daughter."

"Oh, my God. Oh, Maddy. I'm so sorry. I didn't know. I had no idea. Lorraine didn't say anything!"

"No, nor would she. She lets me decide who to tell."

"How?"

"A diving accident, ten years ago. She was at a neighbor's pool and went headfirst into the shallow end. We'd had a fight that morning. The last words I said to her as she went out the door were 'And don't think I'm making your goddamn bed again!'" She shook her head, remembering. "I thought I would lose my mind, at first. Seriously. I felt like I'd just realized the world was made of glass, you know? Thin as a lightbulb, and every step you took was at your own peril. And then, only a couple of weeks after Molly died, I signed up to take tap-dancing lessons. I'd always wanted to, but I'd never had the courage."

"Did it help?"

"Well, it was a place to go where there was never any sorrow. Nobody there knew. Nobody there ever said, 'Well, you still have your sons.' It was just nice people who were all terrible dancers—we all goofed up together. I think the instructor must have felt like shooting herself, but she was remarkably patient. On the day that class ended, I went home and asked for a sign for what I should do next. I opened a novel and pointed to a word, and it was **Greece.** So Dan and I went there."

"Huh! So you just . . . blocked it out."

"Oh, God, no. No. Of course not. You can't do that, even if you want to. But what I'm talking about is . . . well, I think that deep sorrow can make for a kind of . . . unloosening. You can get reoriented in a really important way. Losing Molly reminded me of how beautiful life is. I know it's counterintuitive, but it's true. The horrible stuff? I think it's all a necessary part of the great pageantry."

"That's one way to look at it." I heard the bitterness in my voice. I tasted it, too, pooled at the back of my tongue.

"Think about it, Betta. My pain over Molly ended up making me easier with the world and with myself. Don't worry about backsliding—it's all part of the process. But don't worry about feeling good, either. You don't dishonor the one you loved by being happy."

She turned onto her back and stared up at the ceiling. "You know, in Greece, Dan and I took a walk one night down this twisty little street. It was so quiet, and the stars were so clear. And all of a sudden, both of us could feel her there with us. I remember we stopped walking and just looked at each other, and then we embraced. Later, when we talked about it, we agreed that we had felt her . . . beneficence, you know? We had felt her telling us that it was all right, whatever we did, it was all right—that **she** was all right. We really did feel that. She was telling us . . . well, anyway, her death changed our lives for the better, because it brought a kind of awareness, a specific sense of purpose and appreciation we hadn't had before. Would I trade that in order to have her back? In a fraction of a millisecond. But I won't ever have her back. So I have taken this, as her great gift to us." She looked at me. "But. Do I block her out? Never. Do I think of her? Always. In some part of my brain, I think of her every single moment of every single day."

"Yes. That lit place."

"Right. It is like a lit place." She reached over and took my hand. "Now listen to me. I want to tell you one more story, okay? Can you listen to one more story?"

"Yes."

"When Molly was eight years old, she was an avowed atheist. She told her father and me at breakfast one day that she'd thought hard about it, and she just couldn't believe in God. But then about a year later there was a fire in a house a few doors down from us, some electrical wiring problem. There was a big family living there, five kids, and everybody died—the whole family, they didn't get out. It bothered Molly a lot, especially at nighttime—she'd been friends with the little girl her age. She would think about all those people she'd never see again, how they went to bed that night, you know, and then . . . After about a week, she told us she had renounced her atheism. She said she now believed in God and in heaven. And she said that in heaven, there were cards on which were printed the names of every person on earth. The cards were in God's hands. I'm sure this came from Molly's having heard someone say that very thing, but she added something. She said that written on each card, in real big print, were three words: I LOVE YOU. She found comfort in this, and so did I. I still do."

"Maddy?"

"Yes, sweetheart."

"I saw John. I saw him in that chair right over there."

"Did you?"

"Yes."

"I believe you, Betta."

I started snuffling, and she reached over for a tissue and gave it to me. "Blow," she said, and after I did, she got another tissue and wiped under my nose. "Slob," she said tenderly.

"I don't understand anything."

"Oh, nobody understands anything. We're all just here, blinking in the light like kittens. The older I get, the more I see that nothing makes sense but to try to learn true compassion."

"I'm so glad I found you all again," I said.

"You'll never get rid of us now. You'll have to come on all our expeditions and wait in the waiting room if any of us needs surgery." She yawned and pulled the covers up higher. "Can I sleep with you?"

"No. You kick, if I recall. Do you still kick?"

"So says Dan."

"Right. So get the hell out of here. Tomorrow, do you want a Dutch apple pancake for breakfast or hash browns and eggs and bacon? Or French toast?"

"Yes," she said, and then, kissing my forehead, "Good night."

On a cold afternoon, made bearable by a bright sun, I drove over to Lydia Samuels's retirement home. In addition to the box of letters and the radio, I was bringing a picture I'd cut out of the local weekly the day before. It was of an older couple who lived in the home, dancing. The chairs and tables in the cafeteria had been pushed back. Balloons and streamers were everywhere; one table covered by a sheet held a large plastic punch bowl and a tray of cookies. A couple of aides stood off to the side, beaming. Oftentimes such shots are condescending, patronizing, but that was not the case here: The couple was caught in a graceful turn, and on each of their faces was intelligence and enviable pleasure. I'd thought Lydia might like to have it, or perhaps pass it on to the people featured there, he in his well-cut suit, she in her blue dress, her thick white hair held back by combs studded with pearls.

When I asked for Lydia at the desk, the nurse told me she was in her room and directed me down the hallway to the last door on the right. I knocked softly, then, when I heard nothing in response, more loudly. "Come in!" she said, and I poked my head in, introducing myself.

She stared at me, saying nothing. She was lying in bed in a flannel nightgown, under several blankets. The television was turned on but with no sound—some soap opera, it appeared, an overly made-up woman speaking earnestly to an overly made-up man. Lydia looked paler than when I'd last seen her, and though it was hard to assign a word like **fragile** to one so fiery, her voice was softer, her posture less erect. But her eyes were as brightly focused as before, peremptorily accusatory, and there was about her, even in repose, an air of hectic energy.

"Are you here to fix the television?" she asked. "About time!"

"No." I told her my name again. "I'm the one who bought your house."

She drew back into her pillows. "Oh, no you don't. I have nothing to do with that house anymore. Any problems, you just take to somebody else. Now get out or I'll call the nurse."

I moved toward her. "I'm not having any problems. I just found something I thought you
might want." I pulled the radio from the box.

She reached out eagerly to grab it and inspected it thoroughly—sides, top, bottom. Her
hands trembled and I saw that her nails needed
care—they were overly long, and something was
caked beneath them. "I **told** that Delores I'd left
it behind, but she said, 'Oh, no, no, no.' I knew
it was there! Plug it in, will you?"

I put the box of letters down on the bedside
chair and did as she asked. She immediately
tuned in a talk station to a low volume and then
hid the radio under the covers. "We can't have
these here. Some idiot rule so people don't sue
for electrocuting themselves. Don't you tell a
soul; they'll take it from me. What else have you
got there?" She was almost smiling.

I regretted not bringing her something else: a
little bouquet, instant cocoa, some nice soap.
"Well, that's letters, Lydia, addressed to you.
They were up in the attic."

Her mouth opened, then closed. Then she sat
up straighter and pointed her finger at me. "You
read them, didn't you?"

"I didn't! Well, to be honest, I started to read
one, but I stopped. Anyway, here they are. I
thought you would probably like to have them."

I put the box in her lap, and she stuck her hand
in and pulled out a pile of letters. She stared at

them, unmoving, then laid them on the bed beside her. Then, abruptly, she put them back in the box. "Take them away. I don't want them."

I hesitated, then took the box from her and put it back on the chair. I moved in closer, grabbed hold of the bed rail. I spoke quietly. "I'm sorry for invading your privacy, Lydia, but I must tell you that what I read was very beautiful, and I just thought—"

"He died a long time ago and I died with him. Yes, I did. That same day. My major regret is that I didn't take my own life on the day I heard he lost his. Didn't have the courage then and don't now, either, I'm sorry to say." She gestured outward, toward the hall. "This place is a hellhole, don't you doubt it. A bunch of slobbering, crazy people, tied into their chairs. Visitors looking for money to inherit. That's what's here. Pig slop at every meal, and they wonder why you don't eat. And a staff that can't speak the English language and thinks nothing of leaving a thermometer in your mouth for half an hour **every** single morning!"

I did know about that. I remembered when John was in the hospital and a nurse would run around checking everyone's vital signs and be gone from the bedside for far too long. "You might take it out," I suggested. "You can just take it out after a couple of minutes. If you don't shake it down, it will still register."

"Helpful hints from the ignorant," Lydia said. "You know what they do if you take it out of your mouth? They put it in the other place! And if you take it out of there, they tie your hands!" Her voice had grown loud now.

"Okay," I said, picking up my purse. "Well, I—"

"I don't know what possessed you to bring me those letters. What did you think? That I would be happy to be reminded of him?"

"I did think that."

"Why in the world would that make me happy? To be reminded of all I missed!"

"I'll just take them," I said. "I'll leave my phone number at the desk. If you ever change your mind and want them, call me and I'll bring them over."

"Throw them away!"

"No," I said. "I don't think I will."

I walked out of her room and down the hall. Lydia was right: There were people in the home who were tied into wheelchairs, staring vacantly ahead, lost to themselves and to others. But only some of the people were like that.

There is a story about a Navajo grandfather who once told his grandson, "Two wolves live inside me. One is the bad wolf, full of greed and laziness, full of anger and jealousy and regret. The other is the good wolf, full of joy and compassion and willingness and a great love for the world. All the time, these wolves are fighting inside me." "But grandfather," the boy said. "Which wolf will win?" The grandfather answered, "The one I feed."

John used to talk about finding the soft spot in people, how that was step one. Then came the next step, the harder one, getting them to trust that you would not violate that place. He said patients would often become the most furious just before they were ready to make themselves vulnerable, that you had to withstand the fire in order to earn the cease-fire, and that it was always worth it to do so. He said that inside everyone there was a place that shone. But John's compassion was legendary and his patience far greater than my own. I wouldn't come here again.

Still, I stopped at the desk on the way out and left my number with the indifferent nurse's aide there. She watched with crossed arms and raised brows as I wrote it out. She didn't believe any more than I did that Lydia Samuels would call me to come and see her again, and I doubted she would take much care in putting the information somewhere safe. When I put my hands in my pocket for my gloves, I felt the newspaper picture I'd brought along. I started to take it out to throw it in the trash but changed my mind.

When I got home, I saw Benny standing on my porch. "My mom needs an egg," he said. "Can we borrow one?"

"Of course. Come on in." He followed me in, and I took off my coat and lay it across a kitchen chair, then went to the refrigerator. "Is just one enough?" I asked.

"That's all she said to get, is one." Benny bent down and picked up something from the floor, the newspaper picture. "This fell out of your coat." He looked at the picture. "What is it?"

"Just a picture I liked," I said. "I'm going to put it in my story journal. What **is** the story there, Benny?"

He smoothed the picture out on the table and studied it. "Well, today is her birthday and he gave her a surprise party. And her name is Edna and his is Samuel. No. His name is Garcia."

"Wonderful!" I said. "And how old is Edna today?"

He looked carefully, thought for a moment, then said, "Fifty."

On Saturday morning when Matthew came over to paint the bedroom, he brought along Jovani. "Do you mind if Jovani helps?" he asked when I answered the door. "My other friend couldn't come."

"Of course not." I pulled the door open wider.

Jovani stared triumphantly at Matthew. "I told you," he said. "Is it not?" He came through the door and then stopped to look around the living room. "Niiiicce!" he said, and I said, "Thank you."

"Niiiiicce!" he said again, and again I said thank you.

He turned to face me. "This is very nice house."

"Jovani," Matthew said. "Jesus."

I led them upstairs and helped them set up, laying out newspapers and covering my furniture with sheets, then went out shopping to look for a new outfit while they began stripping off the wallpaper. I'd agreed to have dinner with Tom Bartlett, who'd apparently decided to overlook my behavior at the end of our last time together. And I was glad; I thought we could at least be friends who might enjoy going places together. Tonight, though, he had invited me to his place—he was going to cook dinner. At first I'd hesitated, thinking that **his place** suggested something I wasn't ready for. But then he'd said, "Just **dinner,** Betta," and I'd laughed and agreed.

By the time I got back, a new blouse and sweater in hand, the boys had begun applying long strokes of blue to the walls. I liked the room much better already, and I told them so.

"I am wonder," Jovani said. "If you don't mind, can I ask something?"

"Sure," I said.

"Okay. Why is a woman alone buy a house so big?"

"I just liked it," I said. "It has things I always wanted in a house and never had."

"But . . . so many rooms to be in one person?"

"I doubt I could have found a smaller house that had what this one does. And it was . . . well, it was kind of an impulse buy. You know what that is, right?"

"Of course. But it's too big, the house, not good for you. Your bedroom is far from the door.

Someone come in, and you don't know, you can't hear."

"Jovani!" Matthew said.

"I'm sorry for scare you. But sometimes the truth is want out on you."

The doorbell rang, sparing me from coming up with a response. It was Benny, staring off to the side, deep in thought. When I opened the door, he asked quickly, "Can I come in?"

I opened the door wider, and he stepped into the hall, removed his boots, then headed for "his" chair at the kitchen table, the place he'd begun doing his homework every Wednesday after school before we had dinner. I sat opposite him.

"I've got girl trouble," he said.

"Oh?"

"Yeah. Two of them like me."

"That doesn't sound like too terrible a problem."

"Actually, it is."

I envisioned two girls vying for his attention, then remembered the strong longings I'd felt when I was Benny's age, sitting lovestruck in Mrs. Menafee's fifth-grade classroom. I remembered watching Billy Harris do a math problem at the chalkboard, with his plaid shirt and narrow brown belt and corduroy pants, the comb lines in his hair courtesy of Brylcreem. I'd felt dizzy with a free-floating form of desire, and I wrote **Mrs. Billy Harris** in tiny print on my notebook paper, then quickly erased it. One day, he'd walked me home after school, and afterward I'd lain on my bed with my eyes closed, embracing my teddy bear, trying to think of something to clinch the deal, to win him for my own forever. But the very next day Tish McCollum took him away from me, and that was that. "I'll never love anyone again!" I wailed to my father. "Oh, I think you might," he said.

"So what's happening?" I asked Benny.

"For one thing, they both want to come over. And last time Heather came over, she kissed me. And she's in sixth grade, so. . . ."

"Well!"

"Yeah. My mom doesn't know, because it was in my bedroom."

"**Really!** You brought her to your bedroom?"

"She made me. She said she wanted to see my room, but she only wanted to kiss me."

"Hmmm. Did you like it?"

He grinned. "**I** don't know. But now they both want to come over on Monday after school."

I heard Jovani and Matthew coming downstairs, and Benny quickly looked over at me. "I didn't know anyone was here."

"I don't think they heard anything. That's just my friends Matthew and Jovani. They're doing some painting for me."

They walked into the kitchen, and I made introductions. "Benny just stopped by," I said. "For . . . cookies."

"You make yourself?" Jovani asked. "From nothing?" I nodded. He sat down. "Then I rest here for a while."

"I was just saying I'm having girl trouble," Benny said, and I had to work hard to conceal my delight at his openness.

Jovani leaned in close to him. "You tell me your problem and I tell you **exactly** how do you do."

Benny said nothing.

"For sure," Jovani told him. "If you listen for me your problems women, you become right away happy man."

I threw the butter into the mixing bowl and turned the mixer on.

"Where are you **from**?" Benny asked loudly, speaking above the whirring sounds.

Jovani spoke confidentially. "From the country of love, where the people they know how to enjoy more their lives. You take your girlfriends there. Brazil. You don't have one inch sorry."

I looked at my watch. Two more hours before the first date I'd had in over thirty years.

"I hate to say it," I told Tom. "But you're the better cook."

"Not true," he said. But he was pleased; I saw that he agreed with me.

He was clearing the dishes, preparing to serve dessert—a pie bought at a bakery, I was relieved to see. I didn't want him to really be a better cook than I. He had made us an Indian meal, tandoori chicken, saag paneer, even homemade naan. Though the bad wolf inside me had whispered, "You could do this, **anybody** could do this if they **wanted** to," I was impressed.

We'd eaten dinner in a dining room furnished in a way that reflected his (and I assumed his wife's) taste for the austere. There was a fineness to the lines of the furniture, the room held a great deal of light, and it was pleasantly clean and uncluttered. But the chairs were uncomfortable, designed more to be looked at than sat in.

Nor did I respond to his artwork: a reproduction with a wide swath of mustard yellow against a green background, a print of geometric patterns of thin lines done in colored pencil. His rooms were absent of books but for the few coffee-table books in the living room, older art and photography books, and a newer one featuring the Chicago "Cows on Parade." I'd felt my snobbish self recoil—the Chicago Cows! But that was the one I'd looked at and enjoyed. I saw that what I was really doing was making up reasons why we would never get serious. A man who kept his corn medication in plain sight in the bathroom! I'd told myself. A man who wore an apron, rather than a dishcloth rakishly tucked into the waistline of his pants!

After we finished dessert, I offered to wash the non-dishwasher items. "I'll wash," Tom said, "and you wipe. How's that?"

"Well, I don't know where things go," I said. "Wouldn't it be better if I washed and you wiped?"

He smiled. "You know, I just like to wash better than dry. Do you mind?"

"Not at all," I said, but I was thinking, **Whoa. Stubborn.**

After we did the dishes, we moved to the living

room. "Do you like jazz?" Tom asked, and I said very much. "Coltrane?" he asked, and I said, "Well, **old** Coltrane."

His back was to me, and I could see his exasperation mounting in the way that it stiffened. "**How** old?" he asked.

"How about a different CD?"

"Fine," he said quickly. Oh, what was the matter with me? I was a terrible date. Ungracious and ungrateful. Tense and bitchy.

Tom picked up another CD but then put it down. He crossed the room to sit on the sofa beside me, then leaned over and kissed me, quickly. "There," he said. "Okay?"

I took in a steadying breath, embarrassed by my immediate rapid response.

"'There' what?" I smiled falsely, and tucked a stray piece of hair behind my ear.

"All made up. I think we both need to **relax.** We're just trying to get to know each other, Betta. That's all."

I looked down into my lap. "I know."

"I like you, Betta. I think you're cute."

Cute. Translation: not pretty, not sexy. I imagined telling this story to my rediscovered friends, how in each telling I would make this statement and others just a little more repugnant than they had been. I looked at my watch.

"Time to go home now, huh?" Tom asked.

"I think so. I'm sorry."

"Don't be. I know how hard this is. Believe me."

I drove home full of an agitated emptiness. I would call Lorraine first. I would tell her about how he also told me he had this great idea for a children's book, which to my mind had not been a great idea at all.

I lay in bed thinking of the boyfriends I'd had in college. I wondered what had happened to them. Stevie, the bass player in the rock band who secretly loved the Lettermen's "The Way You Look Tonight." Joel, the handsome blond boy who sent me my first dozen roses. They were so beautiful in their long white box wrapped with a wide red ribbon that I never took them out—I let them blacken there amid the dark green tissue. Bob, the earnest English major with the GTO and the incredible blue-green eyes. If I had found my girlfriends, surely I could find some of them. But first I'd have to really want to. And I didn't really want to. The wife: **Who** is this?

"When you are make gravy, when is time for it the flour?" Jovani asked.

"Pretty early," I said, my back to him. I'd taken the pot roast and the vegetables from the roasting pan and put them into the oven to keep warm. Now I was stirring the drippings, getting ready to make the gravy. I was over for the night, and Jovani and I had decided to make dinner together. Matthew was going to eat with us and then go out with Melanie, apparently in yet another attempt to win her back. "She is viper," Jovani had said, "but he love her. Me, I'm love only gravy."

"It's best to shake the flour up in a jar with milk or water," I said. "Then you don't get lumps."

"Oh, my father make milk gravy. So good."

"Have you guys got milk?"

Jovani opened the refrigerator. "We got beers. One."

"Okay, we'll use water."

Matthew came into the kitchen, drying off his hair with a towel so thin you could see through it.

"Would you set the table?" I asked him.

He laughed. "Set the **table**? Whoa!" But he went to the cupboard and pulled down three plates, one badly chipped, which he placed with care around the lopsided table. He put forks on the right, knives and spoons on the left, then stood back with his hands on his hips to regard his work. "What else?" he asked me.

"Glasses," I said. "And napkins."

"Paper towels?"

"Perfect." Some decent towels, I thought, in earth tones. Dishes. A few cloth napkins. Something to stabilize that kitchen table. Hell, another kitchen table. I'd already fixed up my room as much as I could; I was ready to move to other areas of the house. I had worried at first that I might offend, but the boys seemed to like everything I brought over. Jovani often used the cashmere throw I'd gotten for the foot of my bed. I'd been in the habit of extravagance since John died—since before then, actually. After we got his diagnosis, we came home and wept, both of us. That night, after we went to bed, I said, "Oh, John, what are we going to do?" and he said,

"Well, tomorrow we're going to go out and spend a whole lot of money." It was not true solace, but it had its appeal. I had a gay friend with AIDS in the early eighties, when it was still a death sentence. He ran up every one of his charge cards sky-high when his time was running out. "What are they going to do?" he asked. "Send a **collection** agency after me? I hope they do. I hope they send a cute collection boy." He was in his bathrobe, sitting on the sofa and leafing through a catalog. "Hmmm," he said, "**that's** nice. Oh, wait, I already ordered that. Hey, do you want anything? It's on me." Sure, I told him; you pick. I still had the ivory pie plate he'd selected for me, and every time I used it I thought of him sitting there, swinging his one leg crossed over the other, his watch swimming on his wrist.

While the boys and I ate dinner, the talk turned to Melanie. "You know," I told Matthew, "what you need to do with a girl like that is get her jealous. You're too nice to her."

"Only one problem," Matthew said. "Melanie's not jealous of anyone. She knows she's got it over every girl. Except Demi Moore. She's jealous of her. She's crazy jealous of her. She's afraid of the whole gorgeous-older-woman thing."

"Well, there you go," I said, dragging an excellent curled-up carrot through the equally excellent gravy. "You just need a gorgeous older woman."

"Yeah, but Melanie would have to see her with me."

"Make double date," said Jovani, his mouth full. "You and Melanie with beautiful old woman and her man. Say is your uncle, you have to take them. And then the woman, she is like you in front of **everyone.** Melanie suffer from this, I know."

"That's actually a good idea," I said.

Jovani looked up from mopping his plate. "I am **say.**"

"Yeah, but where's a gorgeous older woman?" Matthew asked. And then, blushing, said, "I mean, you're gorgeous and all, Betta, but—"

"No, I'm not," I said. "But you know what? I know somebody who is. She's my age, but you'd never know it. And she would love nothing better than to be involved in something like this."

"So all we need to do is find a guy for her to go out with."

"I know somebody for that, too."

In the morning I would call Lorraine and Tom. I could hardly wait to hatch the plot. I knew Lorraine would go for it, and I thought Tom could be persuaded to it, especially after he saw Lorraine.

Matthew looked at his watch, then stood quickly. "I've gotta go. I don't want to be late."

"Sit **down,**" Jovani and I said together, and I

added, "**Be** late!" Matthew hesitated, then tore out of the room.

Jovani and I looked at each other, and Jovani shrugged. "Hopeless." He took a last bite of pot roast. "This I am found delicious. Next time, I make you dinner from Brazil. You won't believe."

"That would be great."

He stretched his arms high over his head. "You want watch TV by me?"

"Yes." I liked the way he talked back to the screen, the way he stared wide-eyed and serious-faced at the commercials, then asked, "Is for true?"

"How's the job search going?" I asked after we were settled in the living room, I under my throw on the sofa, he sprawled out in the chair.

"Still nothing. Only temporary. I am so sick of everyone they don't know how I am talented. Even I can sing, did you know?"

"No."

He made some effort at opera, which was terrible.

"Huh," I said.

"I know, not so perfect yet. But believe me, I have other things to make me talent. I can paint."

"Yes, you did a great job on my bedroom."

"No, no, paint like artist. You wait." He went upstairs and came down with a sketchbook. In-side were watercolors: buildings around here and in Chicago, still lifes, a pen-and-ink portrait of a child sitting on a bench. They were exquisite. I looked up at him, the surprise showing on my face.

"I know," he said. "You are amaze."

"I am! Why don't you pursue this, Jovani? These are very good!"

"First, artist must have job."

"Well, I hope you'll try hard to do something with this."

He took the sketchbook back from me and tapped his temple. He had ideas, I supposed he was saying. We turned together to watch an old rerun of **Friends.** Jovani pointed to the screen. "This is us, Betta."

"Close enough," I said.

Long after I'd fallen asleep, I heard the bedroom door open. Then the light turned on, and Melanie stood before me. "Get out of my bed!" She was wearing a tiny white T-shirt and matching underpants, and I noted beneath my anger that her body was extraordinary. Poor Matthew.

"What are you doing?" I looked at the clock. Three-thirty. "This is not your bed; it's mine. Turn out the light."

"It's my bed! It's got your shit on it, but it's my bed. I brought it with me when I moved in!"

"Well, you . . . can just . . . I'm the one paying

rent now. If you want to take your bed, you can do so, but not tonight. Now get out."

Her mouth dropped open, and she started laughing loudly. "Oh. My. God. Are you kidding? Fuck you!" She came over and lay down beside me, pulling the covers over her head.

I yanked the covers down. "Listen. You're going to have to leave. This is my room, and I—"

"Mattie!" she yelled.

"Shhhh!" I said. "Don't you wake him up!"

"Maaaattie!!"

"Stop that! It's not necessary."

She sat up, wide-eyed, and spoke between clenched teeth. "Give me those blankets. I'm freezing."

I pulled them farther away from her. "Go home and get warm, then."

Matthew came into the room, tousle-headed, blinking in the light. He was wearing a T-shirt and blue-and-white-striped underwear, thick white socks. "What's up?" he said sleepily. "Hey, Betta."

"Am I not renting this room?" I asked him.

"Yeah."

"Would you mind asking your uninvited guest to leave?"

"Uninvited?" Melanie shrieked. "Uninvited?! I'm not uninvited! I can come here whenever I want!"

"Melanie," Matthew said.

"Don't even start! Why don't you tell Grandma here about what we did tonight, so she gets it! Or maybe you want me to. Well, first, he fucked me and then I fucked him and then he ~~fucked~~ me. That's how **uninvited** I am!"

I looked at Matthew and he looked at the floor.

"And then I came in to my bed, emphasis on **my,** to sleep."

Matthew continued to stare at the floor. I got out of bed to stand before him, and he looked up at me. "You want me to . . . want me to make her leave?" he asked quietly.

"Like **that** would happen!" Melanie lay back down, pulling the covers emphatically over her. "Get out, both of you."

I could feel myself very close to going over to the bed and dragging Melanie out by her hair. Instead I said, "I'll go home. For tonight. But in the morning, we're going to talk about this, Matthew."

I headed for the stairs, Matthew following me. As we passed Jovani's door it opened and he stood squinting out at us, my cashmere throw over his shoulders. "Why you don't make her go, Matthew?"

Now came Melanie's voice: "Mind your own goddamn business, Jovani!"

Jovani straightened indignantly, then stepped

out into the hall to say loudly, "Listen, Melanie. I am educated man. I don't want fire." He smiled at me. "Good night, Betta." He closed the door quietly.

Maybe he didn't want fire. But I did.

The next morning I called Lorraine. It was early enough that I got her, and late enough that she didn't sound crabby. "I need you to do me a favor," I said.

"Yes?"

"It would involve coming back here again, but I'd buy your ticket."

"I've still got miles. And I can come anytime—I've got no work at the moment. What do you need?"

I told her about Matthew and Melanie, and the impromptu scheme Jovani had come up with. "I'm in," she said. "I love it. All except for the Tom part."

"Well, but I think the double-date idea is really smart. It makes it not so obvious."

"So I have to go out with some jerk? Can't you find another guy?"

"Tom's not a jerk!"

"Well, you haven't make him sound particularly appealing, Betta."

"First of all, I've exaggerated a few things. Second, he's just going to be a . . . prop. And Matthew is **adorable.**"

"Really."

"Yes."

She yawned, then asked in an overly casual way, "How old is he?" If she were a cat, she'd be lying on the windowsill, slit-eyed, flicking her tail.

"Too young for you," I said.

"How young is too young?"

"He's barely over twenty."

"Mmmm! A challenge!"

The last thing poor Matthew needed was another challenge in the world of women. But here was call-waiting. I told Lorraine to make arrangements to come the Friday after Christmas, and to let me know the flight times. I'd straighten her out when she got here.

It was Tom on the other line. "I've got a favor," I said.

"Done," he answered.

Oh, he was a nice man. I needed to loosen up. Next time, I'd sleep with him. I would. Maybe I would.

That night around eight o'clock, too restless to read, I flung down my book, went into the kitchen, poured myself a glass of wine, and downed it quickly, standing at the sink. Then I went upstairs and took off the pajamas I'd put on an hour earlier. I showered, brushed my teeth again, and dressed in black underwear, black pants, and a low-cut green sweater. I applied my makeup with great care. Then I drove over to Tom's house and knocked at the door. When he opened it, I said, "Surprise!"

"Betta!"

I moved in closer. "I brought something for you." All the way over, I'd been thinking about a time I went to John's office at the end of his day. I'd sat in the waiting room wearing nothing but a trench coat. When the last patient had exited, her eyes reddened, a bouquet of Kleenex in her hand, I'd knocked on the door. "One moment, please," John had said, and then, when he'd opened the door and saw me standing there, he'd said, "Betta!" And I'd said, "Surprise!" And I'd come in and waited on his sofa, getting more and more aroused, while he finished making notes. Then I'd stood and dropped the coat.

And that is what I wanted now. I wanted it. Sudden sex, immediate gratification, no prelude.

"What did you bring?" Tom asked, looking around for a package of some kind, I supposed.

"Me."

"Well, that's lovely."

"Well, no. The surprise is . . . can we go up to your bedroom?"

He actually blushed. For a terrible moment, I thought he was going to say, "Well, I'm sorry, Betta, but I've got someone here. I wish you'd called." But he didn't say that. He let me in and gestured, boylike, toward the stairs. I started up.

My heart was racing in the loveliest of ways. And for the first time, there was no ambivalence in me. John used to call me controlling sometimes, even in affection, and I supposed I was. I felt much more comfortable being the one to initiate things. But I was still alive, I still wanted all the things I could have. And here was one of them, an attractive man moving up the steps behind me in the slow and measured way of someone who knew exactly where he was going.

I took off my coat and lay down on his bed. He hesitated, then stretched out beside me. He smiled and stroked my cheek. "This really is a surprise." He dimmed the bedside light. "I'll need to . . . get ready."

At first I was confused, thinking he didn't want to undress before me. But then I realized he meant condoms. I felt deeply embarrassed. I had no diseases! But of course condoms would protect me, too. They were the modern version of walking on the street side. Oh, I hadn't counted on this. I'd forgotten how dangerous the times were, how far from the time when I'd met John. "Okay," I said. "Well, I'll just wait for you!"

"You might get undressed," he said.

I thought of the care with which I'd selected my underwear, how I'd imagined his appreciative eyes on my breasts held just so inside the brilliantly designed brassiere.

"All right," I said.

But it came to me, as I pulled my clothes off and put them in a neat pile on the floor, that all of this was not so much about sex. Despite the racy images I'd revved myself up with on the way over, this was about something else. When I was in sixth grade, I had a textbook that showed two Neanderthals, a man and a woman, standing at the mouth of their cave. Outside a storm raged. Wild animals roamed. Danger was everywhere. The man and woman offered each other a naïve and specific sense of safety. They held hands and stared out at all they seemed to protect each other from, at least for the moment. On their faces were wonder and relief.

At 4 A.M. I heard the clock on my mantel strike again. I lay wrapped in my tangled sheets for a while, then gave up trying to sleep and went downstairs to look for the book I was currently reading.

When Tom had come back to his bed, he'd been wearing a black, hooded bathrobe that I found both ominous and silly-looking. What was he, a boxer? He took off the robe before he got under the covers with me. On his half-erect penis, I saw a yellow condom, and for one brief moment, I felt like vomiting. But then I slid myself beneath him and sighed contentedly, relishing that familiar weight. We kissed, and this was enjoyable. We caressed each other, and this too was enjoyable. And then, when I thought enough time had passed, I tried to signal that I was ready. The problem was, he was not. Nor did he become so. No matter what I did, no matter **what** I did, he did not become so. After a while, he pushed me onto my back, laughed against my shoulder where earlier I had put a bit of perfume, and mumbled, "Sorry." He hesitated, then started to move down, kissing my chest, then my stomach, but I pulled him back up, perhaps a bit too aggressively. "It's all right," I said, and then his phone rang and I felt sure, I was positive, that it was divine intervention, a throwaway favor in the face of scorching humiliation. "Go ahead and get that," I said, and he said, almost at the same time, "I think I'd better answer that."

He'd gone downstairs to talk, ignoring the bedside phone, and I realized that what I did not know about him was vast. How many condoms were left in the box, for example? I'd dressed by the time he returned and refused his offer of a conciliatory glass of wine. I told him I'd see him on Saturday night, when he would be posing as Matthew's uncle.

"I'll call you before then," he'd said. "Maybe we can do something."

I'd answered, brightly and insincerely, "Do!" but I'd thought, **The hell we will.** Then I'd thought, **I will never tell anyone about this.**

I found the book I was looking for on the kitchen table. But before going back upstairs, I went to the Chinese chest and sat before it. I leaned my head against the deep drawer holding those many slips of papers, those words that I wanted so much to understand but, for the most part, could not. "John," I whispered. "I need you." The clock chimed the quarter hour—gently, it seemed to me, even apologetically—but that was all I heard. I looked around the room. The absence of movement was all I saw. Tomorrow, I would be so tired. Already, I was.

Late Wednesday afternoon I lay on the sofa reading. I could hear Benny sighing in the kitchen as he did his homework, and finally I went in to see what the problem was. I hoped he wasn't doing math. Last time I'd helped him, we'd gotten an F.

"Benny?" I said. "How are you doing?"

"Terrible."

"What's up?"

He didn't answer.

I sat in the chair opposite him, reached out to touch his arm.

"Deborah wants to break up with me," he said.

"Deborah?"

"Yeah. My girlfriend."

"The one who—"

"I never told you about her. Because she's the one I really liked, and I just didn't want to tell anybody about her. But we've been together for almost a month, and now she wants to break up with me."

"I'm sorry. Is it because of those other girls?"

"No, she thought that was funny. But there's this other kid? John Hansen? He really likes her? And he talks to her all the time even though he knows she's my girlfriend? She told me a long time ago she can't stand him. But now she likes him and not me anymore. That's what she told me today. And John Hansen was, like, all watching us."

He tapped his pencil rapidly against the table. He looked very close to tears. I supposed I should say something about time healing all wounds, that there would be another girl, that there would be many other girls. Instead, I said, "So . . . you really feel bad."

"Yeah," he said. "And I tried to be, like, so what, but it didn't work." He searched my face.

"Do you think if you fall in love twice, the first one wasn't real?"

"No. It doesn't mean it wasn't real. Most people love more than once in their lives. I think you will, too. And what I believe about love is that any kind is good. And the thing about life is, you never know what's around the next corner."

He sighed deeply. "Betta?"

"Yes?"

"Could you make prime rib tonight?"

I laughed. "Really?"

Finally, he smiled. "Yeah. It's my favorite food."

I stood. "Okay, Benny. Let's go to the grocery store."

As we were putting our coats on, I said, "What do you want with your prime rib?"

"Twice-baked potatoes and Caesar salad. If that's okay."

"It's fine." I grabbed my purse and we ran out to the car. "So, when they ask you what you want to be when you grow up, what do you say, 'Gourmand'?"

"What's that?" He shivered, and I turned up the fan, though all it was blowing out was cold air. **Turn up the steam!** my old-world grandfather used to say, never understanding that you had to let a car warm up first. His impatient genes lived inside me, insisting on repetitions of behavior without regard for logic.

"A gourmand is a food lover," I told Benny. "Is that what you're going to be?"

"Nah. I want to pitch for the Yankees. A-Rod made twenty-five million last year."

As we drove down the street, he leaned back in his seat. "This is awesome," he said. "Deborah could never do this."

Do what? I wanted to ask. **Drive? Cook? Listen to your troubles?** But I just said, "I know. She's really a terrible person."

"See?" he said. "You know that and you never even met her."

"Sometimes," I told Delores, "I feel like I'm forgetting him already. I remember what he looked like, I don't mean that, but certain other things, little things. I just don't remember any-more."

"I know, honey." She reached over to squeeze my hand. "Sorry. Got some egg salad on you."

It was Friday afternoon, and we were out for what Delores had called our annual Christmas lunch. It made for a kind of panic in me, think-ing about what the holiday would be like with-out John. Thanksgiving hadn't even registered; Carol had invited me to come with her and Benny to her sister's house; I'd declined and had spent the day in peaceful solitude. But Christmas was different. So pushy.

"Are you doing anything special on Christmas Day?" Delores asked.

I shook my head, looked down.

"Now listen," she said. "You might want to be alone, and I respect that. But if you don't want to be alone, then you call me, all right?"

"Yes."

"Well, you don't have to call me, I suppose, but I want you to call somebody. Lot of times you can feel like people don't want to be burdened with you at holiday time, but that's not true. Families like to have outsiders over. Keeps 'em from fighting with each other so much."

I took a last bite of potato soup and pushed my bowl away.

Our waitress came over, a too-thin but beautiful, brown-eyed young girl whose hands had trembled as she took our order—first day, she said—and asked if we needed anything else. Both of us declined, and then when we put our money down, I saw we'd both done the same thing—tipped her excessively. "'Tis the season," Delores said. "Every year I say it's not going to get me, and every year it does."

"I know." In my car were two gigantic tins full of cookies. I was on my way over to Matthew and Jovani's. At home there were seven more tins.

Jovani answered the door, visibly upset.

"What wrong?" I asked.

He motioned impatiently for me to come in-side. "I'm tell you the whole story. But short! Be-cause always is the same story."

I followed him into the living room, where Matthew sat reading from one of his textbooks. "Hey, Betta," he said. "What's in the tin?"

I threw the cookies over to him, and he began eating them immediately. "Good!" he said, crumbs flying from his mouth.

Jovani wandered over to him, his hands on his hips, but declined when Matthew held the tin up to him.

"Later, when my stomach it's not volcano," he said.

I sat on the sofa, slid my coat off. "So what happened, Jovani?"

"All right," he said. "You look on my face. What have you find?"

"Well, I . . . I see a very nice-looking young man."

"Do you see on here 'little too much en-thusiasm'?"

I laughed. "No."

"Well, that is why I'm not hire. They think I'm too much enthusiasm."

"It's your shoes," Matthew muttered, not look-ing up. "I keep telling you, man. You can't apply for a job, especially selling men's clothes, wearing sneakers."

Jovani came to sit beside me. "They are not

even looking on my shoes. Only on my face, where I am too much enthusiasm. I am only happy and passionate man, and that they don't like! They want only mannequin, to hang clothes from. To talk to customers like funeral."

From upstairs, I heard the sound of the shower turn off. Melanie, I assumed. I looked over at Matthew, who said in a low voice, "We're all set for Saturday, but just barely. I had to tell her we're going to a really good restaurant in Chicago. Will your friends go along with that?"

"Of course," I said.

"Tonight, I cook," Jovani said. "You come, you won't believe. We having for drink puma's milk. We have **empada,** for main dish is **frango en-sopado,** we have alongside coconut rice, and for dessert Maria bonbons."

"Jovani!" I said.

"Inside me, many surprises," he said. "Nobody see."

"Well, **I** see."

"So maybe you hire me. I make your business blow up."

"You know," I said, "I may just do that. I'm thinking about opening a store. But it would be a store called What a Woman Wants. Do you think you'd like to work there?"

He showed me his palms. "Am I not?" he said. "What she is want?"

I heard the stairs creak, and Melanie came into

the room. She ignored me so completely I almost admired her ability. "I'm ready to go," she told Matthew.

Matthew flipped through his book. "Three more pages to finish the chapter," he said. "Is that okay?"

"**Mat**tie . . ."

He closed the book and went for his jacket.

"Melanie," Jovani said. "Tonight I am cook. Would you like also to join us dinner?"

"No," she said. "I'm busy tonight."

"But thanks," I said, and she turned around to glare at me.

"I was **going** to **say** that."

On Christmas Day I found Lydia in the recreation room, seated in the far back, while the rest of the residents were gathered close around the piano. A tall, older man wearing a burgundy suit was playing with the unbounded voluptuousness of Liberace and singing loudly, his head thrown back. He was still handsome, still had a thick head of beautiful white hair. A sign sat on the piano: BERNSTEIN ENTERTAINMENT. The people sang along, in less-than-robust voices, to "I Saw Mommy Kissing Santa Claus."

I tapped Lydia on the shoulder, and when she turned around and saw me, she frowned. I held up the tin of cookies, and she hesitated, then took it. She pointed to the hall and I wheeled her out there. Over her shoulder, she asked, "Did you **ever hear** such caterwauling? Thank God you got me out of there. Take me to my room."

Once there, she had me station her in the corner. She wore tan pants that were far too short, revealing the same kind of gray knee-socks she'd been wearing last time I saw her. She'd gotten a new pair of sneakers, apparently; they were a startling white, massive-looking on her narrow feet. She wore a man's green plaid flannel shirt, buttoned to the top but still loose around her neck, and her tan cardigan sweater, a bejeweled Christmas tree pinned to it. I knew the pin had not been her doing—many of the residents wore them, so the home must have handed them out. I suspected they had put it on when Lydia wasn't looking. Now she opened the tin and looked inside. "What's this?"

"It's Christmas cookies. I thought you might enjoy them."

She stared at me suspiciously, reptile-like, and I had to restrain myself from grabbing her glasses so I could clean them; they seemed to be begging me. Lydia dug through the cookies, examining this one and that. Her knuckles were huge, arthritic, I thought, and I saw that her hands still trembled. "I suppose **you** want one," she said finally, and I said no, I'd had plenty already.

From down the hall came a man's voice, loudly

chanting, "**Orange** juice! **Orange** juice! **Orange** juice!" He went on and on. Lydia waved her hand in his direction. "Every day. He lives on the other side, with the crazy people. He's just over here because their shower room is having problems again. If they'd hire a decent plumber, they'd get the thing fixed." She popped a tea cake into her mouth, and through her gnarliness, I thought I saw a quick flash of pleasure. "Did you make these?"

"I did."

"Well, I never saw the reason for all the fuss." She pulled her handkerchief from her sleeve and honked her nose.

"Well, one reason is that it's kind of nice to give them away. The other reason is that they taste good."

She nodded, pushing the handkerchief back inside her sleeve. "I suppose they do." She replaced the lid. "Now. What else do you want?"

I laughed. "Nothing."

She was still for a moment, then asked with some irritation, "Why do you keep coming back? You're not going to get a thing from me. And you can't like me."

"Well, Lydia, it isn't easy, but I kind of do." We had a neighbor, when I was growing up, who was generally regarded as impossible. Ball Man, he was called, for the way he would confiscate anything that landed on his lawn. He was an emaciated old guy, stoop-shouldered, bewhiskered with gray stubble, and bald but for a few strands of hair that sometimes were pushed over the top of his head but most often hung at the sides. He wore the same outfit all the time: a T-shirt tucked into too-large dress trousers that were belted high on his waist, and run-down slippers. I saw him only when he came out for the newspaper and the few times he left the house, when he wore a sport coat over his T-shirt and a battered hat with a feather. He fascinated me. I tried to no avail to win him over, leaving butterscotch brownies in his mailbox, ringing his doorbell to ask if he'd like me to pick something up for him at the store, or to rake his leaves, even asking him unlikely questions about whether he'd like to help send our fifth grade to Washington. 'No!' he would say. 'Beat it! Don't come around here anymore! Stop ringing my doorbell!' I never got anywhere with him, but I never stopped trying. "She ought to be a psychiatrist," my father said about me. Instead, I married one. He could do all the work; I could hear all the stories.

Lydia rolled herself closer to her bed. "I'm tired."

"Would you like me to call someone to help you?"

She flung the tin of cookies onto her bed. "Do you think I'm incapable of calling for a nurse? I'll call for a nurse when I'm ready. But for now

I've . . . got a little time." She looked away, then back at me. "Now. I don't know you and you don't know me. What do you propose we talk about?"

"I don't know."

"Let's just play a round of gin rummy."

"I can't do that."

She sat back in her chair. "Why not?"

"I never learned how to play it."

"Well, what can you play?"

"Just crazy eights." It was true. But for that, I had never learned any card games. John had once tried to teach me bridge, but it felt too much like math. And I'd kept looking out the window.

"Well, that's the stupidest thing I've ever heard. And I hear stupid things all the livelong day, believe me."

"Why don't you teach me the game?" I asked.

She frowned, then reached up to rub one eye. "Get the cards. They're in my top drawer. There's some candy bars in there, too. If you'd like."

"Not right now, thanks." I opened her drawer and pulled out a deck of cards. Beneath a pile of Hershey bars, I saw one of the letters I'd brought—she'd kept one. I closed the drawer without comment.

"I'll deal," Lydia said, looking fiercely at me.

I handed her the cards. "Okay."

"Thank you," she said, and quickly cleared her throat.

I sat back in my chair and watched her deal the cards, and inside I felt the spread of a great satisfaction. I knew I would be hard-pressed to explain it to anyone but John. Others might call this futile, a waste of time, masochistic, even. John would call it acknowledging the fact that people truly are all connected, and that we are, at least in some sense, meant to care for one another—all the time, not just in times of catastrophe. He would call visiting a bitter old woman a risk worth taking. I felt as though we were doing it together.

"Hire me, too," Lorraine said. We were driving back from the airport, and I'd told her I was going to hire Jovani if I could ever find a store to rent. He had suggested putting in a wine-and-dessert bar—a sort of female equivalent to a cigar bar. He would manage it. Also, he would sell his artwork there.

"I mean it," Lorraine said. "I'm ready for a radical change."

"Really, you'd come here and help me?"

"I would."

For a moment, I allowed myself the luxury of thinking of Lorraine perhaps even moving here, becoming my roommate once again, going on buying trips with me to Italy, to Greece, to France. But I didn't want to set myself up for disappointment—what were the chances of her doing that, really? It was one thing to help a friend; another to move permanently.

"You should wear that tomorrow night," I said. She looked stunning: a white sweater, elegantly cut tweed pants, soft brown Italian leather shoes.

"Oh, no," she said. "I brought a dress. And some killer heels—they'd better have the sidewalks clear. Should I wear my hair up or down?"

"Up," I said, at the same time as she said, "Down."

"Do both," I said. "Start out with it up."

"Good." She looked at her watch. "I really can't wait to meet him."

"Matthew?"

"Yeah."

"He's adorable."

"You **said.**"

Saturday night Lorraine waited impatiently in the living room for Tom to pick her up. Her black dress was cut low both in the front and in the back but otherwise was quite simple. She wore large diamond studs and a beautiful gold-and-diamond bangle bracelet. (**Real?** I asked, and she said, **That** guy was a **good** one.)

When the doorbell finally rang, I opened it to a nervous Tom, who became even more nervous when he saw Lorraine. For her part, she gave me a tight smile on the way out. I knew what it meant: **When I get back, I'm going to kill you for making me spend time with such a schmuck.** As I shut the door after them, I was already preparing his modest defense.

I made a simple supper of soup and salad, then settled down to read. But I couldn't concentrate; I kept having visions of what I hoped would happen. Finally, at eight-thirty, I called Delores and asked if she'd like to go to a movie. No answer.

I bathed, changed into pajamas, lay in bed and looked at magazines, listened to a couple of CDs, fell asleep, woke up, fell asleep, woke up. At one-fifteen the front door opened, and I heard a car drive away. I turned on my light.

Lorraine came up the stairs, then into my bedroom, holding her shoes in her hand. Her hair was down, her cheeks flushed. "You're awake," she said. "Good."

"So?" I asked.

"I think I'm in looooove."

I sat up higher in bed. "I told you he was adorable!"

"He is **such** a sweetheart! And believe me, Little Miss Melanie is going to go home and do some serious thinking. I was so proud of Matthew; she invited him in after we took them home and he said no, he wanted to go home and study. But then he looked over at me and I put my hand on his thigh. It was great."

"Tell me everything!"

"I will. But first . . . I didn't mean I was in love with Matthew."

Here came the inevitable sarcastic attack on Tom. "All right, fine, Lorraine, I know he's not your type."

"No. I'm serious. I **really** like this guy!" She laughed. "I do! I'm going to see him tomorrow night."

"You . . . what do you mean? You can't do that."

She'd been taking off her earrings, and she stopped. "Why not? You don't care about him, do you? That's what you said."

"I **said . . .** I just said that it was awkward!"

She moved to the bed to sit beside me. "That's not what you said. You have feelings for him? If you do, tell me."

"I don't **know** yet, Lorraine!"

"Well, don't get all pissed off."

"I'm **not!**"

She leaned in closer to me. I could smell scotch on her breath. Her eyes were bloodshot. "You are. You are pissed off."

I looked down, picked at the bedspread. "Where are you going with him?"

"We were going to hear some jazz."

I nodded. I had had no such invitation from him.

"The kind you don't like, Betta, very contemporary stuff in some little club in the city. Did you know he used to play saxophone?"

"Yeah, I remember something like that." I did not. "How do you know I don't like that kind of jazz?"

"Well, because you never did. And also, Tom told me about when he wanted to play Coltrane, and . . ." She looked away from me, and I saw that Tom had told her everything else as well. "Do you want to come with us?" she asked. Still, she would not look at me.

Us. The word was huge.

"Oh, yeah, that would be great." I had a sudden image of the three of us at a nightclub, Lorraine and Tom looking terrific, he in his leather coat, she in her tight sweater, me in my bathrobe and curlers.

She smiled hesitantly, not sure of how I was feeling. I heard my voice growing louder. "You don't know everything about me. You don't know what kind of jazz I like! Things change! You don't even know me anymore!"

"That's not true! I—"

"No, you don't!"

She sighed, reached over to touch my hand, which I immediately pulled away. "Betta. Calm down. I do know you, just as you still know me. Just as we all still know each other—Maddy,

Susanna, you, and I. If you want me not to pursue a relationship with Tom, just . . . I mean, Jesus, **is** that what you want?"

I got out of bed and went into Lorraine's room. I took her suitcase out of the closet and put it on the bed, opened it. Then I began throwing things into it—her robe, a pair of pants, a couple of blouses, her white sweater. She leaned against the doorjamb, watching me. From the corner of my eye, I could see that she had gotten a stain on the left breast of her fancy black dress. **Good.** "What are you doing, Betta?"

I opened the dresser drawer and threw her flannel pajama bottoms into the suitcase, her T-shirt. I threw in her lacy underwear. Maybe Tom would find hers worth looking at. "I am so sick of you," I said.

"You can't be sick of me. You haven't seen me enough to be sick of me."

"I **am** sick of you! I'm sick of you from before! Always lording it over everyone—"

"Lording what over everyone!"

I stopped packing, looked over at her. **"What?"**

I threw in her hairbrush. "You know exactly what I mean, Lorraine. You think you have rights that . . . well, you **don't** think! You just take! You do whatever you want without regard for anyone else's feelings. I had a relationship with Tom, but now you've ruined it!"

"Betta, this isn't fair."

"Let me remind you of something, okay? My husband died. He was the center of my life. He was the one I told everything to, he understood everything, I didn't even have to say it! For so many years, I . . ." I began to cry and Lorraine moved toward me. I held up my hand, traffic-cop style. "No! You have no idea, Lorraine. You don't know what it's like to lose someone like that. It's like being eviscerated! Do you know how hard it is to try to have another relationship after that? Do you know how hard it is to just go **on,** when you've lost someone like that?"

She spoke softly. "No. I don't. You know why? Because I never had that. I never even came close. Now let's play the What's Worse game, you want to play that?" She tossed one earring into the suitcase, then the other. "I think I know something about what you had, Betta. And I think you're lucky. You had someone who protected you from every hard knock and who told you every single day that you were loved. You were so **loved**! I have never had that kind of relationship in my life. And I am scared to death I never will. I'm getting older, okay? And I'm tired. I'm tired of working and I'm tired of being alone. Now I meet someone who . . . he's different, and I think I might finally have a chance to be with someone who can do for me what I've needed most all along. You said you knew right away when you met John that he was the one for you. I felt that way tonight. It was easy being with him! For once, we met in the middle. He's not **afraid** of me—I'm so tired of men being **afraid** of me! I just . . . I have a chance, here. You want to take it from me? Fine. I'll call Tom and tell him I had to go back to Providence. Or maybe you'd like to do that." She pulled off her dress and lay it in the suitcase. She stepped into the pants she'd worn on the plane, then pulled on the white sweater and black boots.

"Lorraine," I said.

She looked at me, her hands on her hips. "What."

"Where are you going?"

"I'll find a hotel in Chicago."

"Don't do that." I sank down onto the bed, and she sat beside me.

"What do you want me to do?" she asked. "Tell me."

"It's not Tom I want," I said. "I know that. And he doesn't want me. We don't work that way together. I know that."

"Maybe you just need more time," Lorraine said. "Maybe if I weren't here . . ."

"How about we go to the airport tomorrow morning," I said, and she stiffened, then nodded.

"No," I said. "Because I want to go back to Boston. You can stay here."

She embraced me and I stared at the wall, my hands at my side.

As a child, I used to dream of flying off to another city on a whim. And now I'd done it. Of course, it didn't feel as glamorous as I used to imagine it, especially since I was using Lorraine's frequent-flyer miles. In those fantasies, I saw myself wrapped in white furs, drinking champagne while lounging in a large white leather seat. Now I was crammed into a middle seat in the next-to-last row, the child next to me drawing on the window with his crayon, the woman on the other side of me complaining over and over about the noise of the engine. But the flight would last only two hours. I closed my eyes.

When I landed, I called my old neighbor Sheila from the airport, asking her to have dinner with me that night. "You're moving back, right?" she said, and I said I didn't know. We agreed to meet at Legal Seafood at seven. When I hung up, I went outside and got into a cab, asking the driver to take me to the Copley Plaza to drop off my bag, then to the Isabella Stewart Gardner Museum.

I stared at the scenery we passed, beloved to me. The ocean, the North End, Faneuil Hall, the fancy shops and outdoor cafés on Newbury Street, the huge red bow put up annually on the office building next to the Pike. I watched a couple walking hand in hand along the Charles, their dog straining at his leash, and I remembered that awful day when I rode home from the hospital with John's suitcase beside me.

When I arrived at the museum, I headed for the courtyard, where I sat on a wall and did not move for what felt like a very long time. I watched different people admiring the flowers there, some obviously tourists, and I felt proud of what was still my city. I remembered attending chamber concerts in the hall upstairs, sitting beside John and closing my eyes, listening hard. Often, we would go afterward to the nearby Museum of Fine Arts and eat dinner in the elegant dining room. I loved how reflective John became after a day of looking at art, how he was so eager to talk about what he had seen that had moved him in one way or another. Going to museums always brought him great comfort; even after he was quite ill, he still loved to go. Art lasted, was the thing. He loved that it lasted.

Remembering this, my eyes filled and I held my gloves up as a makeshift handkerchief. My sounds were small and muffled but obvious. No one paid any attention. It was the way we had become. In a world full of sorrows, this was only one more.

Later in the afternoon, I stood outside the house I used to live in. It had grown very cold. Birds sat puffed up on tree branches; puddles were iced over; even the sky seemed frozen. The people who'd bought the house were home; I could see them moving about inside. I took in a breath, then went up to the door and knocked.

A man with a dramatic receding hairline who appeared to be in his early thirties answered, then looked questioningly at me. "Hello," I said. "My name is Betta Nolan. I used to live here."

"Oh, yes," the man said. "I remember your name. You didn't come to the closing."

"Right. I was wondering . . ."

He stood there, mildly impatient. From behind him came the sounds of someone working in the kitchen, the clangs and bangs of pots and pans, and the rich scent of curry.

"I hope you'll forgive my barging in like this.

But I . . ." I stared past him down the hall. To the left was the kitchen with the large window overlooking the backyard. To the right was John's study, where once I came in, lowered the blinds, and made love to him on the floor. I wanted to see the family room again, where John spent so many of his last hours. And hard as it would be, I also wanted to see our bedroom.

"I wonder," I said. "Would you mind terribly if I looked inside?"

The man hesitated, then said, "For . . . ?"

"Well . . ." I became suddenly furious that I had to ask permission to come into a place where I had lived for so long. "I would actually like to buy it back from you. I made a mistake. I would like to buy it back from you, and I will pay a great deal for it."

"Honey?" A woman's voice, and now a thin, dark-haired woman was standing beside him. "Hello," she said.

"She's the previous owner," the man said.

"Well, for heaven's sake, come in," the woman said, and sent her spouse a dark look, for which I was grateful. "You must be wanting to see what we've done."

"She wants to buy it back," the man said, chuckling, and the woman said, "Charles? Why don't you go and take care of Billy. I'll stay here."

He stared at us, one hand on his hip.

"Go," the woman said. Charles walked off, and

the woman said, "I'm Naomi Appel. Come in. Look around all you want to. It's okay."

I came in, unbuttoned my coat, took a few nervous steps down the hall. "Maybe I could start with the study." Even absent, he would steady me. His papers, neatly arranged on his desk, his favorite photo of us together beside his phone, the leather chair, which, when I'd gotten it for him, had been a major extravagance. Of course they wouldn't be there now. But their ghosts would be.

"Oh, that's not there anymore. We tore down a wall to make the family room bigger. Come, I'll show you. It's wonderful! We changed the wall color to a dark green, and put up—"

"You know," I spoke around a lump in my throat. "Never mind. I guess I . . ." I laughed, embarrassed.

Her eyes softened. "Oh, I thought . . . I just thought you might like to see the improvements. But of course that would be hard for you."

"I'm sorry for disturbing you. I guess this wasn't such a good idea."

She walked me to the door and shivered after she opened it. "If you ever change your mind, you just come on over. Don't pay any attention to Charles."

"All right," I said. "Thank you." I stood still, looking at the wall where we'd hung an oil we bought at the Brickbottom Annual Open Studio sale in Somerville. You could see the faint outline.

"I'm going to close this door right up, okay?" the woman said. "Chilly!"

I stepped outside, then turned to say, "Thank you for letting me look."

"You're very welcome." The door closed on her words.

I moved out to the center of the street so that I could take in the whole house. This is exactly what John and I had done when we bought it, stood in the middle of the street, and a car had narrowly missed hitting John. In our happiness at having found a place we loved so much, we hadn't cared. Now, like a pale echo, a boy raced close by me on a bicycle. Soon he would be a man, then an old man, then gone. I looked up at the sky, darkening and indifferent. Then I went to the corner to look for a cab. I would go and buy a book to read on the plane when I went home. For this was home no longer.

"So, what brings you here?" Sheila asked me, over our martinis.

"I just all of a sudden decided to come. I went to the Gardner. And then I went to see my old house. I didn't look at much, though."

She set her drink down, leaned in closer to me. "Was it awfully hard?"

"Yes."

"**Are** you thinking of moving back?"

"I think maybe that was in the back of my mind. But . . . no. I really like the town I moved to."

"Which is?"

"Oh! Stewart, Illinois. It's not too far from Chicago. I'm sorry I never called to tell you, Sheila."

"Well, frankly, I'm surprised you called now. But I'm glad you did. You're different, Betta. Do you know that? You seem more . . . well, you're warmer. You must be doing well there."

"I am. I've made some new friends. And I've found some old ones." I told her about Maddy, Susanna, and Lorraine.

"Are you seeing anyone?" Sheila asked. She looked down into her drink, toyed with her olive.

"I did go on a date. Didn't work out too well."

"Why not?"

"Oh . . . it's probably too soon."

Sheila leaned her chin on her hand. "You know, Randy has a friend whose wife left him; it was a really bad scene. The man, his name is Vince, met a woman not even a month after his wife left, and fell in love. And he told Randy he just couldn't get straight with it, wasn't it too soon? And you know what Randy said? He said, 'Vince. Don't you think time's a little short for worries like that? Okay, you're not eighty, but you're not thirty, either.' The guy married the woman six months later, and they're so happy."

"Yes, well, but . . . John didn't leave me like that."

"I know," Sheila said. "But at a time like this, I think there's something to be said for taking any good thing that's offered you."

"There is," I said. I smiled at her. "I love your necklace. Where'd you get that?" It was a fine gold chain with alternating stones in the colors of ruby and apple green hanging from it.

She put her hand to her chest. "Do you? I wasn't sure; it's so different."

"That's why I like it."

"After dinner, I'll show you the store. If they have any left, you should get one."

"If they have any left, I'll get more than one."

Back at the hotel, I stood for a long while at the window, looking out at the city. I remembered sitting in Brookline Booksmith shortly after John died, leafing through books about being a widow. I'd felt ashamed of looking at them, as though John's death had been a grievous error I'd made. And I remembered, too, that when I put the books back on the shelf and walked out of the store, I'd had the oddest sensation: I'd felt as though things were falling out of me. Body parts. Whoops, there went my uterus. Now a kidney. A heart to step over. It had scared me a little, how odd this thought was. It had scared me more that there had not been a single person I could think of to talk about it with. That wasn't true anymore. With John, I'd found one kind of love. In the little town I'd moved to, I'd found another.

I sat on the bed and pulled out my cell phone. When Lorraine answered, I told her I'd be coming home tomorrow night. And that if she wanted to live with me and be my work partner, I would be very happy. We'd find another store; I wasn't so crazy about that other one anyway. The parking wasn't good, and that attached apartment was a problem. We'd find something else and it would be much better.

She said nothing.

"Or you could stay in the room I rented at Matthew and Jovani's, if you don't want to live with me. Maybe we're too old now to be roommates."

Silence.

"Lorraine?" I said.

"What?"

"Do you want to? Live with me?"

"There's something . . ."

"Lorraine? Are you **cry**ing?"

"**No,** I'm not **cry**ing."

"Well, what's the matter?"

"You know that place you don't want?"

"Yes?"

"I just rented it. The other person's lease fell through. Tom and I were out walking a while ago, and we went past and the sign was back up and . . . well, I just rented it. Are you mad?"

February 28, the day before our grand opening, I came back from Chicago with more necklaces from an artist I'd found in Pilsen, the Mexican community. I pulled up in front of the shop to see the surprise Jovani had promised me. And received one. For there, stenciled on the window in gold paint, was a large oval of interlocking flowers. In the center was gold script reading WHAT WANTS A WOMAN. I rested my head against the steering wheel, then raised it when I heard a tapping on the passenger window. I rolled down the window. "You saw?" Jovani was smiling, nearly rubbing his hands together with glee.

"I saw. Listen, Jovani—"

"Don't say me! I am happy for do you. And already three people come and buy!"

"Really?"

"**Yes.** Coming by and then they stop and look at the sign. Then they poke inside their heads, 'Are you open yet?' and Delores yell, 'No, but come in, anyway!' One woman, she thinks we are **dating** service."

"Well, right," I said. "Because of the name you put on there."

He looked back at the flowing gold letters. "It's exact what you order, no?"

"No."

"No?"

"**No,** Jovani! It's supposed to be WHAT A WOMAN WANTS!"

"I'm **say**!" He turned around again to look, then covered his mouth with his hands. "Ohh-hhh!"

Delores came to the door and called out to me. "My advice is to leave it up for a while. It certainly attracts attention. The people who've come in all thought it was great."

"Maybe it is kind of interesting," I said.

"You see?" Jovani said. "I have in me late end genius."

"I'm going to run home," I said. "I'll bring back some lunch for us."

Delores waved and went back inside, Jovani at her heels. Lorraine would be back from Indiana soon, where she'd gone to buy antiques. It was hard for me not to want to keep everything in the store for myself: the polka-dotted plates, the persimmon-colored pajamas, the vases of cobalt blue, the rolls of satin ribbon, the miniature oils, the books of poems by Ruth Stone and Chitra Divakaruni and so many others, the novels and short stories, all written by women and stored in bookcases built along either side of the fireplace we'd put in. We had blank suede journals—Benny's idea.

We'd bought things from women potters and quilt artists—Carol, who was now working for me full-time, had found an Amish source in Indiana. We had cards and stationery designed by women, including homemade ones from the three little girls who lived down the street from me—each of these with original drawings and verses. We had whimsical lamps and picture frames, throws so voluptuous you could hold them to your face and sleep standing up. We had a recipe exchange—a big book to add to or make copies from. In another book, people could make recommendations for everything from sitters to sushi. And for five bucks, I'd help husbands write their wives a love letter. In a corner, I had a desk all set up with paper choices and with a drawer full of beautiful fountain pens like the one John used, and full of the black ink he favored.

When I arrived home, I got out the tomato soup I'd made yesterday that would taste even better today. I'd bring some toasted cheese sandwiches, and a bowl full of fruit, plenty of brownies. Benny would be by to help after school, and he liked brownies—he insisted that they be placed front and center at the dessert bar.

I went into the living room, sat on the sofa, and let the quiet engulf me. My mother always used to take a long bath on Christmas Eve, and I would always lie in the hall outside the bathroom in anguished anticipation, wondering how she could possibly take so long when there were presents waiting to be opened. But I saw now that she was savoring the moment **before,** and that was what I was doing now, too. My mother must have imagined my father and me opening our cuff links and doll clothes; I was thinking of the people who might find pleasure in what my store offered—not only in the things but in the ideas they might inspire. I had always wanted to visit a store that functioned as a third place; now I saw that I'd created one. What a whirlwind these last several weeks had been!

What would John have thought of all this? Had I grieved him enough, or in the right way? This was something that gnawed at me; it was the question I wanted most to have answered. As though it might provide me with the answer, I went to the chest and put my hand in the drawer. **Soprano gone, good.** I'd gotten that one before, and still had no idea what it meant. As I had so often when I'd read these words, I wondered what John had been thinking when he wrote them. Was there was a soprano he'd not liked, someone he'd told me about at a time when I hadn't really been listening? It was all too possible. **Okay, John—no bad divas**.

I put the slip back in the drawer and went into the basement to look for a box I could use to carry food in. I'd kept a few of the dish packs from moving and stored them on one of the wooden shelves in the laundry room. I reached up for one and noticed a bit of weight. Startled, I dropped the box and stepped back from it. Was a mouse in there? A **bat**?

I kicked at the corner, and the box moved a few inches. Nothing inside seemed to move, though—at least I heard no scrabbling sounds. Slowly, I lifted the lid and peered inside. There was something in the corner, wrapped in newspaper. Something I'd forgotten to unpack, then, though it was odd that it was in newspaper; I didn't recall the movers using that. In the dim light, I unwrapped a dish. Quite small, and unfamiliar to me. I brought it closer to the high window and looked more carefully at it in the light. It was the green bowl I'd admired in the antiques store so long ago. And at the bottom was a note in John's handwriting: **When you find this, let's have some eggs. (Don't tell the sparrow.)**

I sat on the basement steps, cradling the bowl

in my lap. To think that I might have broken it. And yet, if I had broken it, I'd have it anyway. Having known it, I could keep it in memory, where I might actually appreciate it more.

I thought of the priest who'd told me that many religions hold that it is easier to be closely connected to people we love after death than before. I thought of other elegant contradictions to which we bore continual witness. I thought of rich men who were poor; poor men who were rich; ascetics who lived with nothing so as to have everything. I thought of how "lost love" is a misnomer, for love is never lost at all but only different in appearance, conforming with that well-known law of physics. John used to tell me there was grace in mathematics and romance in physics. In this, as in so many other things, he was exactly right.

The sparrow to which John referred was the one he'd rescued after it had fallen from the nest in our backyard. He'd kept it in a shoe box and fed and nurtured it until it was able to fly away. But how can you let it go? I'd asked, on the day he took the box outside and bent down beside it to nudge the bird toward freedom. He'd shrugged, and smiled up at me. He was squinting, the sun in his eyes, and I remembered thinking he looked so handsome. "There is love in holding," he'd said. "And there is love in letting go."

I went back upstairs to the chest and pulled out the slip I'd just looked at. Right. It did not say **Soprano.** It said everything else.

All the way to the store, pictures of John came to me, truer than any I might have gotten from developing film. I saw him standing with his arms outspread before a large group of people who had come for my surprise fiftieth birthday party, thrown by John at Aujourd'hui with his usual lavish style. I saw him holding Steve and Sara Miner's new baby girl, extending one of his fingers for her tiny hand to hold, and despite our repeated and painful failures at conception, his face was absent of envy and full of love and welcome. I saw him sitting at the edge of a hotel swimming pool, water beaded on his lashes. I saw him grinning broadly from the driver's seat of his first sports car. I saw him standing over the grill, a ruined steak hanging from the tongs.

Then I envisioned John doing something he had often described to me. I saw him as a young man, washing up at the sink after having changed the oil in his car. As he buttoned the sleeves of his fresh shirt, he would decide to wrap a towel around his neck and quickly shave, just in case he met someone at the party. And he would. Me. There I was, waiting, afraid I'd never experience the kind of joy yet to come, but hoping for it just the same.

When I got back to the store, I walked past

two women looking excitedly into the jewelry case. I saw that someone had put her name on the list to rent the retreat space. Apparently, our grand opening had started already, and why not? I carried our lunch into the back room and set out the soup and the sandwiches, the apples and the pears. I arranged them on a table covered by a vintage cloth beautifully embroidered in pinks and greens by someone long gone. The colors were unfaded, still true. I put my hands to the back of my head for a good, hard stretch, then invited everyone to come and get it.

ACKNOWLEDGMENTS

I would like to express my gratitude to my agent, Lisa Bankoff, and to my editor, Kate Medina, for their wisdom, kindness, and care. Thanks too to their assistants, Tina Dubois and Danielle Posen, for the many favors they do for me. My appreciation to my production editor, Beth Pearson, and to Margaret Wimberger, my copy editor for this book, who should be given a gold medal. And so should the art department, for once again creating such a stunning jacket. My writers group offered honest and valuable criticism; I am indebted to Veronica Chapa, Nancy Drew, Pam Todd, and Michele Weldon. My publicist, Kate Blum, is my lifeline when I'm on tour, and I am deeply appreciative of the myriad details she handles on my behalf.

Last, but certainly not least, thanks to Bill Young, my life partner, who shares it all with me and Homer and Cosette—and with Toblance, in spirit, always and forever.

ABOUT THE AUTHOR

ELIZABETH BERG is the author of thirteen novels, including **The New York Times** bestsellers **The Art of Mending, Say When, True to Form, Never Change,** and **Open House,** which was an Oprah's Book Club selection in 2000. **Durable Goods** and **Joy School** were selected as ALA Best Books of the Year, and **Talk Before Sleep** was shortlisted for the ABBY award in 1996. The winner of the 1997 New England Booksellers Award for her work, she is also the author of a nonfiction work, **Escaping into the Open: The Art of Writing True**. She lives in Chicago.